I0544693

15

of the best stories

by
J. S. Kierland

Underground Voices
2014

Published by Underground Voices
Editor contact: Cetywa Powell

ISBN: 978-0-9830456-9-4

Printed in the United States of America.

©2014 by J.S. Kierland. All rights reserved

Sometimes I live in the country,
Sometimes I live in the town,
Sometimes I have a great notion
To jump into the river and drown.
American Folk Song, author unknown

For
Lily, Moira,
Linda and Stella

ACKNOWLEDGEMENTS

COMING APART
Trajectory Literary Journal (Fall, 2013)

TUBA CITY
Playboy Magazine (September, 2003)
July Press Anthology (2004)
Emry's Journal (Spring, 2004)
Colere Literary Review (Spring 2009)
Muse & Stone (aka Teddy Country, 2009)
Lively-Arts.com

UNDER THE CICADAS
Mount Hope Review 3 (Spring 2013)
Lively-Arts.com

DEEP WATER
Threshold Review (Spring 2003)
De La Mancha (2004)
Arizona Literary Review (1992)
International Short Story (1993)
Wising Up Press/Connected (2013)
Lively-Arts.com

TRUE BELIEVERS
Lively-Arts.com (Kindness of Strangers)

PARABLE
Colere Literary Review (Spring 2013)
Lively-Arts.com (Passing)

FENCES
Bryant Literary Review (Running Out)
Cooweescowee Journal (Spring 2014)
Lively-Arts.com (Running Out)

ACKNOWLEDGEMENTS
(cont'd)

ROBOTS
Bryant Literary Review (Spring 2011)
Front Range Review (Spring 2011)
Fiction International (Fall 2013)
Lively-Arts.com

UNSCHEDULED FLIGHTS
Sleet Magazine.com (Fall 2012)
Epiphany Magazine (Fall 2014)

CRATES
Gemini Magazine.com (Dec. 2012)
Feile-Festa (2014)

THE FIRE SEASON
Lively-Arts.com

FULL CIRCLE
Drash Mosaic (Spring 2012)
Lively-Arts.com
Oracle (vol. 8)

MOON CHILDREN
Lively-Arts.com

TABLE OF CONTENTS

SOMETIMES I LIVE IN THE COUNTRY

SOMETIMES I LIVE IN THE TOWN

SOMETIMES I LIVE
IN THE COUNTRY

COMING APART

The long freight switched tracks, turned wide, and the edge of a town rose into view on the flat desert landscape. Breeze leaned out over the rushing ground to look for the water tower. A cluster of buildings appeared, and then the tower with its faded red letters edged into view against the chalked sky. AQUILLA, AZ.

He spread his blanket across the shaking planks, threw in his razor, cell phone, the toothbrush, a small piece of yellow soap, and quickly rolled it into a tight ball. Slipping off his belt, he strapped the blanket over his chest and waited for the train to slow down at the crossing ahead.

A blur of dry desert ground shot by under him and he set himself against the boxcar's open door, measuring the distance. A warm dry wind brushed his face and he felt the train begin to brake. Breeze exhaled, then jumped. Hanging in the air, he waited for the drop, hit the edge of the roadbed, and stumbled out of control along the slope. He fell and a sharp pain ran up his arm and shoulder. The rolled blanket, strapped across his chest, fell open before he could catch it and he came to a sudden stop in the low brush and watched the freight clatter by above his head, waiting for the ground to stop shaking.

When the last car had rumbled past he crawled across the parched earth to retrieve his things. On the other side of the tracks, a lone coyote loped by and stopped to look over at him. They stared at each other for a long time before the coyote turned away and disappeared into the thick weeds that skirted the open field.

Breeze rose up on one knee, slipped the belt back on his jeans, dug his boots into the dry sandy soil, and headed for the cluster of blurred buildings that began to regain their sharpness the closer he got to the water tower. He looked for Pebbles' purple taxi and found it parked in the shade between the bar and the bus station. He poked at the guy sleeping behind the wheel. A startled young Latino looked up and stared numbly back at him.

"Sorry," Breeze said. "I thought you were —"

"Pebbles works the night shift now," the kid mumbled. "Where you want to go?"

"Cartwright's."

"Hell, you can walk that, man. Just go down two blocks and make a —"

"I'd rather you took me there," Breeze snapped, and the kid looked at his torn dusty rolled blanket, glanced over at the empty bus depot, and sat up as Breeze slipped into the backseat. The taxi rumbled to a start and hummed its way down route 60 before turning onto a dirt road.

"You a friend of Pebbles?" the kid asked.

"Since we were knee high."

"You must be Breeze Cartwright."

"You must be Santos."

"Yeah, that's me. Tell me something, amigo. Did my boss really get his name when he was a little kid throwing pebbles at passing cars?"

"That's supposed to be a secret."

"There are no secrets in this town," Santos said with a laugh. "What's his real name anyway?"

"I don't know."

"Now that's funny. Does he know you're back?"

"That's supposed to be a secret too."

"If I don't tell him he'll fire me."

"So much for secrets."

"He's a good man," Santos said quickly.

"That he is and A-men. Is he still on the outs with his crazy brother, the sheriff?"

"I'm not supposed to talk with the passengers about family matters," Santos said, and they both laughed.

"The only thing that changes around here is Pebbles' melon field. It gets wider and longer every day."

"You got that right, sir. The field gets wider and the taxi gets older," Santos giggled and pulled up in front of an old gray clapboard house in desperate need of paint.

Breeze took some money out of his pocket but Santos waved his hand and said, "No, *senor*. You know Pebbles. If I took your money he'd fire me on the spot."

"We sure wouldn't want that," Breeze said, before he was interrupted by the *whap* of a screen door.

Someone on the porch yelled, "Breeeeze," and a woman ran down to the cab.

"Hey, Abby," Santos said.

"Hey, yourself," she said, looking for Breeze's suitcase.

"I checked it at the bus station in Wickenburg," Breeze lied. "I'll pick it up when I get back into town."

"Traveling light again, eh? Just don't tell Ma."

"It's nice seeing you, too," he said.

"You're just in time to help me move her," she sighed.

"That bad?"

"Take it easy you guys," Santos called.

Breeze watched the cab make the turn down the dusty rise, and when he looked back his sister was already on the porch waiting for him.

The house was dark and the musty smell from the swamp cooler hit him. He followed Abby through the living room, past the TV, and the covered exercise bike. They'd moved the leather couch to the other side of the room, and the black and red Navajo pillows had been piled at one end.

Abby glanced back at him, but kept going to the rear of the house where the morning light was brighter. His mother was sitting in a hospital bed set up on the screened in back porch. She lay thin and pale against the puffed white pillows, looking worse than he'd expected. A standing metal pole stood next to the bed with a hook at its top for an IV bottle, but nothing hung from it.

"Hey, Ma," he piped.

The woman opened her eyes and said, "Breeze," in a breathy, surprised way, and they hugged.

Abby stood watching them, made a thumbs up gesture to her mother behind Breeze's back, and the woman smiled. "He just showed up in Pebbles' cab, Ma," she said.

"Let me get a good look at you," his mother said, noticing his torn jeans and scuffed shirt. "This the latest traveling gear?"

"Just the latest Chicago thing," he said, avoiding her disapproving glance. "City people have to be different or they'll bust."

"Glad you got here in one piece," she said.

"Don't I always?" he smiled, rubbing his sore shoulder. "It's all in the game, Ma."

"Let's get these sheets smoothed out," Abby piped and began pulling the ends across the bed into the corners. Breeze lifted his mother from one side to the other, surprised at how light she felt.

When Abby finished, his mother said, "Fix some tea and drag out those oatmeal cookies you've been hiding."

"Maybe Breeze would like some breakfast, Ma."

"No, I had breakfast," he lied again. "Tea's good."

Abby headed for the kitchen and his mother asked, "Did you get my letter?"

He nodded and glanced at the door to make sure his sister had gone into the kitchen. "I didn't answer your letter because I figured Abby would intercept it ... and I didn't want to call."

"I've been waiting for you to just pop in like this."

"You look fine, Ma."

"Ain't fine ... and don't look it either. They cut me open but it didn't do much good. Knew it wouldn't. Now your damn sister keeps dragging me into Phoenix so they can give me a dose of that poison every other week."

"Are you hurting?"

"The pain comes fierce sometimes and both doctors said it'd get meaner before it got better," she wheezed. "Trouble is it's not getting any better."

Her frailness had gotten worse since he'd seen her a few months before when the initial tests came back before Christmas. They hadn't been good. Abby took it hard and insisted she go for the treatments, but she just kept shaking her head, insisting she was "through with it all, especially the *Adeste Fidelis* part."

It'd been her choice and she'd made it, but Abby just refused to accept it. He argued with her and it got so bad that he finally picked up and left before the New Year had even rolled in.

There wasn't much of his mother left now. They'd given her treatments but it didn't look like anything had worked. Thin bony arms in wrinkled skin, shoulder bones protruding from under the sheets, and every few minutes an empty stare popped into her eyes. Looked like she hadn't eaten since he'd left.

"Did you bring it?" his mother asked. He nodded. "I knew I could count on you, son."

"Don't know if there's enough though, Mom."

"Let me see it," she said, and he slipped a plastic bag of dirty looking powder from his denim jacket.

"It'll do," she said. "Ain't much of me left either."

"There's a lot more to it than that, Ma," he said. "I'm still not sure it's the right way to go."

"Then what the hell did you bring it for? I'll do it myself if I have to. All you have to do is fill the needle and I'll do the rest. I don't want you getting into trouble over this."

"Trouble over what?" Abby asked, standing in the doorway with a tray of oatmeal cookies.

"Explain it to her, son. I'm tired of trying."

"Explain what?"

"Mom's just grateful for everything you've done for her," Breeze mumbled, holding the plastic bag behind him.

"What nonsense," Abby said. "She'd do the same for us ... even more."

The woman glared at her from the bed, and said, "Just leave the cookies and go tend that tea."

Abby set the tray on the bed next to her, glanced up at Breeze, and headed back to the kitchen.

"When are you planning all this?" he asked.

"Soon as possible. Right now ... today. I don't want to live like this. Rather get it over with," she mumbled. "I'm miserable."

"Maybe you should try one of these cookies before you go. They're pretty good," he said.

She started to laugh at his little joke, began to cough, and everything seemed to hit at once. Her face cringed in pain and her wasted body shook. Breeze cradled her in his arms to ease the coughing.

"Didn't know it had gotten this bad," he said.

She nodded through her heaving body and tried to say something, but nothing came out except the coughing, and he set her back down on the pillows. The low whistle of the kettle sounded in the kitchen, stopped abruptly, and he stuffed the plastic bag back into his denim jacket.

A flash of motion at the window caught his eye and the purple taxi pulled up to the walkway again. He couldn't tell if Santos was at the wheel, but a heavyset man with a limp got out on the passenger side. The cab pulled away and Abby ran down the porch steps to greet him.

When the screen door slammed his mother wheezed, "Sounds like we got another guest for tea and cookies."

"It's Pebbles," he said, watching Abby throw her arms around the heavyset man's neck and push her body in tight against him. "Looks like Abby's got herself a boyfriend."

"You could call it that," she said.

"What do you call it?"

"Hot panties," she snapped. "One thing's for sure, that boy didn't come for tea and cookies."

"Guess who's here, Breeze?" Abby called from outside.

"This may take a while, Ma," he said.

"I meant what I said about today."

"Let me talk to Pebbles first," he said.

"What do you have to talk to him about?"

"You, Mamma," he said, and managed to get to the front door before Abby reached the porch steps.

When Pebbles saw him he moved past Abby and hugged Breeze, "Welcome back, man," he said. "Good to see you."

"The prodigal returns," Breeze said.

"I read your story in *The Atlantic*. Liked it a lot. You're getting better all the time."

"Story?" Abby squealed. "Why didn't you tell me?"

"Hell, I published six of those suckers last year."

"What about the novel?" Pebbles asked.

"What novel?" Abby squeaked again.

"You better go in and pour that tea for Mom. She could use it," Breeze said. "I have to talk with Pebbles."

"Why can't you do it inside with us?" she whined.

"It's okay, Abby. We'll be right back," Pebbles said. "I've got to check something out at the café anyway."

"He's already had his breakfast," she said, letting the screen door slam behind her.

"What's she so uptight about?" Pebbles asked.

"It's because I showed up out of nowhere. Didn't you know that Abby's a control freak and the main obstacle in this situation?"

Pebbles stopped scratching at his two-day beard, and rocked slowly on his heels in the middle of the road.

"You telling me that Abby didn't know you were coming back?"

"Not unless you told her, Dude."

"Hell, I say nothing to nobody," Pebbles muttered.

"That only gets control freaks even madder."

They walked back down toward route 60 and Pebbles finally asked, "You bring the stuff like I told you?"

"Yeah, I got it," Breeze said.

"Then there's nothing to worry about."

"Except for my sister, your brother, and whether what I brought is enough to do the job."

"That pretty much sums up things," Pebbles said, and they walked in silence down the dusty street.

*

The café was quiet. It was too early in the season for the Mexican pickers to be in town and the regulars had already eaten and gone. They headed for a back booth and the waitress showed up even before they could sit down.

"Coffee, gentlemen?" she asked.

"Yeah," Pebbles said, "tell Carl to cook up some ham and scrambled for me. What do you want, Breeze?"

"I'll have the hash with poached," he said, and the young waitress left for the kitchen. "New, isn't she?"

"Carl's niece. At least that's what he says. I don't care who she is, long as she does the job."

"Just so you know, I'm negotiating with a small publisher in Chicago for that novel you mentioned."

"Does that mean you're going right back?"

"Not necessarily."

"It'll look bad if you do."

"I don't much care how it looks. I just want my Mom to be out of her misery and have her funeral even if it has to be in this dumb town."

"We ought to give her one last blast before she goes," Pebbles said. "Miriam loves parties."

"Yeah, she practically lived for them."

"And hers were always the best," Pebbles said, picking up the mug of coffee the waitress set in front of him.

"Trouble is my Mom doesn't feature waiting around for a party. She wants to leave today."

"Jesus, is she really that bad?" Breeze stared at him. "She never said anything to me about it, and Abby doesn't even talk about your mother anymore."

"Looks like you and Abby have gotten pretty close."

Pebbles looked up in surprise. "You noticed, eh? Been that way since New Year's Eve," he said. "Don't know exactly how it happened, but here we are."

"Just one of those drunken nights, eh?" Breeze asked, and Pebbles shrugged. "She must've been really pissed after I took off. You don't figure she went after my best friend just to put some icing on the cake?"

"Jesus, buddy, is that all you think of me?"

"No, but I know how my sister thinks."

"No one ever called me *icing* before."

"Just writer talk. Don't listen to me."

"But I do listen to you. Always have, man."

The waitress drifted back with their food, coffee refills, and place settings. She smiled at Breeze, and asked, "Can I get you guys anything else?" They shook their heads and watched her walk away.

"Don't worry, man. We'll get through this. Besides, my brother took off for Vegas yesterday. If I know him he'll be gone for the rest of the week."

"That gives us some room," Breeze said.

"Everyone's expecting Miriam to pass anyway."

"Everyone except Abby."

"What do we do next?" Pebbles asked.

"I thought you were the expert." Pebbles shook his head and kept eating. "You are, aren't you?"

"Yeah, I suppose. But it was different back then. It was a foreign country in the middle of a war. The main thing is that I don't want you doing this by yourself. You're just caught up in it like I was when it happened to me. Let's just stick to the plan we have," Pebbles said. "Give me the drugs. If that's what she wants I'll put them into the IV after the Nurse comes and sets her up today."

"How the hell do you get this stuff past the Nurse?"

"I'll figure something," he said with a shrug. "This way even Miriam won't know what's going on. The less people involved the better. All you have to do is drive into Wickenburg with Abby when she does the grocery shopping. She usually goes when the Nurse arrives and won't suspect a thing if you're with her. Try to stall her long enough so I have time to work things out."

Breeze nodded and slipped him the plastic bag under the table. "Hope it's enough," he said. "Don't want this to get ugly."

"I've seen it ugly and it doesn't come out pretty," Pebbles said. Breeze started to ask him what he meant but stopped, and Pebbles said in a quick burst, "You showing up like this is just like a story I heard on my second tour."

"What story's that?" Breeze asked.

"It's about a rich Merchant in Baghdad who decides to throw a dinner party for his friends." Breeze smiled, and Pebbles drawled on. "Anyway, the merchant asks his servant to go to the market and buy a few things he'll need for the dinner. So the servant goes down to the marketplace and sees Death there."

"Death?" Breeze asked with a smile.

"Yeah, and Death gives the servant a weird look that frightens him so much he runs back to his Master without buying a thing. "I saw Death at the market and he gave me a strange look," the frightened servant tells him. The Master doesn't know what to say and the servant asks if he can go to his sister's house in Samarra for a few days to get away. The Merchant agrees and the frightened servant packs a bag and heads for his sister's house in Samarra several miles away."

"Makes sense," Breeze grunted.

"A little while later the Merchant goes down to the marketplace to buy the food for his dinner party, and he sees Death there too. The Merchant asks Death why he frightened his servant earlier that morning."

"I'm so sorry," Death apologized. "I didn't mean to frighten him. I was just surprised to see him because I have an appointment with him tomorrow in Samarra."

Breeze held his smile, but didn't say anything. He'd hurt Pebbles when he called him *icing on the cake* so Pebbles had punched back by referring to him as *Death*.

"That's just Arab fatalism," Breeze finally said. It's their way of removing guilt."

"Yeah," Pebbles nodded. "Good old fatalism."

"We don't believe in death here. It's against our religion. We just suck up the guilt and live with it. Besides, it's not my death, it's my Mom's death and it's her decision to make. We're just helping her."

"Maybe, but it's you I'm worried about not your Mom. She knows what she wants, you don't," Pebbles told him, and went back to eating his ham and eggs.

*

Abby always drove too fast. They'd gone grocery shopping in Wickenburg and he figured she was trying to get back before the visiting Nurse left the house.

"What's your hurry?" he asked.

"I don't want the frozen food and Mom's ice cream to melt before we get back. Besides, I noticed you didn't ask me to stop at the bus station for your suitcase," she said, picking up even more speed. "You didn't bring any bag, did you?" she asked, and waited for his answer. When it didn't come, she said, "What the hell are you doing here, Breeze?"

"She's my mother, too," he said.

"Maybe, but I'm still not up for killing her."

"Did she ask you to kill her?" Abby didn't answer, and he said, "She never told me she'd actually asked you."

"There are lots of things she doesn't tell her son."

They were going 80 in a 50 zone and Breeze leaned over and yelled, "Pull over, I've got to take a piss!"

Abby hit the brakes. They bounced off the road and the pickup rumbled to a stop in front of a large Joshua. "Thanks," Breeze mumbled, and stumbled down the slope to piss on the other side of the narrow tree.

"I still want to know what the hell you're doing here?" Abby yelled out the window.

"I hadn't heard from you and was worried about Mom."

"Why didn't you call ... or write?" she asked, getting out of the truck. "Or at least answer your fucking phone."

"I don't want to get into it with you, Abby," he said, pissing against the tree. "I've got things I have to do."

"What things, Breeze?"

"I left you with her and she hasn't gotten any better. In fact, she's gotten a lot worse."

"That doesn't mean we can't keep trying to save her," Abby yelled back, and stumbled down the slope on the other side of the tree.

"You get any closer you'll get soaked," he drawled.

"This isn't a goddamn men's room," she yelled.

"It's whatever we make it, girl."

"That's always been your trouble, Breeze. You think you're God Almighty!"

"Good old God quit being Almighty a long time ago, Abby," he said, zipping his fly. "Haven't you heard? God retired and He's living in a camper over in Quartzite with a bad drinking problem."

"That's a disgusting thing to say while you're pissing on one of His Joshua trees."

"You coming down here to watch me piss is what's disgusting."

Abby threw her keys at him and they hit his chest and landed in the dry soil between them. He stared back at her for a long moment, picked up the keys, and said, "I'll drive back." She didn't move and he stepped around her to the other side of the truck.

"You are one genuine Sonofabitch!" she snapped.

"It came natural 'cause my sister taught me everything she knew from the bottom up."

"What the hell are you doing here, Breeze?"

"I came back to rescue my boyhood buddy from a fate worse than death, Sister Lady."

It was the one thing Abby hadn't expected and she followed him halfway around the front of the truck yelling, "Stay the hell away from him, you miserable bastard!"

"Giving a man a little *poontang* doesn't give you the right to ruin his entire life."

"Getting married happens to be his idea, wise ass! Go back to Chicago where you belong. Leave us alone!"

Breeze stepped up into the truck, put the key in the ignition and the Chevy roared to a start. Abby kicked the front tire, climbed up into the truck on the passenger side, and sat waiting for him to roll.

"When you doing all this marrying stuff anyway?"

"Soon as I can ... so Mom can be there," she said.

"That old lady can hardly move, never mind go to some hick wedding of yours."

"Then we'll have our hick wedding in the damn house so she doesn't have to move," Abby yelled. "She could use something decent in her life for a change ... all she's got now is some half-assed wandering son. Getting married is the one decent thing I can give her before she goes ... an I'm planning to do just that."

"Yeah, well ... the world according to Abby."

"You Sonofabitch!"

Breeze rolled west on 60 and kept to the speed limit. The desert looked dry and parched, but dark clouds were beginning to roll in over the mountains and it would only be hours before the rain hit.

They drove in silence and he saw the visiting Nurse's Honda pass them on the other side of the road going east back to Wickenburg. He wasn't sure Abby had seen her car because she just kept staring ahead at the flat road that ran straight out in front of them. He'd never seen her like this. Even Pebbles seemed different. It wasn't that either one of them had changed ... but he had. He was the one that had drifted away from them. Now he felt alone in this dry, arid place that he didn't belong to anymore.

*

Breeze pulled the old Chevy in close to the house and he and Abby reached for the groceries at the same time. He headed in with the bags of frozen food and Abby followed with the rest of the groceries. He got to the porch steps and Pebbles opened the front door and ran out to help Abby. Breeze heard her say, "Thanks" and "Is she sleeping?" but he just kept going. He put the load of groceries on the counter and Pebbles shoved in the rest right next to them. They both turned to go and Abby said, "I'll put this stuff away."

Pebbles grunted and followed Breeze back to the living room. "Did you do it?" Breeze asked.

"She's gone," he said, "but it turned ugly."

"Jesus," Breeze mumbled, and headed for the back room. His mother was lying peacefully with one of the Indian pillows from the couch under her head. She looked twenty years younger than she had just a few hours before. The plastic bag on the IV stand had transformed into an empty wrinkle, and he hoped she had gone with a smile. He had tried to give her this one last thing, like flowers on Mother's Day or chocolate in the middle of February, and he began to cry in relief that it was over. She'd gotten what she wanted and he touched the hands folded across her silent chest and kissed her brow. They had been through a lot together and it felt like a part of him had been ripped away in some quick, brutal, clumsy moment.

He wiped his tears, picked up the rolled blanket where he'd left it on the chair, and went back out to the front porch and sat on the stairs next to Pebbles. They listened to Abby putting the groceries away in the kitchen.

Pebbles handed him a fistful of bills. "Santos will take you to the airport," he said. "Grab the red-eye back to Chicago. I'll call you after I deal with Abby."

"I owe you for this, bro."

"You don't owe me anything ... we're family," he said, and handed him back the plastic bag of heroin he'd brought from Chicago. "You can sell it when you get back. It was too risky to use." The refrigerator door closed in the kitchen. "You better get out of here before she figures it all out," Pebbles said. "Don't look back."

Breeze stuffed the plastic bag into his jacket, picked up his rolled blanket, and headed down the dusty road. The mountain clouds had dropped lower into the desert and the air began to smell like rain. He made a quick turn on one of the side streets, and walked toward Pebbles' empty melon field. He'd hide in the tall weeds where he'd seen the coyote, and hop the first freight headed north.

TUBA CITY

The road into the Navajo Nation runs circular through harsh open range. I'd been headed that way for hours, past clusters of mobile homes and modest ranch houses that dotted the wide, stark landscape of chaparral and tumbleweed.

Signs of the modern world popped into view like rising bubbles. A McDonald's appeared, and then a Taco Bell, and I could see a Wells Fargo Bank tucked in among the large mounds of earth that stood like secluded sentinels on either side of the two lane blacktop. A hand-painted sign appeared advertising DINOSAUR TRACKS. It leaned precariously against the burned out shell of an old Ford pickup. Further on a smaller sign read, "GO WARRIORS," and then finally a highway sign came into view saying, Tuba City. A pale horse hung his head solemnly over an old wooden fence and stared out at me as I slowed down to let a pickup truck, filled with firewood, make a wide turn up a dirt road. The horse's eyes stayed with me though, and as I passed, his steady gaze made me feel like an intruder that hadn't earned the right to see these simple things.

Usually these side trips ended with little accomplished except having done a favor for an old friend. The old friend in this case happened to be a man named Teddy Nighthorse whom I'd met in Tucson years ago. I associated Teddy with spring training and our love for baseball. We'd gotten into the habit of meeting in Tucson, at the end of a long winter, and making the rounds together. Usually, we'd run into each other at one of the morning batting practices. We'd lean against the mesh fence and watch the warm-weather ritual of men stepping into a crudely marked box to try and smash a speeding ball with one inch of a round bat.

As a scout for the Arizona Diamondbacks my territory included southern California and an occasional trip up the coast to spy on the Giants. But there were months to go before spring training began so Teddy's sudden phone call surprised me. He asked me to come up and take a peek at a young pitcher, something he'd never done before, so I reluctantly agreed.

Looking at young prospects usually took place in the formal setting of a high school or college game. Baseball scouts showed up to study particular players in the faint hope that they'd be good enough to recruit. There'd be pages of statistics to go through before you arrived. Then you'd have to deal with the particular expectations of the young player and his coach. Isolated cases like Tuba City were less formal and usually you just encouraged the young player and then turned around and went home. So when I made the left on Moenave Street I had the feeling it would be just another turn around day.

I saw Teddy standing under the trees in the middle of the street. He waved me toward a dirt driveway and pointed to a parking place directly in front of a battered dumpster. I began apologizing for being nearly an hour late but Teddy just smiled and said, "Did you bring the equipment?"

"Sure did," I said and opened the trunk to show him. The air had gotten colder, and the first thing I took out was my heavy leather jacket. A group of little Navajo boys surrounded us and stared into the trunk at my array of professional baseball equipment.

"This is just what we need," Teddy said as he picked up the catcher's equipment and opened a fresh box of baseballs. I reached in and grabbed one of the lighter bats and took my speed gun out of its leather case.

By the time I turned around Teddy had already started for the makeshift ball field behind us. I noticed how fit he looked for an older man. His straight white hair and leathery skin gave certain clues to his being somewhere in his sixties or early seventies. He moved slow and easy like an old cat and had probably been an athlete at one time. In all the years I'd known him we had never met outside a ballpark or talked about our past. I came out of the sandlots in the Bronx and Teddy had spent his life on an Indian reservation. That's all we knew about each other. We only talked about big league baseball and the approaching season. In fact, this was the first time I had ever ventured into what we both laughingly referred to as Teddy Country.

The group of nine-year-olds hung in close to us like a flock of colorful birds and helped Teddy carry the catcher's equipment to the broken-down backstop. On a signal from the old man one of the boys took off across Moenave Street and disappeared into a faded white building with a hand-painted sign over its front door that read First Presbyterian Church. I didn't know what the procedure would be but Teddy seemed to have everything under control.

"You did say the kid is left-handed … didn't you?" I asked while Teddy strapped on a chest protector and shin guards.

"Yeah, he's a southpaw and I'm waiting to see what he registers on that speed gun you brought," he said, punching the catcher's mitt.

I held out a shiny white baseball to see which dark-haired little kid would step up and throw the ball at him but they just giggled and backed away.

"I sent one of the kids across the street to get him," Teddy said and I nodded as two of the boys picked up the box of baseballs and carried them out to the recently graded pitcher's mound. Teddy waddled over to the backstop to brush off home plate and fill in the rain-rutted area around the batter's box with his cowboy boots. He seemed nervous and I could hear him telling the boys to stay out of the way.

I looked around at the few rows of stands, in need of paint, that ran the edge of the field along the baselines. I walked slowly across the infield and noticed a large patch of crab grass and weeds had been recently dug out and reseeded. I stepped around it, took out my measuring tape, and waved to one of the little boys to come over and hold the end of it at the top of the pitcher's mound while I unraveled sixty and one half feet to the plate. I smiled over at Teddy still working on the batter's box and said, "This field may not look like much but it's got perfect distance from the mound to home plate."

"I didn't want the kid throwing the wrong distance so I measured and readjusted the whole thing," he said. "The height of the mound was a little trickier but I think we got that about right, too."

I rolled up the tape and glanced out at the school building behind the dumpsters. For the first time I noticed the windows were jammed with people. The left-handed kid had fans. The faces in the windows suddenly turned in unison to look at something through the leafless trees along Moenave Street. That's when I first saw him.

Large, lumbering, and a bit overweight, he had a strong determination in his step as he headed directly for the backstop. His high cheekbones made his round face look even bigger, and a shock of black hair hung straight to his shoulders. He had on a bright red sweatshirt, blue jeans, and torn sneakers that were actually held together with pieces of string. Under his arm he carried an old, flat baseball glove that looked homemade and, as he went past the stands, he playfully rubbed each boy's head with it for good luck.

"This is Nick Costa. The man I told you about," Teddy said. When the kid extended his hand I could hardly grasp it all in mine. His handshake was gentle, almost weak, but his smile was big and strong. "This is Harold Bromley, the kid I wanted you to look at," Teddy said from behind the catcher's mask.

"Everyone around here just calls me Shoe," the kid said.

"That's short for Big Shoe," Teddy added.

"Shoe. That's just fine."

"I've already warmed up."

"Great. Let's get started," I said, and Teddy squatted down behind the plate.

"How old are you?" I asked the kid as we walked out to the mound.

"Almost eighteen," he answered and bent over to take one of the new baseballs out of the box. I watched his every move to see if he had any kind of an injury or handicap, or might be physically compensating for anything, but he moved smoothly around the mound. He flipped the ball to the plate in an easy warm-up motion and when Teddy threw the ball back he caught it as if he'd been doing it his whole life. He threw in another pitch a little faster, and I watched his arm motion to see where he released the ball and where he ended up on the mound after the delivery.

"You gonna put the gun on my fast ball?" he asked with a smile.

"Ever have that done before?"

"No," he said. "Should be fun."

I had never heard anyone refer to the speed gun as *fun* before. Usually you tried to hide the gun from a young kid or even a professional when their speed began to drop late in a game. The big league ballparks had even begun to display the speed of a pitch on the scoreboards. That put more pressure on the pitcher and the batters. But this kid looked at the speed gun as *fun*. I liked his attitude.

It felt like a storm rolling in and I glanced up at the school building. The lights had been turned on making it easier to see the people watching us from the windows.

"Whenever you're ready just let me know," I said, pulling up the collar on my leather jacket.

"Guess I'm ready," the big kid said.

"Just relax and give me a straight fast ball."

"Want me to try an' hit the corner?" he said.

"Why not?" I said and set the speed gun.

The kid nodded at Teddy crouched behind the plate, and he gave him a target on the inside corner for a left-handed batter. The kid went into a short windup and came down hard off the mound. His arm came across his body like a whip, and I heard him grunt as he released the ball. It slammed into the catcher's mitt. When I looked down, the gun read ninety-eight miles an hour. I got a chill just calculating what the kid might do with a good pair of shoes.

"What'd it read?" the kid asked.

"Oh, 'round ninety," I said.

"Did I really hit ninety?"

"Yeah, but you always want to be careful where you throw the ball. That's the important thing. You hung that one a little too far over the plate. You've got natural speed so you want to think about *where* you're throwing the ball rather than how fast."

The kid nodded, and said, "I been working on location with Teddy. But it helps if I have a batter up there."

The kid definitely had the speed so I put down the gun. "I'll get up there for you," I said.

"Thanks," he said.

I walked slowly back down to where Teddy stood with the catcher's mitt and picked up a bat. "How fast did it read, Nick?" he asked.

"Ninety-eight miles an hour," I said.

"I knew it," he replied in a whisper.

I stood at the plate with the bat on my left shoulder and stared out at the kid. He looked big and impressive on the mound. I could feel Teddy crouch down along the inside corner just behind me. The big kid went into his windup and then exploded out of it. I picked up the ball about halfway down the chute and heard it smaaaack into the catcher's mitt. The pitch had good lateral movement on it and slammed in right under my hands across the inside corner.

Teddy flipped the ball back out to the kid and said, "That felt faster than the last one."

"How tall is he?" I asked.

"Almost six-five," Teddy said.

"And his weight?"

"That's a problem. Kid needs structure. A program. I can only do so much. Getting him to lay off the Big Macs and bend over and touch his toes is something else."

I nodded my understanding and looked out at the overweight kid on the mound in the red sweatshirt. Even with what I had just seen he'd be considered for some kind of a contract because we always looked for left-handers with speed. Throwing from the left side is preferred in the big leagues because the right field fences are usually shorter. With good speed and control it's that much harder for a left-handed batter to get around on the ball and pull it down the right field line into the stands. The left-handed pitcher also has the advantage of facing first base and keeping a runner close to the bag. That makes it harder to steal or even get a good lead. It means fewer stolen bases, more double plays, and fewer runs scored by the opposing team. The advantage of having a good left-handed pitcher out on the mound is enormous to a big league team.

"Now I want you to throw the ball on the inside corner about knee-high with the same speed that you just gave me with the last one," I yelled out to him. Whether Shoe knew it or not I had asked for the pitch that either made the major league left-hander or broke him. The kid just smiled, went into his windup, and I tried to concentrate on when and where he released the ball. I only saw the ball when it got close and cut in at knee level along the inside corner. Then heard the BAAAAMMM when it hit the catcher's mitt.

"What kind of pitch did he just throw?" I asked.

"A splitter."

"He got anything else?"

"I got him working a fork ball but it's not ready."

"What about a change-up?"

"He's got one but it needs work. He doesn't throw it with the same exact motion that he uses with the fast ball so a good hitter could read it and know it's coming."

"I'd still like to see it."

"Get ready," he said.

Shoe took the sign from Teddy, and I watched him go into his windup. He came out of it with a slight hitch so I adjusted my swing and hit a screaming line drive down the right field line. He looked stunned when the ball caromed off the building out in right field. Three of the younger kids ran out to retrieve it.

"He's just got a different direction in his windup when he throws his change-up. He comes into it from further out on the mound," I said. "Have him work on keeping his arm motion in tight and it'll make all the difference especially if he uses it with the splitter."

Teddy smiled and said, "Check."

"I can get one of the coaches to work with him. Show him how to throw a few different change-ups."

"That'll help," Teddy said.

"I'd like to see how he looks with a right-handed batter in there," I said. "Sometimes that kind of thing can be an enormous problem. I've even seen it break a good left-hander."

"This kid doesn't have that kind of problem," he muttered.

I stepped over home plate and put the bat up on my right shoulder to see how he'd deal with me from the other side. He leaned forward and I could feel Teddy go into a crouch behind me.

Then the kid did something I had never seen in all my years in baseball. He flipped that weird homemade

33

baseball glove onto his left hand and went into his windup from the other side. Before I realized what had happened he fired a knee-high pitch straight down the middle at about ninety-five miles an hour with his *right* arm.

"What the hell did that kid just do?" I asked.

"I wanted you to see it rather than try and explain it," Teddy said, flipping the ball back out to the mound.

"Does he have the same control from both sides?"

"Yeah, but I think he's faster from the left."

"Let's see his splitter from the right side," I said in quiet shock. Teddy knelt down. The kid took the sign, went into his windup, and spun out of it in a red blur. I picked up the ball somewhere near home plate and watched it hook sharply in under the narrow part of the bat and slaaaam into the catcher's mitt. The row of dark-haired kids in the stands cheered wildly.

"Put a jacket on him. We're finished for now," I said.

"Sure you've seen enough?"

"It's getting cold. I don't want him to tighten up. Besides, what else is there?"

"He's a pretty good fielder. Ain't a bad hitter either."

I held up my hands, smiled numbly at him, and he trotted out to tell the kid that he could go and get a hamburger or just head home. The tryout had ended. What I'd just seen could turn the game of baseball upside down and inside out. Take it up another notch. A pitcher like that could double his output of pitches per game simply by being able to throw the ball over ninety miles an hour with either arm, and also have an advantage over the switch-hitters. I didn't think there were any rules in the book to cover it and at this point I didn't care.

I could see Teddy talking with him out on the mound before they headed back towards me. The kid stuck out his hand and I took it. "Thanks for coming, Mr. Costa," he said. "Nice meeting you."

"I'll be in touch," I said, "but you'll probably have to come down to Phoenix for a few days."

The kid didn't answer but Teddy nodded and said, "I made appointments with some other scouts, Nick." I must've looked surprised because he followed up quickly with, "I didn't know whether the powers down in Phoenix were open for a new pitcher like Shoe here."

"They're always open for left-handers with speed," I said, not mentioning the incredible fact that the kid threw from both sides.

"There's a storm coming in. You better put your jacket on before you tighten up," Teddy said, and the kid threw a halfhearted wave to the both of us and headed back across the street to the church.

"What scouts did you make appointments with?" I asked and tried not to sound annoyed.

"Tom Purvis and Steve Merton," Teddy said and looked away. Then he handed me back the catcher's mask and said, "The kid doesn't think he did very well."

"He did fine. Better than fine."

"That line drive you hit made him think he failed the tryout."

"Did you tell him I knew his change-up was coming?"

"Yeah, but he didn't believe me."

"The young ones are like that," I said and tried to change the subject. "How big a foot does he really have?"

"Twelve ... twelve and a half wide and still growing."

Teddy started to take off the catcher's gear and I said, "Tell him I'll set up a tryout for him down in Phoenix right away. I'm not sure the pitching coach is in town but I could get the owner to come out and take a look."

Teddy didn't answer. When he finished taking off the shin guards we started back across the infield together. I had never talked business with Teddy before and I felt uncomfortable. Things weren't the same in Tuba City as they were in Tucson. I didn't know what to say. Teddy's silence seemed to make the situation clear and I couldn't help feeling betrayed by what I'd thought was an old friend.

"I think this kid should be on the Arizona team," I said as casually as I could. "It's where he belongs."

"Because he's an Indian?" Teddy said.

I hesitated and then said, "No, because he's a Navajo."

Teddy smiled and looked at me with the same kind of suspicious stare that the pale horse had given me on the way in. I felt even more like the intruding outsider as I waited for his answer.

"I've got to do what's right for the kid," he said.

I had to be careful of what I came up with here. The tryout had been the shortest and fastest I'd ever conducted. Something told me that Teddy knew it'd go that way even before I arrived. He'd dragged me all the way up to Tuba City just to put me into a bidding situation with the competition.

I opened the trunk of the car in silence. Teddy dropped in the catcher's equipment while one of the boys put back the box of baseballs. I repacked the speed gun, slid in the bat, and stood there for a long, uncertain moment in front of the open trunk. Teddy didn't look at me. When he started to close the trunk I stopped him and took out my checkbook. "The kid deserves a deal," I said, and quickly wrote out my personal check to Harold "Big Shoe" Bromley for two thousand dollars. On the back of the check I wrote, "I knew your change-up was coming otherwise I wouldn't have gotten near it."

I handed the check to Teddy and said, "Cancel those appointments you have with Tom and Steve. I'll set up the Phoenix tryout as fast as I can."

Teddy looked at my personal check and smiled at what I had written on the back. "I really never made those appointments with Tom and Steve," he said, but didn't crack his usual smile.

"Then why did you tell me you did?" I asked.

"I needed to give the kid something," he said, staring down at the check. "Something real. Something of value." He stopped talking and looked up at me. "This kid needs that," he said. "All these kids need that."

I began to understand what had just happened. I might be an outsider in Tuba City but Teddy was an outsider too. He'd always been an outsider. And for the first time I knew that was the look I'd seen in his eyes before. "Make sure the kid gets a new pair of shoes and a baseball glove with some of that money," I said. "But don't cash it until Thursday."

He laughed and seemed to relax. Then he waved my check in the air and said, "This'll make the kid happy. He can call himself a pro now."

"It'll make me happy too," I said and handed the Navajo kids the box of baseballs they had just put back into the trunk.

"You don't have to do that," Teddy said.

I gave the kids a couple of bats to go with the balls and said, "Let's just say it's an investment for the future and leave it at that." The row of dark-haired boys looked up expectantly for Teddy's approval.

"I'm going to need your help with this kid," I said.

"I'm glad you understand that," he answered.

I started to get into the car but then extended my hand, and it surprised Teddy because in all the years we had known each other we never shook hands. The big Navajo smile came across his chiseled face and he opened his arms and embraced me. For the first time since we'd met I felt close to him. A friend.

"We'll see you in Phoenix," he said.

I started the car and the kids ran down Moenave Street, waving their new bats and balls. I made the turn, headed out past the burned out pickup, and the "GO WARRIORS" sign while the pale horse nibbled contentedly on the sagebrush. If my luck held I'd make the low desert before the storm hit.

UNDER THE CICADAS

Teddy finished cutting the weeds that had crept up the walk and into his old tomato patch behind the house. He hung the whacker in the shed, slipped out of his work gloves, and saw Cody coaxing the big bay through the far gate. The boy tied his horse to the end post, checked to make sure his fly was zipped, and lowered his new cowboy straw against the glare of the August sun. Teddy had told him to "stay away from the proceedings," but he'd shown up anyway ... in his cowboy boots.

Cody's father had been one of Teddy's backers through a tedious eight years in Congress. Teddy had always counted on Old Fritz for that extra bag of cash he needed to win an election. Fritz had it, gave it, and expected things for it. Teddy made sure the open cattle range continued as the modern rancher's credo, and that water remained at what Fritz referred to as "a fair price." When the old man died everyone assumed that Teddy would retire, become Mayor, and adopt Cody. Teddy kept the little house and the land Fritz had given him along the southern edge of the Schumacher ranch, became the town's mayor, but never adopted Cody. No one did.

"Mr. Mayor," Cody yelled across the yard. Teddy looked up in a faked surprise. "He here yet?" Teddy shook his head. "Think he'll show?"

"If you showed ... I guess he will."

"I'm just surprised *he's* not here ... it's getting late," Cody said, ignoring the sarcasm.

"Lawyers are always late, son. They don't like looking hungry. It's undignified."

A low cloud of dust rose along the outer road and Earl's white 250 Ford truck rushed into view between the trees. The slow crescendo of clicking cicadas began to rise and their steady hum enveloped the yard. "Sure you want to hang around for this?" Teddy yelled over the cicadas' clicking. "I'm just going to feel him out."

"Thought I might help you push the load."

"Nobody pushes Big Earl," Teddy said, watching the white truck race up the dirt road while another wave from the cicadas rushed over them in the August heat.

"We're giving him an awesome deal no matter how you cut it," Cody yelled back, and headed for the house.

Teddy shook his head at the boy's remark and waited for the white truck to pull into the driveway. Big Earl stepped out and sauntered across the yard. He walked with a slight stoop but Teddy still had to reach up to shake his hand. "Isn't that Cody's bay?" Earl asked.

"Certainly is," Teddy mumbled, as their boots thumped across the porch. "Can I get you some iced tea?"

"That would do fine," Earl said.

Teddy opened the small fridge behind the screen. "I can stiffen it up, if you'd like."

"Just the tea," Earl said, grasping the frosted glass before Teddy could pour any bourbon into it.

"Hope you don't think I'm trying to talk you into anything here, Counselor," Teddy said, lacing his own tea with the bourbon and ice.

"Hell no," the big man said. "I figure you've got a lot on your mind these days and need some answers."

Teddy liked that about Big Earl. He got right to the point. In his way he saved more sweat, grime, and bullshit than anyone he'd ever known. He cut to the bone by just speaking his mind. Most people in town were God-fearing Christians that believed in those pretty Biblical words printed on thin paper. They had put up with Earl's straight talk for years because if they got into trouble it was Earl they wanted to defend them and they paid plenty for the privilege.

Big Earl never cared much about how the truth got to the table just as long as it managed to get there. Teddy respected that about the big guy and admitted that whenever the platter of truth showed up at his end he just passed it on to the person sitting next to him.

"I figure you're looking for some free advice from a good defense lawyer," Earl said.

Teddy gave out a big laugh and a short nod. "You've got me cold," he said.

"This whole thing's really up to you," Earl told him.

Cody came into the room, glanced over at Teddy, and sat down. "What're they saying down at the courthouse?" Teddy asked, ignoring the kid.

"That the whole thing's about a few people having a meeting and forgetting to get a permit," Earl said. "It's just their way of trying to brush it under the carpet to protect you. Trouble is, it keeps blowing back out at them." Big Earl laughed at his own joke and looked over at the kid, and said, "The fact that the meeting was held at two in the morning on federal property with over a hundred people attending is why it keeps blowing back out from under that carpet."

"They can't prove it," Cody said, jumping up.

"Were you there, son?" Earl asked.

"Yeah, I was there," the kid said, and seemed glad someone had finally asked him outside of the courthouse.

"Did anyone see you there?"

"Sure," Cody admitted. "I invited a few people over to my ranch ... private property. And I can prove it."

There was an uncomfortable silence, and Big Earl finally said, "Several noteworthy witnesses say otherwise, including two ministers and a police officer. They say it was not your property and that the number of people that were there couldn't possibly fit into your living room. That means the prosecutor will be questioning your ability to count ... and to know where you are at any given time of the day or night." The kid looked sullen and sat down again. "Even if what you say is true," Earl went on, "this thing could turn into a circus. It's close to that now. Why don't you just pay the fine and hope the damn thing fades into everlasting County paper work?"

"If we do that then we admit we did it," Cody said.

"They might just take it as a *beau geste.*"

The kid looked confused, and Teddy quickly asked, "You think they really might, Earl?"

"Don't know. Paying the fine will at least take the smell off it a bit."

The cicadas stopped their high clicking and the three men listened to the ice hitting the side of Earl's glass as he took another slug of the cold tea. Earl leaned back and said, "There's a firm down in Phoenix that specializes —"

"We don't want outsiders in this," Cody said.

"You ought to get the best, son," Earl told him.

"We decided to keep it in the family," Teddy said, glancing over at Cody. "Less publicity the better. But we wanted your opinion before we went any further."

"I just gave you my opinion."

"You don't think there's a lawyer here that could —"

"Call Phoenix and be done with it," Earl insisted. "They have more experience with these things, and you'll need that if Singleton is prosecuting."

Teddy poured some more tea into Earl's glass, and said, "Singleton's given the case over to his assistant."

"Singleton's assistant isn't ready for anything like this. He just got out of law school ... barely passed the bar. He couldn't argue a traffic ticket."

Teddy watched the change of expression come into Earl's eyes when he figured out they'd played a political card to keep the regular prosecuting attorney off the case. "Could be a break for your side though," Earl admitted. "But be careful. These things can backfire."

"How's that?" Cody asked.

"Sometimes young enthusiasm goes a long way. The kid may be inexperienced, but he's not dumb. He might dig a lot deeper than his boss. And if he gets together with one of those hotshot reporters on *The Courier* the whole thing could blow out of control. If that boy starts to dig he might find all kinds of things. Your relationship with Cody, how you got this house, and the ranch itself would be open for investigation."

"That's none of their business," Cody said.

"Exactly," Earl said. "There are lots of questions people don't ask because they don't want to hear the answers. But it's situations like this that force them to ask those questions. It's one thing to be thrown out of office, Teddy, but it's something else if they throw the *both* of you in jail along with it. I think you should bring in the Phoenix boys," Earl said again. "They're straight and fast. They'll do a quick plea bargain and it'll be over."

The room got quiet and Cody headed for the door in a rush. "Be right back," he yelled over his shoulder.

"What's that kid up to?" Big Earl asked.

"You got me," Teddy said with a shrug. "He does the craziest things. I can't figure him out anymore."

"No one ever expected you to. He's damaged goods and you know it." Teddy looked up in surprise. It was unusual for Big Earl to reveal his hand like that. "Does he know how bad a situation he's in?" Earl asked. "If he knowingly lied to a Grand Jury about where —"

"I think he's beginning to figure that out."

"Are you holding something back on me, Teddy?" Earl took in a deep breath. "Did you drag me out here to ask if I was up to taking your case?"

"I just wanted your opinion before we did anything."

"I didn't think *anyone* in this town gave a rat's ass about my opinion ... except in the courtroom."

"This town doesn't *like* hearing the truth, Earl. I'm different. I just don't like spreading it around. Truth can be toxic to a politician."

Earl finished his tea and listened to the cicadas. "How do you stand those bugs hanging over you like that?" he asked. "They're so noisy I can't hear myself think."

"They show up a few weeks in the dog-days, make a lot of clatter, then disappear for the rest of the year."

"They're a goddamn menace," Earl said.

"Maybe, but the old man *gave* me this property and I figure I got a pretty good deal," Teddy said.

"An even better deal is to get the best lawyer you can and crawl out of this mess you're in."

"Are you that lawyer, Earl?" Teddy asked.

"In this town ... probably," the big man said, "but I still think you should make that call to Phoenix."

"That's an honest answer."

"I happen to know the prosecution has pictures of the license plates of everyone attending that meeting. They know who was there because *they* were there. You broke the law and they caught you. It's as simple as that."

"I couldn't resist," Teddy mumbled. "There were a lot of votes out there that night."

"Maybe, but the voters that weren't out there are the ones that can vote you out of office for what you did."

"That's already been suggested. Someone's trying to make an example of me. But it wasn't like that. I was worried about Cody so I went along. Those ranchers down Dewey way got him convinced the Latino's are taking over the county ... and that the world will end if they do."

"That crowd thinks terrorists and drug dealers are in their coffee beans."

"That's not all. Somebody's been sneaking on to the ranches at night and gunning their cows. They don't steal them ... just shoot 'em up and leave 'em to die. It's got them spooked."

"Have they reported it?" Earl asked.

"Hell, no. They're fighting mad and determined to take care of it themselves ... and in their own way."

"Hope there isn't some stray fruit picker hanging around or their next meeting might turn into a lynching."

"Jesus, I never looked at it that way."

Big Earl saw a movement out the window. Cody was heading for the back door with a large white box. "What's that kid up to?" Earl asked again.

"Damned if I know," Teddy muttered in a low moan.

"He's lied to a Grand Jury and been caught at it. Does he understand what that means?"

"I tried explaining it to him but he's got his own sense of justice. His world comes cut and dried."

"Like shooting cows?"

"Jesus, you don't think —"

"You better find a law firm … and fast, Teddy."

Cody burst into the room with the big white box under his arm. "Don't want you thinking we dragged you out here just to pick your brain, sir," he said to Earl as if he'd been rehearsing it in the back room.

Big Earl glanced at Teddy, put down his ice tea, and opened the box. A rush of smooth black material slipped out over his arm. Teddy knew exactly what it was but hadn't expected Cody to go that far. He reached out to catch the material before it hit the floor and shoved a business envelope into Earl's hand. "Congratulations," he muttered. "Should've given you this earlier." Earl stared down at the envelope and the material on his arm. "Read it," Teddy said. "It's signed and delivered."

"The Governor's office," Earl muttered, opening the envelope and taking out the letter. "He's appointed me the County's new criminal-court judge."

"Said he knew you."

"Yeah, we suffered through law school together," Earl muttered, refolding the letter and stuffing it back into the long envelope. "Too bad the Governor's headed for jail. That's what happens out here when you marry into money.

You're either thrown on a boring bank board and get caught fiddling with loan votes like he did, or you get elected and sent off to D.C. Either way ... you lose," he said, glancing at Teddy.

"We were the ones that recommended you," Cody said in a rush as if he hadn't heard anything Earl had just said. "Try it on, try it on," the kid insisted, lifting the rest of the black cloth out of the box and holding it up.

"Thank you," Earl mumbled, putting his arms through the large openings.

"You'll get used to it," Cody said, smoothing the purple stripes that ran up the edge of the bloused sleeves.

Teddy could see the suspicion creeping back into Earl's eyes again. "I don't know what to say," the tall man mumbled, staring down at the robe that turned him into a judge.

"Don't say anything," Teddy said. "You've got the job and no one can take it from you."

"That's the system," Cody said. "All legal like."

Earl looked uncomfortable, shifting in the robe until it finally fell into place across his shoulders. "I better call Bobbie and tell her," he said.

"Of course, use the phone in the bedroom," Teddy said, pointing toward the back of the house.

When the bedroom door closed, Cody whispered across the room, "Who the hell is Bobbie?"

"His wife," Teddy whispered. "You pushed too hard and too fast, kid. I told you I'd handle this but —"

"I don't hear anything in there," Cody said, moving closer to the door to listen.

"That's 'cause he's not talking to anybody, so get away from that door. He's in there trying to figure this thing out. Earl's nobody's fool. He picked up on that Singleton move like a hound dog, and you bringing in that goddamn robe just made things worse. I told you lawyers don't like looking hungry. You can't force something like this on a guy like Earl. Jesus, I had no idea he went to school with the Governor. He's probably right about that bastard going to jail too. Harvard Law, my ass."

"We just did him a favor, for Christ's sake."

"You don't do favors for guys like Big Earl. You've got to make guys like that think they're doing *you* the favor," Teddy said, pouring more tea and hitting it with a large splash of bourbon. "Just leave me alone with him. Maybe I can salvage this thing."

"I can't believe he's not on the phone in there," Cody said, listening at the bedroom door again. "No Harvard guy turns down being a judge. It's unpatriotic."

"We're sliding on black ice here, boy. And we been on it ever since you put that damn cross up at the meeting."

"Those people take that cross stuff serious, Teddy. That's why they were in their white robes. They love crosses. Besides, you said it was all about votes!"

"You didn't have to set the goddamned thing on fire!"

"The guys on the fire truck told me it was okay."

Cody heard something move in the bedroom and jumped away from the door, knocking over a small side table next to the stuffed chair. Magazines flew across the floor and Cody tried picking them up before Earl got to the door. The large man rushed back into the room with the opened robe swirling around him. "Think I'll try some of that bourbon now," he said, grabbing the bottle of Wild Turkey and pouring it into his iced tea.

"Did you get Bobbie?" Teddy asked.

"She didn't quite believe it," Earl said, gulping the tea. "She never liked the Governor and he knew it, so she can't quite figure why he'd do something like this for me. She's got this idea that they'll assign me to this dumb Ku Klux Klan case that you're tied up in. She thinks the whole thing's going to be a fast trial. Open and shut." Cody glanced at Teddy, but didn't move. "What's got her curiosity going is this first-time judge, first-time prosecutor thing. It puts the trial in an almost automatic appeal situation. Like the whole thing is being set up. Thrown to the appeals court down in Phoenix. That's what the defense is counting on." He gave out a sudden laugh, and said, "I forgot to mention the robe to her, Cody. Sorry about that. She would've gotten a kick out of it."

"That's all right, sir," Cody mumbled.

"Of course, I could recuse myself and they'd have to appoint another judge," Earl went on. "Or we could keep this little meeting of ours a secret ... like it never happened."

"That's the best idea you've had all day," Teddy said, glancing over at Cody picking up the magazines.

"I suppose we could work out some general terms right now and get that out of the way," Earl said. "Bobbie's been wanting to move out this way for a long time. I told her you had some ranch property up for sale at a great price, Cody. She jumped at it. Those six or seven acres of bottomland you've got tucked up against Teddy's place ought to do fine. A thousand dollars an acre sounded pretty reasonable to her."

"Hell, that bottomland's worth a lot more than —"

"We'll have to make the deal before the trial date's set. She'll pay cash, of course."

"It's a great spot for a house," Teddy said quickly, trying to cover Cody's confusion. "She'll love it out here. Maybe I can even pick up a few horses for you."

"That might make it messy. Everything's got to be legal and at least look above board."

"Of course," Teddy agreed. "I'll have the lawyers get the sale papers out to you immediately," he said, smiling over at Cody.

Big Earl slipped out of the robe and folded it back into the white box. "Thank you, son. This was a beautiful thought ... and kind of you," he said, heading for the door.

"I'll go down and report to the courthouse with this letter while you get that land agreement postdated."

"No problem," Teddy said, stepping out into the yard with Big Earl under a crescendo of cicadas. "I didn't have anything to do with this robe business, Earl," he yelled over the cicadas' clicking.

"I know," Earl said, handing the white box back to him. "That kid will drag us all down if we let him. He's crazy stupid. You think he bought that robe in the same place they make the Klan's white ones?" Earl jumped into the truck before Teddy could answer. The low growl of the engine blended into the high clicking sounds over them. "Tell that kid I'll buy my own uniform for the job. It comes with the territory."

Earl's truck started for the road and Teddy turned back toward the house with the white box under his arm. Halfway across the yard he saw Cody coming at him with the double-barreled shotgun. Teddy looked back toward Earl's truck but it had already made the turn on to the main road. He made a quick run for the shed but Cody cut him off and Teddy raised the white box with the judge's robe in it for protection.

Earl heard the explosion and thought he'd blown a tire, but the truck held the road. The clicking waves from the cicadas rose in a quick tremendous roar and he slowed the truck down to listen. When the shotgun's second round came the clicking stopped in a deafening silence. Earl picked up speed, reached the main road, and made the turn for home to show Bobbie the Governor's letter. After they discussed it he'd drive down to the courthouse and get his first assignment.

ARIZONA PIE

The early morning light hit the window and Pearce carried his clothes downstairs to dress in front of the potbellied stove. Throwing his denim jacket over the TV, he slipped into a red flannel shirt and pulled on his jeans. He opened the front closet, took out an extra denim jacket, and reached up to the top shelf for the cowboy hats. Plopping the brown hat on his head, he dusted the black one across his sleeve, looked into the clouded mirror next to the front door, hesitated, but then pulled on his boots.

The thin ice crunched along the frosted path when he stepped into the morning chill. A sheep dog's nervous bark echoed across the cobblestones. A coyote had probably slipped into the neighborhood looking for a quick kill. The horses on the hill remained quiet. Whatever prowled the streets had decided to stay on the other side of town where the sun began to break through the mist.

Pearce lifted the heavy plastic off the motorcycle and its chrome gave off a ghostly glow in the early light. He took hold of the dark leather seat and steadied it. His brother had bought the cycle at a police auction. A cream line snaked across its maroon fender, ran down along the gas tank, and back over the glistening wheels in a never-ending turn. It was an Electra Glide that the cycle mags had tabbed the *Panhead*. He mounted her, released the break, and rolled down Hill Street. At the county road he kicked it into gear, roared down the mountain, and headed for the low desert.

*

Pearce rolled into the parking lot fifteen minutes ahead of schedule, curled the Harley under the shade of a Palos Verde and stared up at the razor wire that ran the top of the high wall. A guard in the tower pointed down at the dusty road where a bus with bars on its windows rolled toward them. It veered into the parking lot, made a wide turn, and pulled up at the prison entrance. A string of men stepped out in single file. Shoulders bent, hands cuffed. They were herded toward a gate and disappeared into its deep shadows. The rows of pickup trucks began to open. People headed for the gate as the guards led another group out of the prison toward the empty bus. Some of the women began to wave. A few of the men peeled off the line spreading their arms to catch the children that ran at them. Speaking in whispers, they walked back to the pickups. Pearce moved in closer to study the rest of the men. One of them lowered his head and Pearce recognized his brother. Cropped hair, short steps, and ten years thinner.

The rest of the men waited in line to be checked off the guard's list before disappearing into the bus. Pearce had gotten in so close he could almost touch them. He started to tell the guard that he'd come to pick up his brother but Chino's raspy voice shot out at him. "Don't listen to anything that shit says. I'm about to rip his heart out."

"Thought you might like a lift home," Pearce said, moving down the line of men. "Brought your Panhead."

"Fuck off!"

When he'd gotten in close, Chino reached out to grab him but the Latino next to him stepped in to cut him off. "You ain't even off the premises and you're trying to get back in," the Latino said.

"I don't need no fucking lift," Chino rasped.

"He's trying to be your friend," the man drawled, stuffing a folded piece of paper into Chino's pocket.

"You got a problem, Safford?" a guard shouted.

"My brother, sir," Chino said.

"You're either on the bus or off the bus," the guard said. "It's a lift to Phoenix, not a family picnic."

Pearce shoved the black cowboy hat into Chino's hand. His brother took it, reshaped the brim, and slipped it on his head. It didn't fit because of the short-cropped hair, so he cocked it down over his forehead.

"Bring anything else with you besides my denim, my Harley, and my hat?" he asked.

Pearce opened his jacket to show him the pint of Wild Turkey he had stowed in his belt. Chino quickly covered the bottle with his hat before the guard could see it. "Still as crazy as ever," he said. He leaned back, whispered something to the Latino, and headed across the parking lot with Pearce. "Take care, boys," he yelled to the men getting on the bus.

"We'll keep a light on for you," the guard yelled back.

"Fuck you, pension boy," Chino muttered as Pearce flipped him his denim jacket. "I got to wash out this ten year prison shit, bro. First time you see some pines ... pull over. I'll finish the Wild Turkey, kick in your kidneys, and leave you to die."

"Can't do that. The guys are waiting for us up in Jerome ... betting big numbers. We owe it to them."

"They're giving odds on me killing you?"

"The numbers are posted all over town."

"Who's the favorite?"

"Right now ... you're eight to five. Last week you were two to one."

"That's because I'm an ex-con," Chino said, slipping the pint of Wild Turkey out of Pearce's belt.

"How about stopping at Pinnacle Peak? We'll get steak and eggs ... and those biscuits you like."

"Just as long as I don't have to stand in a fucking line," Chino said, sliding onto the seat behind his brother. He took one last look at the men getting on the bus and the Harley exploded to a start.

*

Chino had sensed it even before they reached the interstate. More traffic, more trucks, and a lot more mobile homes dotted the landscape. Miles of desert filled with chain-restaurants, shopping centers, and gas stations. Even his secret dirt paths had been paved. They'd left nothing untouched. The guards and the new cons had told him about the great changes going on outside, but he refused to believe them until now. He felt like he'd been in a terrible accident. Thrown through a windshield and into a place he vaguely recognized. There'd been war in the Mideast, social upheavals, three presidents, four governors, and a new millennium. The world had changed on him.

By the time they hit the interstate the clear desert morning had grown warmer. They rolled north at eighty miles an hour, skirting endless lines of lumbering RV's with names like Bounder and EZ Spirit. Neon signs seemed to erupt out of the desert like wild flowers: Gasoline, Casinos, Golf, and Family Dining. Pearce pushed the Harley into the fast lane and Chino could see the valley up ahead. The whole landscape seemed to lift out of the desert like a broken spoke, with rivers of freeways, houses, and golf courses.

"Where the hell are we?" he yelled over the wind.

"Phoenix," Pearce yelled back. "Got big, eh?"

"Where'd they all come from?"

"Back East, California, Midwest. Nice homes. Big cars. Golf courses, swimming pools, and malls."

Chino took a quick sip of the Wild Turkey and stared at the spectacle. Pearce moved into the right lane and headed north. Traffic merged and they rolled across the concrete ribbon and down past towers of glass. The traffic thinned as they headed up into the mountains and the scattered sentinels of saguaro began to disappear. A new kind of light seemed to glare through the polluted air and endless sky. He needed to do something fast if he didn't want to be crushed in it like a piece of road-kill.

*

By the time Mackey had gotten to work the breakfast bunch were already at the counter. Liberty, the waitress, filled their coffee mugs in the tense silence. Woo Woo Hutchins sat at the end of the counter eating his seven flapjacks on two plates. J.J. Fitz sat next to him cutting into his three-egg omelet. Slade Perkins slumped at the other end piercing his bright yellow egg yokes until they ran into the fries. Two-Bear Jones sat between them eating his biscuits with the usual side order of burnt bacon.

Several new customers sat in the booths. It'd taken Mackey months to get used to them and the packed tourist buses that descended on the cafe every afternoon with people she'd never seen before. She'd reluctantly signed contracts with a couple of Phoenix travel agents to serve the daily invasion that rolled through on their way to the red cliffs of Sedona. Her lunches consisted of soup, hot dogs, burgers, a variety of sandwiches, and her special Arizona pies. The pies had become so popular that they began putting on extra buses just for the lunch crowd that came up the mountain for those large crisp crusts that draped over bubbling baked vegetables and meats.

Some of the newspapers and magazines, even a few TV stations, had tried to get her recipe. Pearce hadn't helped the situation when he decided to tell them "that it all depended on what the local boys brought in that morning. Sometimes they used coyote, maybe even venison or elk. Bear meat if they got lucky, but mostly just healthy Arizona beef." Pearce's *confession* turned the pies into an instant Arizona legend, even though the only real mystery was in Mackey's rich buttery crust. But Pearce's hype had worked and her pies sold by the dozens. In fact, that particular morning was the first time Pearce had missed a shift since the cafe had opened.

54

Mackey's only connection with Pearce's brother was from a variety of stories the boys told about him before he was captured and sent to prison. Like her Arizona pies, the Safford family's escapades had risen into the eerie realm of myth. One of the more popular myths was that one of Chino's ex-girlfriends just happened to be in the bank when he decided to rob it.

The sheriff assigned his deputy, Big Donny Buckeye, to bring Chino in. Big Donny's wife had once run away because he had a tendency to beat her on Friday nights. Chino took her in one Saturday morning and convinced her to go with him to Vegas. A few days later he rolled back into town alone. Donny never saw his wife again and Chino refused to tell him where she was. So it was payback time. Legally. A bullet through Chino's head was Donny's simple plan.

The sheriff knew that if it happened that way it'd make a nice statement to anyone else planning to violate the county's banking system. But Pearce led the feds to Chino before Donny had a chance to kill him. The great Arizona manhunt came to a sudden end at a mountain cave the brothers used in the hunting season. The feds got Chino, a five-day supply of food, a fifth of Wild Turkey, and Pearce got his brother's undying hatred for turning him in.

A new wave of breakfast orders arrived and Mackey loaded a pile of dirty dishes into the washer. Pushing her dark red tresses up under the white cook's hat, she acknowledged the anxious glances from a few of the breakfast bunch as they went out the door. Then she picked up the batch of new orders and started pouring more eggs onto the sizzling griddle.

*

Mackey felt it as she poured herself another cup of coffee and sprayed perfume on her hands to take away the smell of the onions. The place had finally emptied. The tables still held the last of the dirty dishes, and Liberty had vanished. She stared out at the empty street, took off her apron, and opened the front door. Faint sounds of shouting hung in the dry air. Halfway up the hill she saw the crowd of men moving together like some strange, confused beast. She climbed the old stone steps and watched the burly men swaying in their numbing dance. The staccato shouting became clearer as she got closer.

Liberty crouched in a doorway like a frightened animal.

"I couldn't stop them!" she wailed, nodding towards the circle of men shouting at each other. "It's Chino. He's back!" she said, stumbling across the cobbled street. "I went to the cops but they just laughed at me. Said they had bets on the fight like everybody else."

"Go back to the cafe," Mackey said.

The circle of men began to push their way up the hill toward the Holy Family Church. The crowd's outer crust had shifted positions and she could see Pearce being thrown up against the church wall by a hunched figure ramming him with his head. The struggle seemed to grow with the crowd's shouting. Mackey moved along the edge of the circle trying to push past a little man with greasy hair they called Clumsy Clyde. He pushed Mackey away without looking up. She pushed in again. Clyde turned to hit her but then stopped when he saw it was Mackey. He started to say something but then ran to another opening. Mackey shouldered her way in toward the center. The closer she got the louder the yelling became. Pearce's bloodied face lifted up over the crowd. A deep gash sliced over his left eye but a contented smile lit his face as he swung at someone he had in a headlock. They made such a tight ball she could hardly tell one from the other. One of the men leaned in to try and separate the combatants, but the rest pulled him away.

Mackey squeezed in closer as the struggle roared on in front of her. Another bloodied head popped into view at her feet. This one had cuts over both eyes and a large blue lump on his left cheek. His body looked powerful in the tight bloodied t-shirt that had been partially torn off his back. A surprised look came into his eyes when he saw Mackey staring down at him.

"YOU'RE LATE, YOU SONOFABITCH!" she yelled at him. The men took a step back when they heard her, and Chino stared up into Mackey's cold blue stare. "The lunch crowd's been here and gone," she said. "The dirty dishes are still on the tables! How you figure the work gets done if you two are out here playing tough guy with each other?"

"Who is this broad?" Chino yelled back.

"Two-Bear, you and Slade load these clowns into my pickup. Take them down to the clinic. When the doc finishes stitching I want both of them back up here. That means no celebrating until those tables are cleared and cleaned!"

"Yes, ma'am," the huge man said, helping the combatants to their feet. Chino pushed him away but he could barely get to his knees by himself.

"Let 'em fight, Mackey! We'll clean up for you when they finish!" Woo Woo yelled from the back, and a chorus of agreement rose from the crowd.

"You got any idea what time it is?" Mackey yelled.

"Hell," Chino said, still trying to get up. "Who gives a shit what time it is?"

"I give a shit! Settle your grudges on your own time! Right now it's Arizona pie time! Get your asses in gear," Mackey said, and the men cleared a path for her.

"Who the hell are you anyway, the goddamned sheriff?"

Mackey stopped to look back at Chino. "I'm the reason you're still not in jail, Mr. Safford," she said, pushing her way back through the crowd. Chino watched her long, shapely legs disappear among the gaggle of men's boots, her perfume still hanging in the air.

"Where the hell did that come from?"

"That's the boss," Pearce said. "You better do what she says or there'll be no living with her."

"Living with her?"

"You don't think they let you out into the real world on your looks, do you? That's the lady that gave you a job," Pearce said, pulling his brother to his feet.

"What's all this bullshit about Arizona pies?"

"Pickup's in back of the church," Two-Bear said. "Mackey said to take you both into the —"

"I don't need any stitches," Chino said.

"If Mackey says you need stitches you better get stitches whether you need them or not," Two-Bear said, leading the way through the crowd to the truck.

"What the hell's got into you guys?" Chino asked the men filing past him. "You telling me this fight's over cause some woman's pissed about her goddamn pies? This fight's not over till I say it is."

"Fight's over, Chino. You lost. So did I," Two-Bear said, heading for Mackey's truck.

"What do you mean, I lost ... *you* lost?"

"I bet on you that's what it means."

"How much did you lose?" Pearce asked.

"Two-hundred and fifty bucks," Two-Bear said. "I thought sure you'd take him over the falls."

"You didn't lose," Chino said. "Don't payoff."

"It's already paid," the big man said. "Things aren't like they used to be. You pay your bets right off now. Nobody trusts nobody anymore. We had Curley hold the money. Bets poured in from all over. Must've been thousands."

"I still don't believe some broad can just walk in —"

"Leave it lie, bro."

"Suppose I don't want to?"

"You don't have any choice."

Blood ran down Chino's cheek from the cut over
his eye and he wiped it away with his sore hand. Two-Bear
helped him into the back of Mackey's old Ford pickup and
the blood from over his eye dripped along the paint-scraped
truck bed.

*

Mackey went in the back way, turned on the kitchen
lights, and started the coffee. Someone was knocking on the
front window. To her surprise, Chino was waiting for her.
His bandaged eye looked a lot worse in the early morning
light.

"Where's Pearce?" he asked, looking around.

"Trying to shave his swollen face," she said, handing
him the work sheet and the keys. "You'll be the one to open
every morning." He nodded as he glanced down at the piece
of paper. "It's important that those things on the list are
ready when we get here." She began breaking eggs into an
aluminum bowl. "Couple of dozen usually does it for
starters. Just put them in the fridge when you're finished."

"Sounds easy enough."

"Sorry, I didn't ask if you'd ever done it before."

"Break eggs? Did it when Pearce and I went
hunting. I always made breakfast," he said, beginning to
break the eggs into the bowl with one hand. "Want them
whipped?" he asked.

"Yes, please. That covers the scrambled eggs and
omelets. The rest I cook to order."

"What else you got?" he asked.

"Pancake batter's in this dispenser," she told him.
"Just make sure there's enough. Pearce usually checks it
before we leave for the day."

"How long's my brother been into this kitchen
work?" he asked, in a sarcastic way. Mackey didn't answer.
When he finished with the eggs, he looked up. She pointed

to the garbage pail near the door. He carried over the broken shells. "I could use a bigger bowl. They'll whip better."

She got him a larger bowl out of the cabinet. "The only other thing is to have the tables and booths ready for Liberty. She's always late. Poor thing can't help herself." Mackey pulled out one of the deep drawers to show him where they kept the utensils and napkins. "I get in about six," she said. "I make the first batch of coffee and heat the grill. Pearce gets in about six-thirty. Then we're ready to roll."

He poured the eggs into the larger bowl. "Do you put a little cold water in like the French?" he asked.

"The Breakfast Bunch don't care much about the French. Besides, they don't like anything they eat or drink to be watered down." He laughed, and the sudden pain made him put his hand up to his bandaged eye. "Is that hurting you?" she asked.

"Not enough to miss my first day of work."

"How many stitches?"

"Fifteen. Twenty-two between us."

"That some kind of record?"

"It is for us," he said, taking out a handful of knives, forks, and spoons to place along the counter with a paper napkin under each set.

"Is the room we got you all right?" Mackey asked.

"I slept okay ... if that's what you mean."

"It's the best we could do on short notice. Has a private entrance so we thought —"

"It'll do," he said.

"Don't put the cafe's front lights on too early or they'll be knocking on the door to get in. That means you have to set up the booths with just the kitchen lights on."

She felt a sudden relief when she heard Pearce's boots on the gravel at the back door. He stumbled in with a baseball cap slanted down over his eyes to hide his swollen face. "How's it going?" he asked, glancing over at his brother folding napkins.

"Real good," Mackey said. "You didn't tell me he used to cook breakfast for you."

"Chino whipped up the best goddamn omelet in the forest," he said in a loud voice so his brother could hear him. "When those mule deer smelled Chino's cooking they headed right for our campfire. Soon as they showed, we'd shoot 'em and go home early. Never had to leave camp. Ain't that so, bro?"

"Something like that," Chino said from the dark.

"That's what the old man used to tell everybody. Made us hunt even harder. We'd stay out there until we had something to bring home just to prove him right. He knew all the tricks."

"Yeah, old Winslow was one clever sonofabitch," Chino said from the darkness.

"I haven't told Chino about the days off yet. You can clue him in on all that after the breakfast rush."

"Will do," Pearce said.

"Almost time to open," Mackey said. "Whole town will be here just to see how the combatants fared after the war."

"More like a dumb dance," came out of the darkness.

*

The pickup bounced its way through the thin pines. Pearce drove along the edge, avoiding the deep ruts where the heavy rains had cut into the scarred road. They bounced into the last turn before heading up over the tree line.

"What the hell we doing here?" Chino asked, rubbing the new skin over his left eye.

Pearce pulled the truck in close to the barbed wire and jumped out. Chino followed him up to the faded wooden sign. SAFFORD MINE - DANGER - STAY

61

OUT. Pearce lifted the rusted metal bar on the gate so he could park next to the broken sluice that zigzagged across the hill.

Chino looked in at the piles of rock and ragged shafts that sunk down beyond the daylight. That hole had always frightened him. He could taste the dirt on his lips, and the ache in his lower back just thinking about hauling those heavy stones he hated so much. Pearce gunned the truck up the steep hill inside the barbed wire. When he turned off the motor the incredible silence came back. "I hate this place," Chino muttered.

"Give me a hand with this," Pearce said, untying the ropes around the piece of canvas in the back of the truck.

"Last thing this place needs is another rock."

"Yeah, but let's just slide it on down anyway so we can lift it out," Pearce said. Chino reached in from the other side and they slid the covered piece of stone down over the truck bed. Chino could see the stains on the canvas where he'd bled from the cut over his eye. "It goes up there between those scrub oaks on the ridge," Pearce said, angling his end toward the edge of the truck.

Chino took hold of the canvas and they stumbled across the edge of the hill, into the small clump of trees, then down on their knees to lower it into position.

"That's one heavy sonofabitch," Chino muttered.

"I've been waiting for you to get out of prison before I did this," Pearce said. "Now that you're here I can forget all about this godforsaken hill. This is the end of it," he said, uncovering a polished red rock tombstone. It had a curled design along its top with the name WINSLOW SAFFORD chiseled across its middle in large, deep letters. Near the base of it were the words:

> Cast a cold eye
> On life, on death,
> Horseman, pass by

The two men stared down at it. "You telling me the old man's buried up here somewhere?" Chino asked.

"You're kneeling on him," Pearce said. Chino looked down then quickly hopped off the grave. "This is where he wanted to be. I just waited until you got back before setting the stone. I figured old Winslow would've wanted it that way."

"You mean he's not buried over in Bagdad with Ma?"

"That's where everyone thinks he is. I paid off the guy at the funeral parlor. The only place he wanted to be was right here," Pearce said, lifting the stone up on its end so he could shift it inch by inch to a spot he had dug between the trees. When he got there Chino helped him lift the stone onto the two rebars that he'd set years before.

"You forgot to date the damn thing," Chino said.

"He handed me a piece of paper with this stuff written on it, and then pointed to the spot. Don't think he cared much about the date. The spot was everything to the old man."

"What the hell does it mean?" Chino said, taking a closer look at the words carved into the headstone.

"Never could figure it out," Pearce said.

"Horseman, pass by. No *Trespassing* I guess."

"He didn't tell me. I didn't ask."

"It's funny."

"What's funny about it?"

"I thought you dragged me up here to find out where I buried those tomato cans."

"What tomato cans?"

"The ones with all that missing money," Chino said, glancing suspiciously around the hill. "I just hid enough to give me a head start when I got out."

Pearce watched the slight smile break in Chino's eyes. "You saying that crap about missing money was true?"

"True as a cold rain, bro."

"The old man would've loved it."

"Yeah, he would've done that little dance of his," Chino said, doing a quick double step in imitation of their father. "I knew they'd put me away. I just wanted to protect my end."

"You think the money's still here?"

"It is unless it walked away."

"What're you planning to do with it?"

"Invest. Make a lot of money for the both of us, bro. That's the way the old man would've wanted it. Sticking together. We got our differences but we're blood."

"The Safford motto," Pearce said, looking down at the unsettled ground around the tree. "Now that old Winslow's got his fancy cut stone. It's finally over."

"That's right. It's takeoff time," Chino said.

"You can't go anywhere. You're on parole."

"That's the trouble. Everything's so fucking clear you can see right through it."

"Maybe. But it's the way it is."

"Does that include you too?"

"I'm not on parole."

"Don't look that way to me, bro," he said. "Right now, Mackey's got custody of the both of us."

"What the hell does Mackey have to do with it?"

Chino kicked at the loose dirt along the edge of Winslow's grave, then smoothed it over with his boot. He let his brother's sudden anger hang in the breeze that edged its way up through the pines.

"Mackey don't need me or you," Pearce said.

"That's what I been trying to tell you. The woman gives you a job, room, board, and beds you down. After awhile that gets to be like prison, bro. It's time you broke out. Let loose. We're not getting any younger. Sixty is coming at us like a freight train." Pearce stared back at him from the other side of the shaded tombstone. "I figure you need a change of scenery. No guards. No roll calls. No lines. No dishes. No Arizona pies. Let's just get out of here, bro. They've shoved Arizona so deep into the chute it's already in the past and doesn't know it."

The caw of a raven drifted up through the trees. Pearce could feel his brother's whiskey stare. "What've you got planned?" he asked.

Chino put his arm around his brother's shoulder. "First thing is those old tomato cans," he said.

"You buried them up here?"

"This goddamned mine's the only place I could think of. If you remember ... there wasn't much time to spare."

"You think they're still up here?"

"I haven't told a soul."

"And now you're about to make a withdrawal."

"That's it. Close the account."

"Sure you remember where you buried them?"

"Get the shovel. I'll meet you on the other side of that big ass rock," Chino said, heading up the hill. Pearce watched his brother go around the wide cluster of mesquite, and head back to get the shovel.

When Chino located the three boulders, he started digging. He'd buried the money in heavy plastic freezer bags, stuffed them into cans, and buried them upside down so they wouldn't fill with water. "They're only about two feet down. I was in a hurry," he said.

After digging about ten holes around the rocks, Chino remembered he had stretched a string between the inside of the boulders to form an equilateral triangle. He buried the fourth can directly between the others. They began to uncover the earth along the inside of the boulder until they hit the rusted edge of a large can. Chino stopped digging and Pearce carefully pulled out the remains. He could see the money, wrapped inside the plastic, and smiled up at his brother. Once they had found the first can it was easy to calculate where the others were. The middle one had slipped down a few feet where the soil had washed away. Part of the can had actually been exposed and all they had to do was put the shovel under it and angle it out.

The old Three Dog Night tune, *One Man Band*, blared in Chino's head as he sang and danced between the boulders, hugging the bags of money. Pearce liked to remember his brother this way and waited for Chino's dance to end. Then they tore the bags open and did a quick count.

"All there?" Pearce asked.

"About twenty-five thousand looks numbered," he said. "They've probably got that pack on file somewhere. Have to get rid of it."

"What about the rest?"

"Looks good," he said, separating the piles.

"I'll hide the bulk of it in the truck," Pearce said, carrying the stacks of money up the hill. When he glanced back he saw a dull white smoke rising from between the boulders where his brother was burning the short stack of traceable money.

*

Jerome hung on the edge of a mountain. It'd been an old mining-town gone copper dry. Many of its houses had collapsed over the years with the shifting earth, sliding down the mountain to join the slag heaps in the washes below. Those that were left hung tenaciously along the cracked streets like broken boxes forgotten in time. Woo Woo Hutchins, Slade Perkins, and Two-Bear Jones walked the cobble street and headed for the Spirit Room at the end of the block. Jenny, the barmaid, handed each of them three fingers of bourbon and pointed at the makeshift table in the middle of the room. A piece of plywood had been placed over the pool table where the Safford brothers were passing out tortilla chips and *cerveza fría* to their guests. Then Perkins asked about Mackey and a silence hit the room. "No women invited," Chino said, and the boys settled in to drink their cold beers.

Old J.J. Fitz, a paunchy, red-faced Irishman, got up on the semi-carpeted bandstand to propose a toast. "To the dear lads and the free beer," he said. The gang roared and carried him over to the makeshift table. He stood among the chips and *salsa*, in his soiled boots, waiting for quiet. Then he raised his sweating bottle of beer and said, "I want to propose a goddamned toast while I'm still able to speak coherently!" He lifted the Corona over his head as if he was about to pour it on himself. "To the dear, dear Safford boys." A wild cheer rose out of the crowd and the frustrated old man had to stomp on the table to quiet them. "To the Safford boys," he said in a flourish. "They're what Arizona used to be!" The men howled and barked at him. "Arizona and the Safford Boys are all about the same goddamned thing," Fitzey said. "Love, loyalty, friendship, and the best a man can be. So here's to the Safford Boys and to old Arizoney!" Then he blurted in a rapid fire of spit and speech, "To every blessed one of thee, and to all in peril on the sea!" The gang roared their approval and pulled the old man down, passing him from one to the other like a stuffed laundry bag.

Pearce reached up with the rest and heaved Fitzey into the next breach of waiting arms. Then his eye caught a glimpse of someone standing between the parked cars across the street. They watched each other through the wild tumult of getting J.J. back on his feet. Any movement of Pearce's head made the figure in the street seem to disappear into the deep shadows along the stonewall.

More Corona was opened in a fever of shouting and laughter, but Pearce could only feel the emptiness in the staring eyes from across the street. Somehow it had gotten all turned around. He couldn't explain it to her, or to himself. They hadn't been alone since Chino arrived. Even their day off seemed to run into the rest of the week. Nights had become a simple routine of brushing teeth then falling asleep. No practical jokes, no midnight discussions, or loud sex. Their rough, desperate kisses had been replaced with simple *goodnights*.

Pearce wanted to tell her how he'd fallen in love the first time he saw her get out of the car with the California plates, and that he wanted to marry her and have all those babies that danced in her eyes. He stared out at the figure in the shadows, listening to the babble that flew around him like frightened birds. Woo Woo leaned over to grab the last piece of limp pizza. "Hey, Pearce, you drunk or just flying in another orbit?" he asked. "There's nothing out there. It's all in here." Pearce forced a laugh and took a slug of the cold beer.

"This time we're going all the way, bro," Chino said.

Pearce lifted his bottle in a silent toast and glanced out the window again. The street was empty, and he wondered if anyone had been out there at all.

*

Tom Watkins, the parole officer in Cottonwood, read Mackey's progress reports on Chino. He'd even gotten a pay raise. Chino took Watkins' compliments graciously, swore he had no known association with any convicted criminals in the past week, shook the parole officer's hand, promised to "keep up the good work," then headed back to the truck.

Work in the cafe had gotten harder and they were all feeling the strain. An extra tour bus had been added on Saturdays, and the Arizona pies became even more popular. Chino was convinced that Arizona's population boom, the land sales, and the disappearing desert were all Mackey's fault. His intolerance toward her had solidified into a hatred he barely managed to cover with that quick smile he now gave his brother slumped half-asleep behind the wheel.

"Can I buy you breakfast?" he said, shading his eyes against the low morning sun.

"Where to?" Pearce asked.

"How about the Omelet Shack in Sedona. Haven't been there in awhile," he said.

Pearce nodded and they headed towards the great red buttes that had remained unchanged in the ten years Chino had been gone. As they got closer he could see where the new homes had been built behind the mini-malls and the blur of advertising signs. Pearce pulled the pickup into one of the long parking lots, and they rolled toward the wide wooden structure with the curled sign across its front.

"See that guy behind you?" Chino asked.

Pearce turned to see a man sitting behind the wheel of an old Chevy. "I think he's one of the guys I'm supposed to meet. Something tells me he's changed his mind."

"About what?"

"Wait here until I get back. If the guy in the truck decides to follow me, hang with him," Chino said.

"What about breakfast?"

"We'll do it when I get back."

Chino slipped out of the truck. He'd picked this place because of the low lights, dark stained tables, and tourist trade. Ramon was sitting alone in the back, and he slid into the booth with the sharp-featured Latino.

"How's it been going?"

"I don't exactly miss prison."

"Want a beer?" Ramon asked.

"Yeah, I could use one," Chino said, glancing around.

"Looking for something, *amigo*?"

"I thought you'd be with —"

"He couldn't make it," Ramon said.

"Is he the one sitting out in the Chevy?"

"Yeah ... doesn't want to be seen with ex-cons."

"Did he give you the piece?"

"Did you bring the money?"

"Yeah," Chino said.

"I checked out the place. They're on the ninth floor. There are three elevators and a way to get out through the underground parking lot ... just like he said."

"Did he give you the remote?"

"He won't give us nothing until he gets paid, *amigo*. After that I'll test the remote to make sure it works." Ramon smiled. "You trust me, don't you?"

Just as Chino started to answer a waitress showed up and said, "You want to order?"

"Bring me one of those," Chino said, pointing at the Carta Blanca.

"How's Tom Watkins doing?"

"You know him?"

"He used to be my parole officer in Guadalupe."

Chino took a long brown envelope out of his jacket and dropped it on the table. "That's thirty grand," he said.

Ramon quickly stuffed the envelope into his shirt. "I'll get started right away," he said. "It's the perfect time. The tourists are buying everything in sight." He smiled, and slid several folded pieces of paper toward Chino. "This is a breakdown of the whole operation. Second to second. Once we get into the final phase it shouldn't take more than two minutes. Memorize the floor plans, the steps, the timing. Then burn it. It'll go down a week from today. That's when they bring in the Christmas shipment."

"That's a lot of money I just gave you."

"No. What we're *getting* is a lot of money. If you're worried we can forget the whole thing. No hard feelings."

"Have you figured out how we'll get the stuff across the border?"

"All taken care of. We'll drive to Lukeville and cross there. I'll meet you in Penasco later that afternoon," he said, sliding a couple of passports across the table. Chino covered them when he saw the waitress coming with the beer.

When she left he opened one of the passports and looked down at his picture with someone else's name under it. He opened the other one to look down at Pearce's picture over another strange name. "Don't forget to sign them," Ramon said. "And be sure to use the same names on the passport."

"What's next?"

"I pay this guy. Get the remote and check it out."

"And the incidentals?"

"Taken care of," Ramon said, throwing some money on the table. "You sure your brother's up for all this?"

"He'll be fine," Chino said.

"Then we better get out of here."

"You know how to get in touch with me?"

"Same way we been doing, *amigo*. Just give me a couple of days," he said, putting his index finger into the top of the beer bottle and heading for the door.

*

Pearce recognized the Latino walking across the parking lot with the bottle hanging from his finger. The heavyset man in the Chevy started the truck, the Latino jumped in, and they rolled across the blacktop and out into the bustling Sedona traffic.

Chino came out a few minutes later. "I just made that investment," he said, taking out the passports and flipping them on the dashboard. Pearce stared down at the pictures they had taken a few weeks before. "These little items spell freedom. With a capital F," Chino said.

"Who the hell is Elliot Sanders?"

"Elliot who?"

Pearce shoved the passport at him.

"It's just our cover for awhile," Chino said.

"You bought a whole deal here."

71

"You'll be third man on the swing ... with a full cut. I need you on this, bro. I got no one else."

"Let me think about it," Pearce said.

"There's no time for that."

"I've got to be able to pull out anytime I want."

Chino didn't move. "Okay," he finally said. "But when you see how easy this lays you'll get comfortable with it."

"No guns," Pearce said.

Chino took a deep breath. "There has to be at least one. It's safer that way."

"No guns, or you can forget about me."

He waited for Pearce to say something else, but he didn't. "Things like this don't come along every day," Chino said, shoving the phony passports into his pocket. "I just can't walk around with that number under me anymore."

"Is it that bad?" Pearce asked.

"Yeah," Chino said. "I'm starting to hate *myself*. I have to get out or I'll do something crazy."

Sedona's red rocks faded into the rearview mirror, breaking into odd-shaped pieces. Pearce listened to his brother breathing heavily next to him.

"Okay, no guns," Chino finally said, and they drove back up the mountain to Jerome in silence.

*

Mackey didn't expect it to happen so fast. She'd picked up a professional stove at a Flagstaff auction, ordered a brand new refrigerator, got a dishwasher from Phoenix, and found a rebuilt freezer in Cottonwood. Then four shiny buses reading, ARIZONA PIE COUNTRY, descended on the cafe the next Saturday. The tour operators had filled two extras. The mayor, the police chief, and the rest of the town didn't know how to react to the sudden windfall. Mackey had to run around hiring busboys out of the bars to clear the tables.

Every customer wanted an Arizona pie. When they ran out they filled in with hamburgers, hot dogs, and chicken salad. The town police had to wave other tourists through the winding streets and out the other end because there was nowhere to park. Mackey finally hung the CLOSED sign on the front door.

"I'll go down to the supermarket. Pick up what I can for tomorrow," Pearce said. "You get the crusts going. We need a shitload of new supplies."

"Don't ever let me run out of pies again," she said.

"I told Chino to come back and uncrate that rebuilt freezer. While the pies are baking we'll get it running," he said. "All I need is some cash for the new supplies."

"Want a list?"

"Hell, no. Arizona pies run in my head," he said, opening the cash drawer. He gave a low, hard whistle at the money they'd taken in. Few hundred ought to get what we need," he said, emptying the cash on the counter. "We'll take the rest down to the night deposit when I get back."

"Don't have time to count money until I have those crusts ready for tomorrow," Mackey said, shoveling the cash into a floppy gray bag. "The bank can wait. The pies can't."

By the time she looked up, Pearce had already crossed the street and disappeared over the hill. At first she didn't realize another face had been staring back at her until she saw the tire iron in his hand.

"Pearce told me you needed some help unpacking that new freezer," he yelled through the window.

She took a quick breath and laughed. "Chino ... didn't see you there. I'm sorry we had to drag you back after all that craziness today. I'll pay you extra time."

"That's all right," he shrugged, and headed for the large crate. "If I'd done this a week ago we wouldn't have had to work so goddamn hard today."

"Sorry. I just didn't expect it to double like that."

Chino checked the over-sized crate and Mackey went into the kitchen, lined her spices across the counter, and took out all the flour she had left. A loud squeal of ripping nails burst through the cafe. She looked up to see Chino ripping off the top of the crate, jamming the tire iron down into it.

She wondered if he had stopped at the Spirit Room for a few drinks before he got there. When he drank she could see the anger in his eyes, and it frightened her. There'd usually be the smell of mints on his breath to go with it.

"Might as well use this wood for the fireplace," he said, holding up the pieces of sharp edged slats that he'd ripped from the crate.

"It'll make good kindling."

"I'll throw it out back," he said, and she caught the smell of mint as he went by. She set the large aluminum bowl on the counter and began mixing the dough. The broken pieces of wood hit the pavement with a crash just outside the back door. "I'll carry that stuff up to the house before we leave tomorrow," he said, coming back in.

"Where you going?" she asked.

"Didn't Pearce tell you?" he asked. "He's taking me down to Phoenix after work. I have a meeting at the state parole board early Monday morning. We figured it'd be easier staying down in Phoenix the night before."

"Sounds like you're getting to meet the higher-ups."

"One parole officer's the same as another. They stamp them out on a cookie-cutter," he said.

"I thought you liked Tom Watkins."

"They're all the same."

"Long as you're going down to Phoenix you can take the pickup. Get some supplies while you're there."

"We're taking the Harley. Motor needs work."

"I thought you did your own tuning."

74

"Needs an expert to look it over. Especially after so many years just sitting around."

Mackey nodded, pushing a large ball of dough across the board. There'd been a lot of incoming phone calls for Chino but she hadn't been suspicious until he'd mentioned going to Phoenix. She and Pearce hadn't spent their day off together since he'd arrived. It'd taken her a long time to understand Pearce's determination to get his brother out of prison, but as the weeks went by she sensed something deeper between them. They seemed to be locked into something she didn't understand. When she looked up Chino was standing in front of her, slapping the tire iron in his hand. "We'll move the freezer when Pearce gets back," he said.

She pulled back, and said, "Thanks for opening the crate. Sorry we had to pull you out of the bar." He glanced down at the tire iron in his hand, and slipped it behind him.

"I wasn't at the bar," he said. "Just heading up to the house." Mackey threw another lump of dough onto the long plastic sheet. "Don't worry," he said. "We'll have that freezer running before we leave tomorrow."

"This place just rolls along," she sighed, catching his eye before he looked away.

"You're right about that. Only trouble is it could roll right over you," he said. "Work's getting too hard ... hours too long," he said in that hard tone he had whenever he drank too much. Mackey could see the tire iron swinging back and forth behind him. "Nothing's worth your life," he said.

"I'm working hard to put some money away," she said. "That's why I pay good money for the work. Guess I expect too much. If it's too tough ... maybe you should get another job."

He stopped breathing and just stood there. The iron bar behind him swung back and forth like an off centered pendulum. "What're you going to do with all this money you're making?"

"Buy some land," she said.

"That's ranching. Cattle, horses, and stacks of feed for the winter. Your own rodeo."

"It's what your brother wants," she said, lining up the balls of pie dough. "Someone has to take care of Pearce."

"Wages and aspirin don't sound like Pearce to me."

"Maybe you don't know him anymore," she said. He dropped the tire iron on the counter and she jumped. It rolled to a stop and she glanced up into his whiskey stare.

"You in love with him?"

"I've been in love with Pearce even before I laid eyes on him," she said, slapping the balls of dough through the sprinkled flour. "We go together. Perfect fit."

"Guess you didn't plan on me showing up, eh?"

"I don't plan on anything," she said.

"I can see it in your eyes, honey. You're not sure whether he loves you or just did all this to get me out."

It was the way he said it that hurt Mackey. Like he was laughing, and knew something she didn't.

"Guess I'll go get a drink," he said, opening the door. "By the way, thanks for those good reports to my parole officer." When Mackey looked up again he was gone.

*

They hit Phoenix just before dark. Pearce left Chino at the Circle K and walked down the street to pick up the U-Haul he'd reserved the week before. He drove the truck to the deserted corner in the motel's parking lot, opened the back, slid out the ramp, and waited for Chino to roll the Harley up into the truck. They tied it to the side panels, closed the back, and checked in.

Pearce went out to pick up a couple of burgers and beers before they went over the map again. Chino turned on the TV to watch a hockey game and fell asleep before the last period. Pearce flipped through the channels fighting the urge to call Mackey. She was probably working through the night. He didn't want to lie to her again so he checked the alarm for the third time, and then fell asleep with the TV still on.

He heard Chino in the shower when the alarm went off so he got dressed and went out to find a couple of coffees. When he got back Chino had almost finished wiping down the room.

"Don't touch anything," he said.

"It'll be squeaky clean by the time the maid gets through anyway," Pearce said.

"The less they know, the better."

"I checked the truck. It's working fine."

"All we have to do is put out the DO NOT DISTURB sign and slip on the coveralls."

"We're about a half hour ahead," Pearce said.

"What's it like out?"

"Cool. No wind. Should be an easy ride to the border."

"Let's go. The less we're seen the better," Chino said, grabbing the overnight bag.

Pearce wiped both doorknobs with a hand towel then glanced down along the outside corridor. The passageway looked shapeless in the half-light. Long shadows hung against the walls. He jammed the door with his foot, so they could walk out without touching anything, and then finally let it close behind him.

Chino opened the truck's back door and Pearce jumped up with him. They slipped into the baggy gray coveralls. Pearce zipped up his front, then handed his brother one of the matching caps. Ramon had insisted they wear them even though Pearce had been against it. Now that they had put them on he realized how professional and nondescript the uniforms made them look. The Latino knew the game. Pearce began to sense how well the operation had been planned. He hardly had to think about what to do next.

He pulled down the truck's back ramp, checked the parking lot, and signaled Chino to come down on the Harley. He jumped on as Chino kicked it to a start. They were twenty minutes ahead of schedule.

Ramon was waiting for them, ready to go, which seemed to relax Chino. "Let's set up now," the Latino said.

They slipped on the work gloves, loaded the signs and ropes, and took the elevator to the ninth floor. Ramon opened the elevator's control box while Pearce and Chino set the plastic barriers and caution tape. Then they put the large OUT OF ORDER sign in front of the middle elevator.

"What about the guy downstairs?" Chino asked.

Ramon pulled a remote out of his coveralls. "Works like a dream," he said. "I've already set the signs on the main floor. All we have to do is wait for his signal."

"Let's make sure we're ready for them," Chino said.

Ramon closed the doors with the remote, and turned the elevator off with the key. Chino opened the stepladder and began taking out the ceiling panels. When he had enough of the top opened, he climbed out into the elevator shaft and reached back to help Pearce up. They stood together on top of the elevator holding the steel cables as a thin ray of daylight drifted over them from above.

Pearce waited for Ramon to lift the ladder up onto the top of the elevator. They balanced it between them as the cables hummed through the elevator shaft. The faint sound of women's voices drifted through the emptiness as the office workers began to arrive. Pearce leaned out over the edge to watch the elevator in the next shaft rise from floor to floor, and then drop to the bottom again.

"Did he tell you which side they'd use?" Chino asked.

Ramon pointed to the other shaft. "They always take the same elevator, and that's where he'll put them. They won't suspect a thing. When he gives the signal we're into the two-minute drill. The faster we get out of here the better. I'll meet you on the other side of the border. Don't forget the masks. Every detail helps."

Chino took the ski masks out of his coveralls and gave one to Pearce. The operation began to shift into an eerie rhythm of its own. Ramon checked his watch as Chino stared down at the disappearing elevator in the next shaft.

A telephone rang. Its sharp sound cut through the soft whirring of the sliding cables. One ring. Two rings. Three. Then it stopped. "They're here," Ramon said.

Pearce leaned out to look down the other shaft and wondered why it took so long. Then he saw the top of it moving up through the thin ray of sunlight. Time seemed suspended as the elevator crept towards them.

Ramon aimed the remote along the wall. The elevator came to a smooth stop just between the eighth and ninth floors. Pearce lifted one of the panels off the top, and Chino shoved his head and arm into the lighted space.

"Freeze or you're fucking dead!" he yelled.

The two men were facing the elevator door. One of them reached for the alarm but then stopped, and the moment seemed endless. Chino dropped into the elevator, shoving both men against the back wall, and Pearce covered the door.

The larger man held a small zippered bag with a lock on it. Chino tore it out of his hand and flipped it up to Ramon, standing at the top of the elevator. "Put your hands where I can see them," Chino said to the man, patting him down and pulling a .38 out of the guy's pocket.

Pearce took the gun, raised his hand, and a roll of duct tape flew down. He caught it cleanly, flipped the gun to Ramon, and began taping the men's hands and legs. He pressed the rest over their mouths and eyes turning them into what looked like manikins.

"Forty-five seconds," Ramon said, leaning into the elevator with the ladder. Pearce caught the end of it, set it, and tapped Chino on the shoulder before starting to climb out. When he looked back he could see Chino going through both men's pockets. He had pulled out another black bag from the little guy's jacket. The man's breathing got faster. Pearce watched as Chino stuffed the black bag into his coveralls.

"Thirty seconds," Ramon's voice echoed through the shaft. When Pearce got to the top he turned to help Chino out. Ramon had already crossed the open shaft.

"Fifteen seconds."

Pearce waited for Chino, and stretched across the shaft to the other elevator where Ramon waited for them. The cadence kept clicking in his head. It'd gotten to nine seconds when he saw Ramon putting the key back into the elevator panel.

Pearce couldn't remember whether he had shouted, "Noooooo," or just imagined it. A blinding light flashed behind him and a sharp crackling sound echoed through the open shaft. By the time he turned back Chino was hanging between the cables in a suspended ring of fire and smoke. He leaned out to catch him and felt the rush of heat pour out of his body as he lowered him into the elevator.

"You didn't wait for my signal, you sonofabitch!" Pearce yelled, and felt the floor dropping as he pulled Chino's mask off to look down at the twisted expression on his brother's face. Ramon was mumbling prayers in Spanish. When the elevator stopped they lifted Chino to his feet and dragged him out into the garage. Pearce ran to the Panhead, kicked it to a start, and swung it around to where Ramon held Chino against the wall. "Sit him up behind me," he said, and Ramon wrapped Chino's arms around Pearce's neck so he could grab his hands. Pearce shoved it into gear with his other hand and took off into the morning glare. He kept to the backstreets, made a quick left in front of the oncoming traffic, and rolled up the street that edged the motel's parking lot. The open U-Haul stood in the corner where they'd left it. He drove the motorcycle straight up the ramp into the truck and turned off the ignition. Chino hadn't moved.

Straddling the seat, Pearce turned to ease Chino onto the floor. His eyes were closed and his head rolled easily in the bend of Pearce's arm. "We made it, bro," he whispered, and Chino's head fell back onto the truck bed. He slipped out of the coveralls, tied the Electra Glide to the side panels, then jumped down and slid the ramp back into position so he could close up the truck.

The scream of sirens got closer as he walked to the motel's office to drop off the room keys. He put on a pair of sunglasses to cover his stinging eyes, and stared numbly at the printer spitting out the receipt.

*

The U-Haul groaned up the dirt road and Pearce squeezed the wheel to keep from sliding into the deep ruts. He made the last turn and gunned the truck in close to the broken wooden sign. SAFFORD MINE - DANGER - STAY OUT. Then he backed the truck up until the mineshaft's gaping mouth filled the mirrors. When he opened the truck a pungent smell of burnt flesh hit him. He took a deep breath, lowered the ramp, and looked out across the valley. The sky had turned a snow gray with only a few hours of light left.

Moving up the truck's ramp he tried not to look at his brother's body slumped in the corner. He set the cycle's kickstand, undid the bunji cords, wound the ropes into a large loop, then hooked all of it onto the back. Setting himself, he lifted Chino in a quick upward motion, put him on the seat and straddled the cycle. He swung the kickstand with his boot and the burnt smell of his brother's flesh filled his head. He began to cry as he rolled him forward to the edge of the truck. Then he pushed the front wheel over a small hump so they could roll down the ramp. The cycle swung wildly, slid off the ramp, and threw them into the rust-colored dust.

The entrance to the mine gaped at him from twenty feet away and his shoulder throbbed. He crawled out from under the cycle. Chino's body lay sprawled up against the broken sluice. Fresh blood glistened on the boards where Chino had landed. This time when he tried to pick up his brother the pain in his shoulder stopped him.

He dragged Chino into the mine with his good arm, leaned him up against a wooden pole, and staggered back up the incline to the Electra Glide. The maroon paint had been scratched and the chrome had been dented but it could still roll. He guided it down into the mine, curling it between the stanchions, and leaned it against the center pole.

The dampness made him shudder and the pain shot across his shoulder as he headed up the slope. This time when he lifted Chino he heard something fall, and he stared down at the black flannel bag that Chino had taken from the little man in the elevator. When he pulled the drawstring the polished jewels tumbled into his palm in glittering colors. There were diamonds, rubies, and emeralds. He shook out some more and a large sapphire tumbled over the rest like a blue beacon in the half-light. Pearce stared at the glittering rocks in his hand trying to put a price on them. They could be worth hundreds of thousands. He squeezed the jewels in his fist and funneled them back into the bag. "We hit the jackpot, bro," he said, sitting down next to Chino. They sat like that for a long time, leaning against each other, shadows deepening as the daylight faded in the dusty air along the jagged entrance. He reached over to take his brother in his arms. His lungs filled with the after burn on Chino's clothing. "Just remember the good times, bro. You, me, and the old man," he said, stuffing the bag of jewels back into Chino's pocket. "I never wanted any of it. I was planning to tell you that when we hit the border," he muttered, trying not to cry. "Jesus, what happened to us?"

The fading light turned the mine's row of pillars into lines of sentinels. He took hold of Chino's arms and dragged him in deeper to where he'd left the motorcycle. His shoulder felt worse as he cradled his brother's body and lifted him up onto the seat. He shoved Chino's boots into the stirrups and clicked on the cycle's front headlight. The beam bent along the mine's dark walls, lighting the serpentine path.

"Don't look back, bro," he said, grabbing the nylon ropes and wrapping them around the old wooden posts. He backed out on his hands and knees and tied the ropes to the truck. A dull silence hung over the mountain. It'd gotten colder. He could see all the way to the other side where a thin sliver of light glowed against the old man's tombstone.

Pearce climbed into the truck, turned the key, and the motor rumbled to a start. He let the truck roll until he felt the pull of the ropes behind him. Then he pressed hard on the gas pedal. When he couldn't see the ropes anymore he let the weight of the truck take him over the incline and heard a low rumble behind him. A shower of rocks bounced around him and a cloud of dust thickened across the windshield. The truck began to slide. His foot jammed down on the brake and he waited for the sound of the falling rocks to subside. Then he stepped out into the dusty air and looked up at where the earth had buckled along the ridge. Large boulders had rolled down off the top, covering the entrance and the old man's sign. The sluice and barbed wire were gone too.

He waited until the dust settled before starting to dig his way back under the truck to untie the ropes. Cursing his bleeding hands, he began to clear some of the large boulders that blocked the old road. When he started the truck again he didn't look back until he was well below the tree line.

The snow began to dance in the headlights making little webs on the windshield. He thought about Mackey's fresh baked Arizona pies as he waited to make the last turn. The cafe's lights were still on so he parked across the street and trudged through the thickening snow. Mackey was at the counter, spreading dough over a line of unfinished pies. He tapped on the back window but she kept working. He hit it harder and she looked up and smiled when she saw his face pressed against the window.

DEEP WATER

He waited until his grandfather took the oars before sliding the skiff into the water and jumping in for a perfect start. The old man nodded his approval and began to row through the glassy water toward the dark island that edged the shadows on the other side. They headed for the dead tree where the light wouldn't hit for hours. He reached for the paddle, dipped it into the dark water at the stern, and angled the boat toward the black mound where the fallen tree barely broke the surface.

He held the rod while the old man tied his special bait of worms and silver fish just above the hook. Then standing straight up in the boat, the old man lobbed his line just below the sunken tree and let it run out in a clear buzz until the fish broke the surface.

"You got him, Grandpa!" he yelled before it turned.

The old man stiffened at the sudden weight, pulled at the line, and the large bass flopped into the boat. Billy took the pole, while his grandfather lifted the flapping fish from the bottom of the boat and carefully angled the hook out of its mouth. Then Billy took the fish in his arms, curled it in against his chest, leaned over the edge, and let the fish slide back into the water.

"If you *have* to catch them then you're not fishing," the old man would say, and Billy would watch the quivering fish disappear back down into its secret world.

Drifting out into the deeper part of the lake the old man tied a heavier weight on the line to work the bottom. That's when Billy took a long gulp of the canteen's metal tasting water and settled back to watch the early light rise out of the silence.

No matter how many times he thought about the old man he always remembered the one fish that hit so hard. It cut in close and the old man had to let out a lot of line. It turned to fight and his grandfather leaned forward to shorten his grip. Billy lunged into the bow, stumbling over the bait bucket, and had to grab the back of the old man's jacket to keep him from tripping over the oars. His grandfather's legs tightened like posts as he bent to keep the sagging line from disappearing under the boat. The fish came up thrashing and Billy caught the large wriggling bass in midair with its greens and blues sparkling in the shimmering light that jumped off the lake.

"He's a beauty, Grandpa," Billy said, squeezing the fish against his chest.

"He's caught deep though," the old man said, opening the bass's mouth, trying to unhook him. "Can't reach it," he said. "We'll have to take him."

"My hand's smaller," Billy said. "I'll get it."

The old man held the fish's mouth open and Billy reached down into it. Bony ridges scraped along the back of his hand. He pushed further down into the yawning mouth, feeling the taut line where the bait wriggled just above his grandfather's special knot. The fish's cold, sticky insides chilled the tips of his fingers but the hook stayed just beyond them. If he jerked the line it would pull the fish apart, so he let go and eased his hand out of its gaping mouth. The old man stared down at the fish and opened his jackknife.

"I could try again, Grandpa."

"He took it too deep, Billy. Can't put him back like that. Wouldn't be fair."

"I know," the kid said and the old man cut the line. "Does this mean he'll die?"

"We all have to die, son," he said, and began packing up his old metal box.

"Are we going back so soon?"

His grandfather began rowing towards the dock even before the sun had reached halfway across the lake. The bass flopped at his feet as they slid over the water, cutting through the long shadows that reached down off the high trees that ran the lake like dark fingers. Billy sprinkled fresh water over the flopping fish until the skiff finally bumped to a stop at the dock.

The old man cleaned the big bass and they stopped off in town and gave it to the one-eyed cook at the diner. The cook invited them to eat with him but the old man declined. They got back into the car and headed home.

"I'll be going away for awhile," the old man said. "You can take the poles. Go fishing whenever you want."

"Where you going?"

"Oh, not far. I just won't be able to fish for awhile." He started to say something else but stopped. They sat quiet, listening to the drone of the old Chevy. It'd be their last time out together. After that came the church, the cemetery, and the long ride back in the limousine.

A few days later his father handed him the old man's fishing poles. He slid his legacy into a dark corner of the closet and waited for a time that never seemed to come. The years passed until he could barely see the fishing pole's worn handles behind the hanging clothes that had gotten longer with each passing year. Whenever he did notice the poles he'd sense the big open-mouthed bass on his hand again and think about his grandfather drifting on a lake somewhere, fishing the deep water.

TRUE BELIEVERS

Billy pulled his denim collar up against the sudden prairie breeze and opened the hood on the steaming old Woody. He grabbed the faded army blanket, wrapped the end around his hand, opened the hot radiator cap, and let the steam hiss out into the cool morning.

A slim teenaged girl slid out of the passenger seat, numbly pulled a comb through her auburn hair, and sat down on a white washed rock in the morning sun.

"What the hell we doing here, Billy?" she mumbled.

"Busted fan belt."

"Hell, just get another one."

"You think it's easy picking up a fan belt when you're on the front of every goddamn newspaper in three states?"

"I'm hungry."

"You're always hungry, Char."

"Least you picked the right place to bust something," she said, looking around at the empty parking lot.

A tan van with faded decals covering half its windows clattered across the black top toward them. The doors flew open and three little boys exploded from its void and swarmed around Billy's old Woody. A large bulky man in baggy shorts and torn tennis shoes struggled out of the driver's seat, and a small, thin woman in a bright yellow raincoat followed them.

"Haven't seen an old Woody like that in years," the man bellowed. "My uncle had one when I was a kid. Loved it. Uncle passed on but he took such good care of it I bet it's still chugging along somewhere on the prairie. This might even be it. Where'd you find this thing, son?"

The man stuck his head under the hood next to Billy and the woman in the yellow slicker sensed Billy's annoyance and said, "Let's go on up to the restaurant and get started, honey. This way, kids," she called in a high cracked voice. "Time to eat." The children cheered and ran toward the glass doors with the golden arches.

"If you belonged to Triple A they'd have you rolling in no time," the man yelled over his shoulder, and trotted after the wedge of children dodging and screeching around the plastic yellow raincoat.

"Asshole," Billy muttered.

"I'm going in for a Mac Muffin," Charlene said. "Want one?" Billy shrugged and waited until the last little boy darted in behind the glass doors before he moved to the loaded van and popped its hood.

"What the hell you doing?" Charlene asked.

"We need a fan belt, Char. Hand me that blanket."

"You want a Mac Muffin, or not?"

"Get some water for the radiator, and make sure those assholes don't come strolling out here 'til I finish getting this belt off their van."

"Does that mean you want a Mac Muffin, or not?"

"Just don't forget the water ... better get two large."

When Charlene got to the front door she looked back at Billy holding the van's fan belt over his head like an oval snake he'd just wrestled into submission. She laughed at how silly he looked, opened the glass door, and moved into the bright colors of the restaurant. The bulky man in the tennis shoes stood at the counter, ordering things in a booming voice. His wife stood behind him and kept adding to the order while their squealing kids pulled paper napkins out of the dispensers and threw them at each other. Charlene edged back to the window to check on Billy, now doubled over in the old Woody again.

She sensed someone staring at her in the gold tinted mirror. A soldier sat on a duffel bag holding a handmade sign with VIRGINIA scrawled across it. He smiled when he saw her and she noticed his short cut hair, streaked from the sun, sticking out under his cap.

"Name's Alden, ma'am. Corporal. U.S. Marines."

"I think my daddy was a Marine," she said.

"What's your name?"

"My name's Morse," she said.

"Moss. That's pretty. What's your last name?"

"That is my last name, silly."

The bulky man and his family moved toward them carrying assorted containers. The little boys chased each other and his wife tried to keep them from knocking him over. He raised the carton of food over his head, and said, "We'd give you a lift, Corporal, but you can see there's not much room at the inn."

"Appreciate the thought," the Marine said, holding the glass door open while the five of them swept out into the parking lot again.

"You looking for a ride?" Charlene asked.

"Yes ma'am," he said, pointing at his VIRGINIA sign.

"I thought sure you'd have your own car," she said. "You being in uniform, an all."

He smiled at her odd reasoning, and said, "And I thought you belonged with that family out there."

"I wouldn't be caught dead with them," she snapped.

"Takes all kinds to make a world, ma'am," he said.

"My mamma used to say that to me all the time."

"You never did tell me your first name."

"Marilyn," she said quickly.

"Marilyn Morse. That's a lovely name."

"Makes my initials M.M., like Marilyn Monroe and those little candies!" Charlene said, and they both laughed.

"I'm headed east," he said, holding up the sign.

"You from California?"

"I was stationed out there."

"I knew it," she said, looking up into his blue eyes. "I think me and my brother are headed east."

"I'd sure be grateful for a lift, ma'am."

"'Scuse me, I have to get a couple of egg Mac Muffins. Two please," she said to the boy behind the counter. "And two large cokes, an two large waters to cool off that silly old car. You want a Mac Muffin?" she asked Alden. "My brother doesn't stop much, if you know what I mean."

"I can go a long way without eating, ma'am."

"Guess that's part of your training, an all."

Reaching for the bag of Mac Muffins she noticed a discarded newspaper on the counter. Its headline read, **BILLY THE KID CRIME SPREE. THREE STATES.** She shoved the paper under her arm and waited for Alden to pick up his duffel bag.

"I hope your brother won't mind me tagging along."

"Oh, he won't," she said, glancing toward the old Woody where Billy sat watching the family in the van eating their Big Macs and fries.

*

It wasn't until Charlene was halfway across the parking lot that Billy realized she was walking with the Marine. He sensed a trap, licked his dry lips, and edged down behind the steering wheel. The van next to him coughed to a start and the man yelled, "Hope you get your car fixed, son. I'm sure glad you kids picked up that Marine. God bless you!" The van jerked backwards, turned toward the highway, and jolted forward with arms, legs, and hands waving from the windows. The Marine waved back and Charlene shifted the package in her arms.

"Who's he?" Billy asked.

Charlene smiled over at the Marine and said, "This is my brother, Stanley. What'd you say your name was?"

"Alden. Sure glad to meet you," he said.

Charlene leaned into the station wagon and handed Billy the containers. "What's this?" Billy grunted.

"Water for the car, silly. And I told Mr. Alden he could come along with us for a ways," she added quickly. "He's going east too."

"East is a big place," Billy said, and got out to pour the containers of cold water into the radiator.

"He's been to Hollywood," Charlene said.

"I just stopped there for a few days."

"How long you in for?" Billy asked.

"He just got out," Charlene answered.

"You sure know a lot about this guy."

"I sure could use a hitch, sir," Alden said quickly.

"How come the Marines don't fly you home?"

"I wanted to take my time and see this great country of ours. Talk to people. Help out."

Billy grunted, threw the empty containers on the ground, and got back in the car. He turned the ignition and the car hummed to a start. Charlene nudged Alden and said, "We better get going." She opened the back door and he threw in his duffel. Than she handed the Mac Muffins to Billy and bounced into the front seat next to him, slipping the newspaper under the seat. Billy caught the move and she nodded at him.

He pulled out one of the Cokes, pushed in a plastic straw, and listened to the fan belt whirl. His body ached and he reached for his stash of pills. It was time for the smooth orange one. He slipped it into his mouth and took a gulp of the Coke.

"This is a neat old car," the Marine said as they picked up speed and took the inside lane.

Up ahead the tan van had pulled to the side of the road. Steam poured out of its engine and arms waved from the windows like a doomed centipede caught on its back. The large man in the torn tennis shoes tried to flag them down but Billy roared past him, and Alden watched as the island of people faded behind them on the long empty road.

"You from back east?" Billy asked.

"No, just heading for where it all began," he said.

"Where what began?"

"This great country of ours."

"You get to kill anybody?"

"No," Alden said, and Billy looked up at him in the rearview mirror. "I was headed for Special Forces though."

"That sounds real nice," Charlene smiled.

Billy moved the old Woody past a flat bed truck loaded with bales of hay and they rolled into a town with gray painted houses on either side of the street. Then the pill hit hard and Billy felt his body go limp.

"Hey, Buddy, can you drive?" he asked.

"Sure," Alden said. "Haven't used a stick-shift in awhile but I'll give it a try."

Billy pulled off the road. "If you get into any trouble, just holler," he said, changing places with Alden and slipping into the backseat. He pushed the Marine's duffel out of the way, pulled the army blanket up over his head, closed his eyes, and gave in to the smooth orange pill. The Woody jerked forward in a shudder of gears.

"Pay no mind, she does that all the time," Charlene said in a little girl's voice.

"Looks like we're going to need some gas," Alden said, as they rolled back out on the road behind a tractor.

Billy could hear their voices but the words rushed together at him under the blanket. The drone of the motor ran through his tired body and he eased into the crease of the back seat and let himself fall into the void.

*

Billy tried to move but the army blanket had twisted around his arm and caught him. When he shifted his body a crack of light broke across his eyes. He squinted and tried to block the bright stream coming in along the top of the window. They had stopped. He fought the blanket, pushed his arms free, and then realized he was alone. Lifting himself up he looked out to where the sun glared in a straight sharp line through the window. He could barely see the water through the high weeds, where a hazy figure stared back at him. They were parked in an open field and the only road out was the one they'd come in on. A few cars moved across it in a silent parade, but the field itself was empty. He reached for the sawed-off shotgun under the seat and felt the newspaper Charlene had jammed in there. Shoving the paper out of the way, he pulled out the gun, opened the door, and crawled out into the dust to peek over the front fender. The staring figure had gone and he wondered if anything had been there at all.

*

Alden's words came in a rush. They were hush-words, secret words. Words he'd never spoken before. "The Brass took us out on maneuvers," he said. "Short notice. Full equipment. The copters dropped us in the desert at 2200."

"Sounds scary," Charlene said, squinting through the glare coming off the river.

"Our orders were to move into position and take the objective."

"Where's 2200?" she asked, but he just kept staring at the river.

"We were being trained for a strategic target, issued live ammunition, and told to expect combat conditions. I jumped out of the copter and hung close to my buddies. It was so dark you couldn't see the ground, and so hot I was soaked in my own sweat. We hung in tight formation but the C.O. kept ordering us to spread out. Then there was nothing. Not a sound. I turned to stone. Felt like hours. Then something brushed my leg. I looked down and saw all these eyes staring up at me. Then I felt something behind me." He took a deep breath. "The eyes were everywhere. Going and coming until they'd surrounded me."

"What'd you do?" Charlene asked with a shiver.

"I raised my rifle and fired. There was a tremendous howling. Someone yelled. Then a whole lot more gunfire and yapping started. It all went haywire." They both sat quiet and finally he said, "They put me on trial."

"What for?"

"One Marine dead, two wounded, and a whole lot of coyotes shot up real bad."

"Coyotes?"

"They discharged me because I kept telling them He was testing me."

"Who'd do a thing like that to you?"

"God," he said, staring out over the river.

"Did you tell them God did it?" He didn't answer and she reached out to touch him. "What'd your girlfriend do?"

"I don't have a girlfriend, ma'am," he muttered.

"I don't believe it. You don't have a car and you don't have a girlfriend?"

"No, ma'am. All I've got is a mission."

"What's that?"

"A promise to God that I'd bring peace to His world."

They stared out at the shining river in silence letting Alden's simple words hang in the humid air, and Charlene finally said, "Well, at least you know what you want to do with your life, an all."

"A lot of men have tried to bring peace to the world. Men much greater than I could ever be."

"You mean like the president?" she asked.

"Men like Ghandi and Jesus Christ."

"Sounds to me like you just want to be a preacher. I know lots of guys want to be preachers. If you're good at it you can make a lot of money. Friend of mine —"

"I don't want money. I just want to stop people from killing each other."

"That's all right, I guess. It's just like me wanting to be a movie star," she said, moving toward him. He looked surprised and thought she might be making fun of him. "You put your mind to it you can do anything you want," she said. "It's a free country, an all, isn't it?"

"OH, GOD, PLEASE HELP ME," he shouted, and fell to his knees.

Charlene looked around to see if anyone had heard him, and whispered, "What you going on like this for?" Alden closed his eyes and pressed his hands together in prayer. "All you have to do is believe, an everything will turn out just fine," Charlene said. "For someone who wants to be a preacher you're off to a real poor start."

"It's not that easy," he said, swaying back and forth. "You've got to believe, accept, let yourself be delivered."

"Hell, anybody can be a preacher or a movie star if they want it enough," Charlene insisted.

"OUR WORLD IS HEADING DOWN A SLIPPERY SLOPE," Alden shouted. "WE'RE LOSING CHRIST'S TEACHING, FALLING INTO THE ABYSS!" He stopped to look out over the river, and a low angry growl came out of him. "God has summoned me for the good of the many. Called me to save the world, and I have given myself to His bidding." His deep voice rose over the riverbank and his body fell forward on the slope.

"I think that's real nice," Charlene mumbled, and he grabbed her around the waist and buried his face against her belly. "You crying?" she asked, stiffening against the slope to keep from falling backwards. He began to mutter something against her belly, and the warmth of his moving mouth ran down her thighs. "Next thing you'll be speaking in tongues, or making miracles," she said in short breaths.

"My God, my God," Alden pleaded, but the rest got lost and muffled against her. The tension in Charlene's thighs grew tighter. His mouth pressed in even closer against her and she trembled in the breeze coming off the river. The slope began to blur and she had to hold his head to keep from falling. Her knees bent and she felt a strange heat rush up between her legs. Her breathing came in short bursts, and a weakness hit her legs. He'd stopped mumbling and his head had dropped lower. She tried lifting him back but her arms had gone numb.

"I WANT TO BELIEVE! OH, GOD, I'VE GOT TO BELIEVE!" he yelled. The light floating sensation took her again and he began to sound further away. "You've made me want to do it," he cried, staring up at her. She tried to answer but couldn't, and steadied herself against him.

"I didn't mean to upset you," he said.

"I'm just fine. Really I am," she mumbled, but the incredible lightness in her body stayed with her as they climbed the hill. Billy was waiting at the top and she smoothed her dress and wondered if he'd seen what had happened to her on the slope.

"Where the hell are we?" Billy yelled down at them.

"Mississippi River," Alden shouted. "Illinois side."

"I got to talk with you, Char," Billy said, strutting along the top of the bluff. When she finally caught up with him he snapped, "What's with this guy?"

"He wants to be a preacher, but he's scared."

"Scared? He's a Marine for Christ sake."

"Don't make any difference if you're scared."

Billy jerked his shoulders and kicked a rusty beer can over the edge of the bluff and they watched it bounce down the slope toward the river.

"What's in that newspaper you shoved under the seat?"

"It's just dumb stuff about you kidnapping me and that maybe I'm dead. But I'm not dead, am I?" Billy kicked at the ground and another roll of dust flew into the air, and she glanced over at Alden.

"Why the hell did you have to pick him up?"

"So he could spell you at the wheel, silly. Besides, they're not looking for a Marine driving an old wagon."

"He got any money?"

"He filled the tank while you were asleep."

"I figured he'd spring for that. I just don't like uniforms. Don't trust them."

"No one even looks twice at us with him driving."

"How much money you figure he's got?" Billy asked.

She shrugged, and they walked back to the car. "He's got this thing about God though. It's kind of crazy."

"Don't like him much. Smiling and calling me, Sir, all the time."

"He's harmless, long as he keeps driving."

"An buying the gas," Billy said with a laugh.

Alden was sitting on the old Woody's fender staring out at the Mississippi like a man transfixed. "You just keep driving, Buddy. You're doing great," Billy said, and when Alden looked up at him Billy could see how changed he was. His face and eyes seemed to beam in the bright low glare coming off the river.

Charlene settled into the front seat and Alden started the motor. "If we can find 64 it'll take us right into Chicago," he said. Charlene stretched out in the seat and pulled her dress up to let the afternoon sun hit her legs. She closed her eyes, thought about what had happened on the slope, and edged her dress up a little higher.

*

Alden caught a quick glimpse of the white structure through the trees, felt a sharp, gulping ache in his chest, and the whole thing began to float in front of him. He looked for a sign in the bursts of sunlight shooting through the trees and saw the cross above the door.

The old Woody bounced off the blacktop and headed up a gutted dirt road. Charlene lay curled in the front seat and Billy snored under the army blanket in the back. When Alden finally reached the gleaming white building he eased in close to its white steps. A small sign hung on the front door. The letters had been crudely chalked on a flat piece of wood and he squinted through the glare to read the circle of words, **CLOSED - NO DELIVERIES.**

Alden stared at the sign and fought the pressure growing along the top of his head. His legs bent under the force and he fell to his knees to face the blinding glare coming off the white lacquered front door. He began to pray through his tears. Despite what the sign said, he'd been delivered.

*

Billy sensed the stillness in the air and peeked out from under the ragged army blanket. Everything was bathed in a white light and he noticed the carved wooden cross over the door. That same floating figure he'd seen at the river seemed to be there too, rolling back and forth in front of him.

"Hey, Char," he whispered, poking her. "Take a look at this."

Charlene groaned, "What's he doing now?"

"He's down on his knees and —"

"Oh, shit," she said, falling back on the seat again.

Alden's head was tilted upward, staring at the crude wooden cross over the door. His lips moved but there was no sound. "Hey, Buddy, what the hell you doing?" Billy called, looking around to see where he'd taken them. "We can't stay here," he said. "Marilyn will be wanting to eat again soon." Alden turned on his knees and his lips bent into a smile. He stared into the late sun, rocking from side to side on the top step, making his head flare in the fading sun.

"I know who you are and what you've done," he said.

Billy looked around to see if anyone had heard him. "She's not your sister and her name isn't Marilyn. You're Billy The Kid! Picture's in all the papers and on TV," Alden said, staring into the sun. "They think you kidnapped her … killed her."

"Nobody's been killed! 'Specially her!" Billy said. "We just took some money."

"And now you've led me to this eternal light … a place of goodness. You've led me to God Himself! You're my deliverers. My archangels." Then he lowered his voice, and said, "Kneel with me, boy … you need salvation."

"I don't need nothing," Billy muttered, looking around to see if anyone was watching them.

Alden reached up, grabbed him by the neck, and Billy felt a sharp pain in his knees when he hit the wooden steps. He could hear him mumbling and moaning, and when he tried to get up Alden's thumbs pressed in behind his ears.

"SAVE YOUR SINNING ANGEL, LORD! SAVE HIM," Alden shouted. "Keep this boy from harm. Protect him from the worldly fears that surround us." Billy tried to move but when he did the pressure on his head got worse. "LIFT YOUR SINNER, LORD!" Alden yelled at the last piece of fading sun. "HELP HIM OVERCOME THIS ADVERSITY OF SPIRIT AND MIND." Alden looked out across the empty field, bathed in the late sun, and began to sing:

> "You can ease your load,
> Down this sorrow road,
> If you take my God's hand,
> And a-walk this land."

The pressure behind Billy's ears gave way and the sounds of Alden's singing crackled and exploded in his head. When the singing stopped he looked up at the Marine glowing at the top of the stairs in the last remnants of the sun. Alden raised his head into the fading light and shouted, "CHARLENE SKINNER AND BILLY CAREW ARE THE ANGELS THAT BROUGHT ME TO THIS HOLY PLACE WHERE WE WILL PUT UP THE HIGHEST TRANSMITTER WE CAN FIND TO SEND OUT YOUR MESSAGE TO THE WORLD!" Then he rose up and said, "Get up, Billy. The Lord's calling us! It's our time! THE GATES ARE OPENING," he shouted at the dimming sky, and turned the large brass knobs on the little church's glossy white door.

"Why the hell did you tell him who we were, Billy?" Charlene asked, rubbing the sleep from her eyes.

"I didn't. He must've read it in that newspaper you left under the seat. Or God told him," Billy said, heading after Alden.

"WHERE YOU GOING?" Charlene yelled, but Billy kept going. "Crazy ... you're both nuts!" she mumbled, and headed back to the car.

*

A white metal cross, cut crudely from the hood of a Ford Mustang, hung prominently above the preacher's nook. The large piece of metal glowed in the filtered light that came through a lone window facing the highway. Alden fell to his knees and stared up at the cross. "This rugged piece of metal has saved you, Billy," he said, and his words rushed around the long empty room. "It's a new life ... a second chance."

Billy moved into the room, staring up at the glowing white cross.

"Do you hear Him calling you, Billy?"

"I guess," came the weak answer.

"That's all God asks."

Billy stared up at the high buffed simonized cross but all he heard were the passing cars out on the road.

"Let's get outta here," Charlene whispered from behind him, as the last of the light faded into the shadows.

"Be quiet, I'm trying to hear God," Billy whispered.

"Hell," Charlene hissed, and a wooossh of pellets roared past Billy, catching Alden in the back of the head. A sudden gush of blood sprayed across the white metal cross and Alden's body jerked forward, and sprawled into the preacher's nook.

The smell of gunshot hung in the air and Billy let out a low moan. "Shit, Charlene, I told you to leave that gun alone."

"There's no way I'm going back to that dumb Juvie Hall with those weird women and loser guards." Billy stared at her as if she were some stranger they had picked up on the road. "HE KNEW WHO WE WERE, BILLY!" she yelled at him.

"Yeah, I know," he muttered, taking the gun from her and hobbling out into the buzz of crickets and mosquitoes to see if anyone had heard the shot. The long gutted road was empty. Nothing moved.

"How 'bout us stopping for a burger and some fries?" she asked, holding out a handful of money.

Billy slid the gun back under the seat, turned on the old Woody's motor, and listened to the new fan belt hum. "No more hitchers," he said. "They complicate things."

"Yeah, I know. But at least this one got to go where he wanted. That's all that really counts."

"I don't think he cares much about where he is now."

"Whatever," she said bracing her feet on the shaking dashboard while Billy drove the old Woody back up the gutted dirt road toward the highway.

PARABLE

The young Doctor hung his framed Harvard Medical degree on the office wall while the Church elders set up a long table in the front vestibule. He and his wife, an intensive care nurse, had just arrived from Boston to start the first medical practice in the history of the town. The mayor and minister stood at the front door greeting the parishioners, who had come with their casseroles, roast chicken, chili, corn bread, and pies. They were there to meet the new young physician and his wife. The doctor's gray eyes, a little too far apart, maintained a constant look of surprise as he tried to remember the names and faces of every one that came to shake his hand and welcome them.

The festivities had hardly gotten underway when a man was rushed into the vestibule as an emergency case. The Doctor quickly diagnosed the patient as being in cardiac arrest while his own heart pounded so hard he could barely hear his wife calling out the patient's weakening condition.

The townspeople knelt on the hard wood floor and the Minister led them in an Our Father, while the young Doctor worked on the man's chest. When the Doctor glanced up for some reaction from his patient he was surprised to see that the man was a Native American. High cheekbones, dark rolling eyes, and long gray-black hair that spread across the pale green pillow like a web of fine silk. A perfectly shaped white feather, a small beaded pouch, and a Silver Star medal had all been woven together into his hair to form a simple headpiece.

The Doctor jolted the Indian's chest and listened to his wife's readings over the low hum of the parishioners' prayers. Nothing seemed to work. Desperate, he applied an anesthesia, cut open the man's heaving chest, pulled out his heart and held it in his hands. The dripping organ spread through his fingers like a wet sponge and he muttered a prayer as the final seconds of the Indian's life began to rush away.

Around the large room, the gathered knelt in silence while the doctor battled to save the dark skinned man on the table, massaging the heart until the wriggling muscle began to jerk between his fingers again, relieving the strain on the old man's breathing.

Word of the Doctor's emergency victory over certain death spread through the long valley on the late October winds, and the young Doctor went into the Church and fell to his knees, giving thanks to God because he had faced Death and won.

Through the long night, his patient slept peacefully and when he finally wakened the Doctor was at his side. "You're in our new makeshift hospital," he said proudly to the old man. The Indian stared with bottomless eyes at the upside-down bottle dripping into the long plastic tube in his arm. "You're our first patient," the young Doctor told him, but the Indian's eyes never changed their expression.

When the Doctor opened the Indian's chart he was surprised to see that the white feather, beaded pouch, and Silver Medal had been tied across the top of it. He brushed them aside and was amazed to find that his patient was nearly ninety years old. "You're in good shape," the Doctor said, reading through the chart. When the Indian finally looked up his vacant stare seemed to go right through the young Doctor. "Your name is Willy Lone Tree." The Doctor waited for an answer and finally had to ask, "Is that right?"

"You saved me?" the Indian asked in a clear voice.

The Doctor looked down into the dark eyes. "You had a heart attack and I was the attending physician. We were lucky."

The Indian reached up to touch his head and looked perplexed. The Doctor untied the white feather, beaded pouch, and Silver Star from the medical chart and laid them in the old man's wrinkled hands.

"What are those things?" the doctor asked.

The old man took in a deep breath and said, "The silver medal is mine. The pouch belonged to my father and the feather to his father. They wore them on their Death Day. I wore them on mine so they'd know who I was when they saw me."

"But you didn't die."

"They're waiting for me on the hill."

The old man seemed so assured. Confident. No questions, no fear, not even an acknowledgement of coming through the ordeal alive.

The young Doctor didn't quite understand what the old man was trying to tell him, but each day he came back to watch over his patient, prescribing medicines, diet, making sure there wasn't any strain on him. When the medical release was signed he made sure the old man's future appointments were verified and that he had all the medicines he'd need for the critical days ahead. The Indian nodded, took the packets of pills, signed the forms, and drove away in his pickup. That same evening the old Indian climbed the north side of a nearby hill in the shadowed rain and hung himself from an oak tree.

The Doctor was confused and hurt when the elders told him what the old man had done. He went across to the Church, thinking of the struggle they'd had with Death, and began to pray like he'd never prayed before. Hours later, the caretaker had to call the Doctor's wife to come and take him home so they could close the church.

Months later, when the first snow hit the valley, an Indian woman arrived at the Doctor's office. She stood stiffly in front of his desk, snow melting in her black hair, and reached into her bag to pull out the white feather, beaded pouch, and the old man's Silver Medal. They'd been woven into a long piece of the old man's hair. The woman stared down at them for a long moment, laid the odd pieces across the Doctor's cluttered desk, and walked out.

Flurries of snow danced across the window while the young Doctor stared down at the old Indian's headpiece on his desk. He finally picked up the pieces and draped them over the medical degree he'd hung when he'd arrived. Staring up at the Indian's odd set of pieces, hanging on his medical degree, the Doctor smiled as he began to understand what his patient had wanted. Now he would wear the long white feather, the beaded pouch, and the silver medal when his time came.

FENCES

When the deep shadows finally came in, he sprung out of the cluster of junipers and made a run for the mountain's stark cliffs. He'd come down from the rim country, circling the ranches that flickered in the growing darkness. This flat open country hadn't given him much protection and the only way he could get to the mountain was to jump the fences that covered the darkening pastures.

*

Brenny pulled the pickup in close to the swing gate. His back stiffened as his legs took the rise. A gentle rain began to cover his face and he opened the gate. Stoner, the new dog, got up and wagged his tail. Brenny patted him on the rump, and leaned over into the back of the truck to check on Busher and Chloe. Boog and Skeeter didn't budge. He didn't like the monsoon season. The dogs tended to get lazy.

"Pretty soon, guys," he whispered, and drove onto the ranch. He got back out to lift the wires over the end-post and secure the gate again. In a few minutes they'd be at the bunkhouse and he'd get a hot breakfast before starting out.

Ed Ruttner, the ranch manager, appeared in the headlights, and Brenny had to drive around him to park in the back. Ruttner was at the truck's front door before it even stopped.

"Bad business," he muttered.

"It's only bad business when you start using the place for a playground," Brenny said.

"They're all over the place. Execs and their wives ... one of them even brought a Nanny for their kids."

"They still in bed?"

"They're getting Ostrow up now."

"I could use some pancakes."

"Jesus, Brenny. Ostrow's pissed. He's expecting you to get out on this right away. We're trying to keep it under wraps." Brenny reached in between the dogs to pull out the blankets and saddle while Ruttner picked up the empty thermos. "I'll get you some fresh coffee," he said. "Sorry you won't have time for breakfast. Didn't mean to spoil your birthday. Mary sounded angry when she answered the phone."

Brenny's wife had taken Ed's emergency call. The job had finally become a strain between them. She kept telling Brenny that he was spending too much time out on the trail. When he denied it, she surprised him with a packet of torn off calendar pages. Every time he went out she had colored in the days with a red crayon, like he'd been missing-in-action.

"Yeah, I can understand my wife being angry," he finally said to Ruttner. "We were going to celebrate my big fives. Guess it'll have to wait."

"I tried not to drag you out here," Ruttner said. "Even tried taking care of it myself. We waited for the cat to come back but she never showed."

"How do you know it's a female?"

"Well, hell, one of our calves is ripped to shreds. You know how messy lion cubs can get. Trees are clawed up too."

Brenny knew the female. He had left her alone because she'd never gone after the stock. He hadn't seen her for months. She'd probably gone into heat or even had a litter. She might've run into a problem feeding her cubs and went after a cow to make it easier.

One of the cowboys opened the stable door. They'd already taken out his horse. Old Dusty stood in the barn's dim light. Brenny set the blanket and swung the saddle on her. He'd almost finished tightening the cinches when Ostrow showed up in pressed jeans, bright plaid shirt, and a new ranch hat covered with a fitted piece of shiny plastic to keep off the rain. Brenny figured he'd probably bought new boots for the occasion too because he moved toward him in a slow and stiff motion.

"We don't like this business anymore than you do," Ostrow said in a tone that made Dusty take a nervous step backwards. "I've been trying to keep a cap on things until you got here."

"I'm just heading out to look at the damage," Brenny said, and another young cowboy handed him his thermos and a package of sweet rolls. Brenny led Dusty out into the light rain and they headed for the truck to get the rest of his gear. Ostrow kept pace with him through the muddy driveway.

"This is probably just a lot of bullshit to you, Hartrey," he said, in that same annoying tone.

"Things like this happen out here," Brenny replied.

"My execs work their ass off all year and look forward to coming out to the ranch, having a good time, and getting some work done at the same time. I don't want anything to get in their way."

"Mountain lions come and go. They eat, sleep, drink, and have their cubs. Last thing they want is to run into a vacationing Corporate Executive," Brenny said, dragging his old saddlebag out of the truck and reaching back for his Winchester.

"I want that damn lion out of the way, and if you can't do it I'll get someone who can. I expect results, Mr. Hartrey," Ostrow said, and started back to the barn.

Tritech had acquired Webb Ranch for intensive corporate meetings: a lot of city dudes flying in from all over the country for seminars, fishing, and horseback riding. Ostrow didn't want his Executives' fun ruined by some mountain lion getting in too close to the lodge.

Brenny watched the little man walk away in the rain. He felt like quitting but knew it'd only take a few hours to replace him. Up to this point he'd been the sole protector of the Webb Ranch for nearly twenty years. In his own way he'd kept the balance. The cattle grazed, the mountain lions had their young, grew old, and moved on. The original owner had hired him to protect the cattle, but times had changed. Now the Corporation was in charge. They were sending him out to kill a lion so the Executive's families could feel safe. Three of Tritech's calves had been ripped apart and Ostrow wanted the lion's ass, which meant six feet of fur to hang on some office wall in Dallas.

The pink light of sunrise barely began to break across the sky. Brenny slipped the rifle through the worn leather scabbard and let the dogs out of the truck. They ran across the driveway, sniffing and pissing on the corners of the bunkhouse. The soft drizzle began to let up as they made their way to the fence. He heard Boog's low growl, warning the new dog to stay in close. The sounds of morning melted into Dusty's clopping steps and the squeak of the saddle. Brenny began feeling good again. There were a whole lot of noes waiting for him out there. No phones, no wife, no home, no Ostrow, nada. Once he passed through that fence, rode through the grove of trees along the edge of the pond, he'd be alone again. The only true peace he knew anymore.

*

An early glow broke over the mountains as Brenny headed for the pasture where the feasting ravens had gathered. He turned the horse, clucked at the dogs, and headed straight for the shade. He tied Skeeter, Busher, Chloe, and the new dog, Stoner, to separate trees so they wouldn't get in the way. He and Boog didn't have much time. The cat had probably hung around the kill for the past few nights, and headed off in a different direction each time. There were always a lot of tracks around a carcass. Boog's job was to find the freshest one.

When they approached the kill, the ravens squawked and flew into the trees. Boog sniffed at the carcass, looking for a track. The ground around the dead calf had been torn up just like Ruttner had said. When Brenny glanced over at the birds he saw where the trees had been clawed. The marks were too high for lion cubs and female pumas rarely did anything like that.

Boog moved easily through the grass and Brenny followed him to a second dead calf. This kill was even older. Insects had taken over. Boog high-stepped around it, sniffing the ground, whining in frustration. It was difficult to pick up an old scent in this weather even for a good strike dog like Boog.

When they started back he lost sight of the dog in the tall August weeds. Then he heard him bark and a raven took flight. Brenny stopped to look for the carcass. The calf's head barely stuck out of the grass. The Webb Ranch brand, a W with a wavy line under it, had been clearly marked on the calf's quarters. Boog circled the carcass. Brenny froze so he wouldn't destroy any tracks the dog might find. When he looked down he saw the fresh paw prints all around him. Going and coming. The lion had come back to the kill several times.

Brenny kneeled in the wet soil to get a closer look. The dampness seeped through his jeans as he took out his reading glasses. The kill had been made about fifteen or twenty yards away then dragged into the dense brush. He guessed, from the size of the tracks, that a male lion had done the damage. The cat made the kill with a blow to the neck, and followed it with a spine severing bite. He had to be big. It took great strength to drag that large a calf into the brush and hide it.

A transient male was probably moving through the territory. He made the first kill, and the female must have stumbled onto it with her cubs. The male returned, saw it'd been eaten, and went searching for another kill. He was young and looking for a territory to settle down in. These days that became harder to do for the lion. There was too much development going on. The ranchers were selling out and track houses were pouring in with man-made waterfalls and pools. Land was running out. Solitary predators like the puma were being forced into a smaller territory where there was less game. In the end, this transient cat would have to fight for territory somewhere down the line.

Boog's sharp cry bit the morning air. The other dogs barked back. Brenny got up stiffly, making his way around the dead calf to the other side of the high brush. He caught up with the dog where the high weeds ended. Boog's dark tail waved as he stood protecting a small patch of matted grass.

"What you got, boy?"

Brenny knelt, put his arm around the dog, and stared at the fresh print between Boog's front paws. If the lion had been in that close he must've heard the dogs barking. Still, with a fresh new track like that the dogs could probably catch up with him before he bedded down in the heat of the day.

"Good boy," Brenny said, patting old Boog. He left his yellow slicker to mark the spot, and headed for the other dogs.

*

Brenny had been up on Dusty for over an hour. Boog trotted along next to him, letting Skeeter lead them up the ridge. Sunlight broke over Simmons Peak and rushed down over the miles of ranches below. The Santa Maria Mountains were caught in a mist but he could see that the sun would eventually win the battle. He hoped the lion's scent wouldn't dry out. The prints moved out of the brush and he had to hang down off the saddle to track them. The spacing between them was bigger than he'd ever seen before.

When he turned to look for the dogs they disappeared around a bend, heading for Granite Mountain and the long rocky washes that ran straight to a peak about eight thousand feet up. He heard a lot of yapping but couldn't distinguish the sounds. The dogs were all barking at once.

He turned his horse in toward the hill, riding her on a sharp angle through the scrub oak. Leaning forward he coaxed Dusty toward the barking and rode the small crest. He wrapped the reins in the brush, took his rifle, and ran to the rim. The barking had become a riot of noise. Chloe had staked out a dead doe. The lion must've jumped her higher up and the struggle had gone down to where the carcass had finally been dragged under some shade trees. It'd been a dangerous kill. The lion couldn't reach the top of the deer's neck so went under it. The deer's flank had been ripped open and was still bleeding.

Brenny heard barking on the other side of a large boulder. He found Boog and Skeeter guarding a juniper tree. When they saw him coming their barking turned into whines. Brenny stopped about thirty feet from the tree, and searched its branches until he found the mountain lion hissing at them from a narrow crotch about half way up. It was the female. He looked around for her cubs, hoped the dogs hadn't killed them, and only then realized that Busher and Stoner were under another tree further down the hill. Two of the female's cubs hung precariously from a scrub oak just out of the reach of his new dog's playful leaps.

"It's all right, Busher," he said. The dog came running to him but Stoner kept leaping at the cubs.

He reached inside his jacket for the package the cowboy had given him in the barn. Busher and Chloe stood watching him undo the rubber bands while Skeeter and Boog came up the hill after them. When the outer package came undone Brenny pulled the last few sticky pieces of wrapping off the sweet rolls and cut off a large piece with his jackknife. The smell of cinnamon sliced the air.

"You first, Skeeter," he said. The dog took the piece of roll from his hand. "Good boy," Brenny whispered, rubbing the dog's ears. Somewhere the lion tracks had crossed one another. The dog had picked up the female's tracks instead of following the large male. "You're still the best, Skeeter," Brenny said. "Anyone could have made a mistake like that."

He gave the rest of the roll to Boog, and cut the next one into thirds for Busher, Chloe, and the young dog, Stoner. The treed lioness looked hungry too and she kept growling to reassure her cubs. The litter had been a strain on her. It might've even been her first. They looked healthy though. She'd done a good job and he knew she wouldn't leave that tree without them.

If he killed her and toted her back to the ranch, the whole matter of satisfying the corporate picnic would be over. He'd be an instant hero and probably get a raise. The only loss would be some lioness wearing a government collar.

"All right, gang," he said. 'We're leaving this lady and her pups alone." The dogs wagged their tails. "Let's get it right this time." Boog started up the hill to where Brenny had tied the horse. The old dog was ready to go again.

*

It took Boog over an hour to find the spot where the tracks had crossed. The dogs moved in tandem, finding the male's smell on the brush and along the rocks. Deer are a lot easier for a dog to follow because they leave a sharp track. The lion has a soft pad and it's harder to see. Skeeter might have been the best track dog in the territory but it was Brenny's job to keep them all moving in the right direction.

When Brenny saw the fresh scratch marks on a large cedar he clucked at the dogs, heading them up along the boulders. The lion they were chasing had to be eight feet or more. Brenny had worked these mountains over twenty years but never saw a cougar that big. The dogs raced past him in a rush, moving toward the peaks. Granite Mountain's the perfect place for a cougar. Enormous rocks tossed together like a petrified salad. Its highest peaks are stark, and the rest of it spreads out across miles of rock.

Brenny cut across a switchback to catch up with the dogs. Boog was waiting for him, but he didn't see the others.

"What's up, boy?" he asked.

The dog stood in front of a barbed-wire fence hidden in the overgrown brush. If they crossed that wire he'd be into a government wildlife area. Dusty cantered easily to where Boog waited. The rest of the dogs were already on the other side.

"You know what happens if we get caught in there. Lots of screaming and threatening," he said to the dog, as he opened the worn saddlebag to take out the clippers. "There's a big buck-ass-fine for cutting government wire." Boog yawned.

Brenny narrowed his eyes against the glare of the sun. He scanned the trails below, making sure there weren't any stray hikers, then snipped the barbed wire and bent it away from the post. He pulled the fence out to let Dusty through, then forced the wire back into place so the cut couldn't be spotted.

*

Storm clouds rolled in over the mountains. The big cat watched the lightning tear through the curving shapes. An intense heat made the air feel heavy and slowed the climbing. He came up on a rim of low juniper and reached in to sweep away the loose rocks. He took a deep breath,

115

smelling the rain in the air. A movement shimmered in the heat below, darting in and out of the brush. Coyote. He slumped down deep under the juniper, into its damp shade, and waited for the storm to hit.

*

Brenny lifted the heavy canteen off the saddle and Boog and Skeeter turned back. The new dog, Stoner, trotted easily behind them. "That rain could cut into our day," Brenny said, pouring water into a pan. Boog moved to drink first. Then Skeeter squeezed in next to him. They drank together in long, loud gulps. The younger dog edged in closer. "You've been pretty good today, boy," Brenny said, pouring some water into his hand. The young dog trotted the last few steps for the earned drink.

When Busher and Chloe didn't show, it usually meant they were getting close to the lion. Brenny poured another handful of water for Stoner, and listened for Busher's bark. The only sound was the flat growl of jet planes leaving their white streaks across the sky over them. Granite Mountain stood directly under the New York to Los Angeles flight pattern. Every hour the businessmen, tourists, and their plastic food trays hurtled over the struggle between man and beast below.

Brenny poured more water into the empty pan. Skeeter took a few gulps before disappearing into the deep shade. Stoner hesitantly approached, drank the rest of the water, then sat at Brenny's feet.

Dusty danced a nervous step as a sudden wind rushed down the mountain. "Easy, girl. Just the rain coming in," he said, as a crooked stick of lightning hit. Brenny counted the seconds before he heard its low rumble. They had about an hour to find the lion or it'd be just another long walk home in the rain.

Stoner whined and the brush began to wave in the breeze. Brenny glanced over at Boog and Skeeter but they didn't move. "You hear something, boy?" Brenny asked the young dog. Stoner turned to stare up at the peak. He barked sharply, waited, and barked again. Boog jumped up to move in next to him. The older dog's ears stiffened, and he started up the trail with the new dog behind him. Brenny grabbed Dusty's reins and they moved out so fast the horse nearly stepped on Skeeter who had run under her to catch up with the others.

*

They were there on top of him and he rolled out from beneath the juniper, catching one of them under the chest. It howled. Then he felt a sharp pain run up along his back leg. The other one had gotten in behind him. Springing to higher ground, he looked back through the flying dust. They weren't coyotes. The smaller one kept barking at him while the other crawled through the dust along the narrow wash. He shrieked at them and their barking stopped. A sharp pain ran up his back leg where it had been ripped open. A quick nausea hit him and he slid between the boulders, looking for a place to hide.

*

Brenny heard the barking but had lost sight of the dogs. When he reached the ridge, just below the steep climb to the top, he had to go around a pair of huge boulders. Boog stood rigid on the other side, guarding something in the wash. Busher was lying dead among a rash of loose stones. He covered the dog's broken body with his jacket and hid her under the juniper. Tying the horse in close to the rocks, he pulled out his Winchester, and noticed the fresh blood. He smeared his fingers in the heavy red splotches and raised them to his mouth. The blood lingered on his tongue and knotted his throat. It was the musty taste of the mountain lion.

He finally caught up with the dogs and they followed the cat's trail up the mountain together. Lightning ripped the low clouds, with splitting roars of thunder behind it. If he stopped now they'd lose the track in the rain. Brenny glanced up at the stark cliffs on the north face and the three dogs ran ahead. Skeeter, his head low, sniffed along the large rock formation leading to the peak. Boog stayed in close, but the new dog dropped back when the cat's high scream rushed down at them.

Brenny took off his slicker, threw it aside, and made a wide turn to come up behind them. The cat had placed himself along a granite wall that split straight to the top of the mountain. If he fired a shot he might force the cat out but didn't want to lose any more dogs. The only other choice was to climb to the peak while they still had the cat trapped.

*

His hind leg pained and he shifted his weight away from the growling dog that paced back and forth in front of him. A brown muzzle snarled in close and he screamed at it in anger. The dog retreated so fast it nearly stumbled off the narrow ledge.

He pulled back as far as he could, waited for the dogs to come in closer, then jumped at the granite wall. His long body arced off the flat stone, catching one of the dogs full on the shoulder. It rolled in the dust and he swiped again. The dog tumbled away. He turned swiftly to face the large black and tan standing his ground. A younger dog stood behind him, whining in the wind.

He leaped up across the boulders. A sharp pain ran through his back leg but he managed to scratch his way out of the cleft. He had another long jump to the far ledge and couldn't be sure if his leg would hold. A drenching rain hit in large heavy drops, turning everything into a blur. He crouched, looked up into the downpour, and jumped.

118

J.S. Kierland

*

The storm hit Brenny just below the deep cleft in the mountain. He took off his boots so he wouldn't slip on the wet algae. His clothes had gotten so heavy he could hardly move. He ripped off his shirt, letting the cool rain bite his bare back and shoulders as he slipped out of his soaked pants. The water gushed across the rocks in a rushing stream, falling off the cliff on the other side. He finally reached the top of the cleft, dropped to his knees, and peeked over the edge. The cougar was gone.

A chill ran through his naked body. Sensing something, he looked up and saw the huge, powerful head staring down at him. He cradled the Winchester and tilted his head toward the sight. Like a pagan god, the lion looked as if he were part of the mountain itself. There'd be no second chance. A blinding light suddenly hit below the ledge, bouncing in a thin blue flash toward his rifle barrel.

A bolt of heat hit Brenny's chest, throwing him backwards into a pool of sizzling water. He felt an incredible thirst, and there was no sound to the hail bouncing off his face. He'd been hit by the lightning and thrown into a gushing stream of rainwater. Pieces of ice were melting on his eyes. Raising himself on his arm, he felt a deep weakness and fell back into the water. A familiar smell moved over him. It was old Boog. He tried to call out to the dog but his strength faded like the rushing water that ran past him and disappeared over the edge.

*

The lion limped across the rocks, waiting to see which way the men on the horses would go. He took a last look at the lifeless form on the lower ledge. The black and tan had crawled up on the man's chest to protect him, and he could smell its panting fear.

119

The line of men had started their final climb to the peak and he heard them urging the horses as he limped down along the other side of the boulders. It'd be slow going because of the bite on his leg, but he'd try to get down the mountain before daylight ran out on him.

SOMETIMES I LIVE IN THE TOWN

J.S. Kierland

ROBOTS

The Major drove north along 95 into the oncoming darkness. The sun hung low over the desert behind him, turning Vegas into a blur of light in his rearview mirror. From here it'd be forty minutes of uninterrupted silence before the electric gates and building C came into view. Each night he prepared himself like a Boy Scout on retreat. His assignments had all become top secret and a different officer put in charge for each one. A minimum of words, the flight plan revealed, then the darkened room for ten hours of flying time. He began to feel like a robot, and finally requested an immediate transfer back to building A. Instead, he was promoted to Major, given a pay raise, and an extra day off each month. Nothing else changed.

His promotion made Nancy happy. The extra money had more than covered Billy's private school for the year, plus the new couch. It also meant he could keep the red Beemer, and she could continue driving the SUV. The extra day off usually came on the weekend when he could catch up on his sleep and watch a football game.

He found flying in a darkened room much more exhausting than the real thing, and missed the freedom of disappearing into the sky without someone monitoring his every move. After his request for a transfer back to Building A had been denied, he asked to be reassigned to the base he had come from in Germany. They ignored that completely and didn't promote him this time, meaning he was going to stay in Building C where they needed him until further notice.

Flying the drones was boring: sitting in a seat over a targeted terrain and watching it on video screens from a few thousand feet up. Color by day, black and white by night. A variety of young sergeants were assigned to sit next to him and work the drone's cameras, but he controlled the plane. That included the 500 lb. bombs and the deadly missiles.

War and surveillance had turned into a video game, unlike flying his beloved F-17 where he was as far above the target as he wanted to be and didn't have to see it, or even think about what he'd hit below. Flying the silent drone was more precise and he could be in as close as he wanted, to see what they were wearing, catch their expressions, and even hear their voices.

Most of the time he followed convoys, or a stranded soldier put in harm's way. He'd maneuver in as close as he could to watch and protect until reinforcements arrived. He had trouble working in such close proximity to the targets, and to the high expectations of the intelligence officers in charge. They never seemed satisfied with anything he did, and yet never complained. There were different agents every night with great expectations for their particular projects. Nothing spoken. He was simply handed his orders and a flight plan.

He began leaving for the job earlier each evening to stop and pray at the little church outside Indian Springs. There were never any priests or people around and he'd arrive and leave alone. Usually, a priest's vestments hung in a corner of the church near the confessional. Several benches, in need of paint, made up a few rows of seats and a large crucifix dominated the copper sandstone altar.

Invariably, a variety of coins had been thrown into the holy water bowl at the front door, probably by gamblers looking for a little luck at the tables back in Vegas. The Major would scoop them out and drop the dripping coins into the little wicker basket on the floor. Then he'd bless himself with the residue of water on his hands, throw a few bucks into the basket on top of the wet coins, pray for a few minutes, and head for the shiny red Beemer he'd parked in the lot outside. His life had turned into these simple rituals. Only the crucifix over the makeshift altar and the priest's ironed vestments hanging in the corner seemed real to him in the weeks that had passed.

The ride through the darkness to Building C went quickly if he found the jazz station that he sometimes got on clear nights when the desert smelled of perfume and sand. Miles Davis' muted trumpet played *SUMMERTIME* and it made him think about a time before he'd been born when jet fighters scorched the sky and the pilot's only challenge was how fast or how high they could fly. Now they had graduated to simple missions and targets. Those old exciting times were gone and only came back when he talked to the older men in worn flight jackets, holding drinks in their fists, and dreaming of walking on the moon.

He came up on the security checkpoint and the lighted gates. The guard knew him but went through the routine of checking his IDs, saluting, and then raising the barrier. More dull repetitive rituals. He rolled into the base at the required fifteen miles an hour and headed for Building C. It was the nondescript tan building, hardly noticeable in the day, and just a dark shadow at night. Large fan palms had been planted along its northern perimeter to lessen the look of the numerous satellite dishes that faced the southern sky.

He parked in his usual spot away from the lighted entrance where his red Beemer would be less noticeable. He grabbed his leather pouch, threw in his sunglasses, locked the car doors, and headed for the building. The cold AC hit him when he stopped to get another check of IDs at the door by someone he hadn't seen before. The buzzer sounded and he went through into the narrow hallway, and down to the cramped room they called the lounge. It was empty and someone had left the TV on. A football game was going and the Redskins were up on the Giants by a field goal.

"Sir," a voice said behind him. He turned and saw another new face. "They're waiting to assign us. I'm Sergeant Davies. I'll be with you tonight." They shook hands and the Major followed him down the hall.

Several extra people were at the table. He had worked with some of them before. Their silence and avoided glances made him look around for the guy who'd be running things on this particular mission. He sensed it'd be the one in plain clothes at the end of the table, dressed in chinos, a Hawaiian shirt, and a desert jacket. He had a nondescript preppy look, probably Ivy League, with a shock of sun burnt hair. Someone he didn't know or want to know. The guy smiled and said, "You're late, Major."

"I'm sorry. It won't happen again," he said stiffly.

"We have a lot to do," the man in the Hawaiian shirt replied, and the usual manila envelopes were handed to him and the Sergeant. The others in the room stared blankly at the protocol. The Major opened his envelope and the Sergeant followed. A black and white picture lay on top of the papers. A man dressed in Arab robes was looking back over his shoulder. The expression had fear in the eyes and a surprised look on his face, like he wasn't sure which way to turn.

"This is Farouk Abdul. He's a top recruiter and one of the higher ups in the organization," the Hawaiian shirt said, keeping the information minimal. It was doubtful he even used the man's real name. The Major studied the picture and the apprehensive eyes staring back at him.

"How old is the picture?" he asked.

The man smiled, and said, "A year at most."

In this game the Major knew how much a man could change in a year. He looked for some clue in the man's face so he could get a quick identity. He saw a small, almost unnoticeable, birthmark along the left line of his jaw. It would have to do. The angle of the picture made it difficult to tell how tall he was, and the loose Arab clothes hid his body and head.

"He's our target," the man in the Hawaiian shirt said. That was it. An evening's work spelled out in three words.

The Major signed the usual pieces of paper under the picture and stood up. The Sergeant rose with him and they both saluted the other men at the table and headed for the interior room behind them.

They took their positions in the large leather chairs and the video screens flickered and lit up. The Sergeant adjusted the focus on his controlled cameras and a brown terrain came into view. The Major thought it was probably Afghanistan, or the run along the Pakistani border. On one screen he could see mountains in the background and even a few houses. He took the controls, gave the signal and felt the drone's power switch over to him. He recognized this particular drone by the easy feel of it. He'd spent an entire night flying it a week earlier, protecting a group of men in a disabled Humvee. Shots had been fired and he'd used two missiles to protect them. It had been a long, boring night but the people in the room seemed satisfied with his work and the positive results he had gotten. Three insurgents were killed and the trails of blood meant several others had been wounded. He liked this drone and felt sure it was the same one he'd used that night.

This new flight plan would take him over a mountainous ridge toward some small houses nestled in along a dirt road that ran down the mountain. It was early morning there and he could feel the men stir in the seats behind him when they saw the houses. The Sergeant zoomed the belly camera in and caught what looked like a covered lump behind one of the houses. The Major maneuvered the drone higher and glided to the other side of the structure where the shape of a car could be seen more clearly under a loose covering. The Hawaiian shirt moved in closer to the TV monitor and stared at the quiet scene. The Major kept the drone in the glare of the sun where it would be less noticeable, and the shadowed mountains also helped conceal it from the houses.

The guy in the Hawaiian shirt looked back at him from the monitor and smiled. He understood what the Major was doing. No one in the room moved and, like large birds of prey, they sat waiting for something to happen.

A door opened and a young man slipped out of the house dressed in Arab robes. He looked carefully up and down the road, checked the mountain passes, then moved to the car. Tugging and pulling at the covering he finally managed to lift it, revealing an old, pale Mercedes touring car. The young man checked the interior and pulled out what looked like used food wrappings. Then he turned, checked the road again, and went back into the house.

"Do you think he saw us?" the Hawaiian shirt asked.

"I don't know," the Major said. "Is he the target?"

"No," the man answered, and continued to stare at the quiet scene on the TV monitor. "But they're getting ready to move." The room got quiet again and he figured the car would be his target and that they'd want the strike to be out on the road somewhere away from the houses. The brass didn't like civilian casualties.

The room stirred when the same man came out again and got in the car. He started the motor and pulled in closer to the house. A woman came out with a covered basket that looked like food for a long trip, and she placed it in the back seat. A *berka* covered her face so there was no way of identifying her, or linking her with the man. She wrapped the cloth even tighter around her head and went back into the house. Everyone in the room stayed riveted to the screen. The door opened again and the woman came back out with a little boy in tow. He was dressed in plain jeans, sneakers, and a t-shirt with something written on it. She opened the back door and lifted the boy up into the Mercedes. He hugged her, and for a moment the *berka* dropped, and she kissed him. The Sergeant tried to zoom in on her face but she pulled the *berka* up again and went back into the house.

The man in the Hawaiian shirt took out some other photos, spread them across the table, and stared at the pictures that he'd probably studied for months. "I don't think that's his wife," he said. "She looked older. Maybe it's his mother."

"Who is the boy?" someone asked.

"I don't know," the man replied.

The screen didn't move. The Sergeant tried another camera to catch the face behind the wheel but the man remained in the car's shadows. The Major watched the door for the man in the picture to come out. There would only be a moment for identification unless he went around the front to get into the passenger seat. The Major was sure the man in the Hawaiian shirt knew that too. The room tensed with the waiting.

The back door opened again and another man in Arab robes came out carrying a small briefcase. He turned to speak to someone inside and then headed for the car. It looked like the same man in the picture that had come out of the envelope. Except now he was laughing as he threw the briefcase into the car and got into the back with the boy. The car pulled away and the men in the room got up and quietly headed for the door, leaving the Major, the Sergeant, and the man in the Hawaiian shirt alone in the room. "Thanks for coming, gentlemen," he muttered as they left.

The Major lifted the drone higher, staying behind the Mercedes so that the mountains covered him. The car drove past the small community of houses and turned north toward the main road. The agent took off his safari jacket and moved in closer to the monitor. "He's our man. You can take him anytime, Sir," he said.

"What about the child?" the Major asked.

The air hung heavy in the air-conditioned room. "What child?" the man asked, keeping his eyes on the monitor.

The Major did not acknowledge the Sergeant's quick glance at him, and said, "I thought civilian casualties —"

"Our target has killed civilians and more," the man answered quickly. "There's a ruthless killer in that car."

The man with the sun burnt hair had still not looked away from the monitor and the three of them watched the Mercedes bounce down the road toward the main highway. "We've been hunting this guy for three years, Major. I can't go back and write another report telling them he got away again. This is exactly what he's done in the past. I was expecting it."

Behavior like this was against the rules and the Major knew that he was in charge of making the choices and decisions. Protecting policies and planes was his ultimate duty. He watched the Mercedes go out past the last house, getting closer to the main road. The man in the Hawaiian shirt finally turned away from the video screens and stared at the two men in the leather chairs. He started to say something but the car on the screen stopped and the Sergeant pointed.

The man in front of them turned back to the monitors. "Watch him," he said. "It may be some kind of trick."

"Are you sure it's him?" the Major asked.

"It's him!" the man said.

The back door on the Mercedes opened and the little boy got out and ran off the road. The man in the back got out to follow him and the camera zoomed in closer. The boy ran to a ditch and pulled down his pants to piss. The man came up behind him and the boy laughed and waved him away. The man laughed with him and stepped back. The Major angled the drone slightly and felt the missile release in his hand. The monitor lit up in colors and a cloud of dust and debris covered the area. Through it he could barely see the Mercedes beginning to race down the road and he flew the drone up over the dark cloud and headed north with the car. He angled the drone again and fired. The silent explosion rocked the video picture. The car lurched off the road, the gas tank blew, and a ball of flame covered the picture. The Major lifted the drone and slid back toward his first strike. The smoke had almost cleared and he could see the dark hole where the missile had hit. He looked toward the ditch for the boy but nothing moved.

"Do you see the kid?" he asked.

"Negative," the Sergeant called.

"Get out," the Hawaiian shirt yelled.

The drone lingered and moved to the other side of the ditch. One of the cameras caught the boy lying on the side of the ditch. He either crawled or had been blown there.

"There's nothing you can do. Get out!"

The man was right and the Major knew it. He lifted the drone and headed for the mountains. There were people running like bugs across the screens. Then the mountain peaks suddenly covered everything. He veered the drone southward and gave the signal. He felt it come back and heard a voice telling him, "Nice work," and he let go. For a few seconds he sat there letting the tension run out through his arms and neck.

"Great shooting, Sir," a voice said next to him. "You might've even saved that kid." When he looked over the Sergeant saluted him. "I never saw anything like it."

"It was a definite kill," the other man said, shuffling papers and pictures off the desk, and stuffing them into an attaché case. He spun the numbered lock, picked up his jacket, and said, "You're absolutely the best, Major. The best." And the door closed.

"I'll be in the lounge, Sir," the Sergeant said.

The Major left the building and went out to wait in the car to be reassigned. The young Sergeant came out to tell him he could go home early. It was still dark. The moon had come up and its pale light covered the desert in a cool

131

glow. The Major swung the car out past the security gates and headed for the highway. He tried not to think of what had happened and clicked on the radio. Bill Evans and strings drifted in around him playing a Faure piece. It had a clear sound to it like the night. The road was empty and he picked up speed, heading for the glow in the sky over Vegas. He'd be home in half an hour.

When he saw the turnoff to the church up ahead he took it, and had to rethink which way to turn in the dark because he had never come up on the church from this side of the highway. He needed to pray.

He slowed down, saw the pile of stones by the church's entrance, and made the turn. It looked different at night. Smaller. He edged the Beemer forward, looking for the parking lot. It was difficult to judge how far he'd come and he thought he'd taken the wrong turn. When he turned off the headlights the old stucco building glowed in the moonlight. He thought he may have come in from another angle, got out of the car, and started walking down what looked like a path to the little church.

He didn't expect to see anyone at that hour and made the turn to open the door, but it wasn't there. It had been ripped off its hinges. What were left of the benches had been piled in a corner. The holy water bowl had been removed and the wicker basket gone. He looked up at the altar where the crucifix used to be, but only the stained image of a cross was left on the copper sandstone.

He looked quickly around for the priest's vestments. They were gone too and he felt cold and alone. The church looked like it had belonged to the desert for a long time. The Major looked for the confessional box where the vestments hung. The oval top had been smashed but the seats were still intact. A lizard looked up at him for a moment and then crawled away under a board. Nothing seemed to move in the cold moonlight. He pushed aside what was left of the torn pieces of curtain on the confessional, mumbled a short prayer, and began talking about what had happened to him and where he'd been. His voice got stronger as he spoke, but only the moonlit night heard him.

UNSCHEDULED FLIGHTS

The roofs on city tenements are flat. They're made that way so you can lie on them during hot summer nights, gaze up at the stars, and take off into a sky that burns brighter than the fire on old men's birthday cakes. These unscheduled flights rush through Earth's orbit, shoulder their way into space, and head out to distant Nebulae and obscure moon paths. They make a wide turn on the far side of Jupiter and return to Earth just in time for the next sunrise.

That man over there, lying near the edge of the roof, has been taking these unscheduled flights for years. He started his space travel off small docks on the Finger Lakes, flew from low straw-roofs in Saigon during the Vietnamese War, and now does most of his unscheduled flying from four and five-story tenements along the eastern seaboard. He's been amply fueled for his trip tonight, by the looks of the empty Jack Daniels bottle lying next to him, and he's been running through his final check before lift off. Eyes wide, hands on chest, body relaxed and ready for that sudden thrust upward. Mental runways cleared, body set at ease, and all systems focused on the simple idea of hurtling up and out into the stars. Any interruption in this process automatically cancels all unscheduled flights in the immediate area.

Unfortunately, the barefoot boy opening the roof's heavy metal door has to be considered one of those interruptions, even though the kid never had that intention when he squeezed out onto the roof in his pajamas. Even worse, in the kid's excitement he raced to the object with the recently used paintbrushes around it, ran his little hands over it, and yelled, "It's dry!"

The man lying in perfect takeoff position heard the kid's shout, which interrupted the countdown, and his unscheduled flight was immediately cancelled.

"That you, Joey?" the man asked, rolling to his knees.

"I didn't know you were still up here, Eli."

"Did you get to talk with your father?"

The kid shook his head. "They only let him use the phone a few times a week," he said. "I guess my Mom and I will have to go up and see him this weekend, but they don't let little kids in so I have to wait outside. Sometimes they let him wave to me from a window."

"Well, let's hope he gets out soon."

"Did you come up here to check on the paint?"

"No, I couldn't sleep and decided to catch this spectacular view instead," Eli said, waiting for the boy to look up at where he was pointing, before he slid the empty whiskey bottle into the deep shadows with his foot. "It's too hot to sleep in those apartments on nights like this," he said. "There's not enough air down there."

"Yeah, I know what you mean. And you were right about the paint too," the kid said, moving his small hand over the long, shiny object again.

"Next few days ... she'll be ready to go," Eli mumbled.

"She looks pretty good right now," the kid said.

"You can't hurry these things, Joey. Lots of details still have to be worked out," Eli insisted, limping over to wipe a smudge off the narrow windshield with his sleeve. "She's the best damn rocket ship I've ever seen. Once she has a name, we'll start a log and begin testing her."

"Why don't we name her after my Mom?"

"Great idea. We'll call her THE LUCY. I'll pick up the letters first thing in the morning," he said, helping the kid roll the wooden rocket ship out into the moonlight so they could look at her from both sides.

Her thick silver paint, and the brass studs that held the black vinyl seat covers in place, gleamed under the

135

crescent moon and gave the bent plywood a glimmer along the silver tail that curved back into the shadows.

They had built her with matching aluminum shafts for strength, added a longer middle bar, and attached wheels soaked in thin summer oil to keep them quiet and fast. The old man found a picture of an instrument panel in a car advertisement and pasted it across the dashboard so that it fit snugly under the steering wheel they'd taken off an abandoned baby carriage.

"You ready to fly this thing?" Eli asked.

"I sure am," the kid answered.

"We'll need tubing and sun filters for that first mission. Venus isn't going to hang around waiting for us. Everything moves out there. Nothing stops. Not ever."

"Are filters hard to find?"

"I've got a line on some," Eli said. "I'll pick them up tomorrow when I get the letters for her name."

The kid climbed into the cockpit in his pajamas to test the wrapped steering wheel they had covered with the left over vinyl from the seat covers.

"How's she feel?"

"Okay, I guess. The seat's sort of hard though."

"We can take care of that. How's she steer?"

"Great," the kid said. "Feels like she wants to fly."

"She's designed that way, but we won't fly her until she's checked out and ready to go."

"When will that be?"

"In the next few days. She'll be all set for the Venus Transit. That's when Venus creeps across the sun in full daylight. You can get the feel of how she runs then."

"That makes me the test pilot."

Eli laughed and said, "You're the only one that can fit in there."

"I know and it makes me feel special," the kid said, turning the wheel in a sharp banking maneuver. "But you can fly her too, Eli. Anytime you want."

"Thanks, but it's my job to teach *you* how to fly. I had to learn all that by myself."

"Was it hard?"

"Learning anything by yourself is hard. It takes longer ... and it's a lot lonelier," he answered, looking up into the stars.

"Did you teach your son Junior how to fly too?"

"Junior? Sure, sure. Long ago when we lived up State. He wasn't as good as you though, Joey."

"Yeah, I'm awesome, I guess."

The man smiled at the kid's assessment, and said, "We've got a perfect sky tonight. You can see out past the moon to Jupiter and Venus."

"To the Cat's Eye."

"Hey ... not quite that far."

"She'll go that far though. An I'll take her back through the Milky Way past Saturn ... my favorite."

"You're in a perfect position for that tonight."

"I've already mapped the whole trip," the kid said, pulling out a crumbled piece of paper with crossing lines and bearings on it. "All I have to do is go."

"That's right, Joey. But each person has his own way of going. You're lucky. You've got a rocket ship to fly and that keeps you focused. The rest is about getting started and knowing where you're headed. That's the hardest part."

"But I've already done all that."

"Looks like you have," Eli acknowledged. "Guess you're all ready to go, eh?"

The kid nodded and stared down at the advertisement for the latest Cadillac instrument panel pasted under the wheel. Eli smiled and said, "What you're doing is good. But the trick is to look up at where you want to go. It's out there, Joey. Out there!"

Joey looked up at where Eli pointed and the star fires spun and expanded over him. His eyes widened and his little hands squeezed the rocket ship's makeshift steering wheel. "It's like I'm lifting off right now," he yelled. "It feels like I'm flying, Eli!"

The old man limped in closer, waving his bony hands in the moonlight, directing the boy. "Just bank her easy and she'll come back on a straight line," he said. "If you have any trouble just hit that red button on your right and she'll make the turn by herself and come in on automatic."

"Okay, here I go."

"Joey," a voice called from behind them. "What are you doing up here? Why aren't you in bed?"

The sound startled the boy and he let go of the steering wheel, turned toward the voice, and his first unscheduled flight was automatically cancelled before he'd even left the Earth's orbit. There was a long uncertain moment and it hung in the night air around them.

"I just flew the rocket ship, Ma," Joey yelled through it. "I'm almost an astronaut! I went up over the city and looked down into the streets. Eli helped me land her."

The slim, half-dressed woman pulled at her nightgown and stared at the little boy and the old man. "This isn't your playtime, Joey. You're supposed to be in bed."

"He's just excited about his new rocket ship, ma'am."

"We're naming her after you, Ma, and in a few days I'll fly out and watch Venus crawl across the sun."

The woman nodded patiently, and said, "You better get back to bed now, Joey. It's what your —"

"It's too hot to sleep down there, Ma. There's not enough air," the boy said, trying to imitate the old man.

"Maybe you better do what your Mom tells you, Joey," Eli said. "Astronauts need their sleep. You shouldn't be flying in your pajamas anyway." The kid groaned, threw down his space map, and headed for the heavy metal door that led to the darkened apartments below. "I'll stow your ship for tonight," Eli called to him, but the kid had already gone.

The frail woman in the nightgown stared at the old man, and said in a low restrained voice, "What the hell are you doing to my son, Eli?"

"Oh, he's just a bit excited about his new rocket ship, ma'am. Once we put numbers and decals on her she'll be all set to go."

"Go where, Eli?" The old man stared back at her, trying to figure out why she kept asking him questions. "You should be ashamed of yourself," she said. "A grown man playing games with a little boy."

"The rocket ship's not a game. It's a tool that'll teach him about space and what's out there," he answered. "Joey gets all excited about that. He even wants to take his rocket ship to school and show the other kids."

"What the hell are you talking about?" she asked again and moved toward him, accidentally kicking something in the shadows. The hip-shaped Jack Daniel's bottle skittered out into the thin milky moonlight between them.

"Is that *your* rocket ship, Eli?" she asked, staring down at the empty whiskey bottle like it had fallen from outer space. "That's not what I want for Joey."

"His rocket ship is different, ma'am."

"Is it? Don't look much different to me than that empty bottle. Neither one is going anywhere. You understand that, Eli? Joey and I don't want your kind of space traveling. We're all we've got and it looks like it's going to be that way for a long time. We don't have any room for these kinds of games in our lives. We can't afford them," she said, stepping over the empty bottle. "First thing tomorrow, I'm telling your son Junior what's going on up here and if he doesn't do something about it, then I will. I'll see to it that you're put away —"

"Joey's a bright boy," Eli said quickly, trying to head her off. "He knows the universe like the back of his hand. Better than any kid I've ever seen. He's a natural. That whole thing out there is part of him and he's part of it. They go together."

"There's too many things between here and out there, Eli," she said, her rising voice running the rooftops. "There are important things right down here and Joey doesn't need some pile of junk for that."

"Just give him a little time, ma'am. Let him be a kid for awhile."

"The last thing my kid needs is nonsense like this," she said, kicking the wooden rocket ship.

"You got it all wrong —"

"No I don't, Eli. You do. I know what's going on up here. You just keep thrashing around in your imaginary Vietnamese jungle, like you've been doing all these years, and keep talking to your Shrinks, but stay the hell away from my son," she yelled. "You got nothin' for him. Nothin' for nobody!" The slam of the heavy metal door rushed at him and the dull erratic sounds of street traffic drifted up from below.

Eli stood alone in the shadows. His son would give him another fatherly lecture and he'd be sent off to his daughter's place with more old luggage, different labels on the six packs, and endless talks without talking.

His body ached and he wasn't sure where he was anymore. One roof began to look like another. The hot humid air closed in around him and he picked up the wooden rocket ship and cradled it in his arms. He shifted the uneven weight and caught the smell of its summer oil and fresh paint. Its bulkiness made him feel off balance and he stopped to pick up the kid's thrown away map of the night sky. He glanced at the map again and stuffed it into his pocket for safekeeping. It was the perfect time to go to

Saturn, or even the Cat's Eye, and he stepped out toward the planets, squeezing the rocket ship in his arms.

Nothing moved on the empty roof. Even the traffic faded into the sudden quiet, and the night sky glittered and spun in the silence. Seconds later the roof's metal door pushed open again. The barefoot boy grunted against the heavy door, and hopped back on to the roof with his pillow.

"I got something for the rocket ship's seat," he called, looking around the empty roof, just seconds after the unscheduled flight had gone. "It'll be perfect!" he yelled, but only the stark silence answered him. He glanced down at the empty paint cans, the brushes, and the spot where the rocket ship had been. Making a quick turn, the little boy looked up into the night sky.

"Eli, Eli, you did it! Take her to the Cat's Eye, Eli," he yelled up at the stars, waving his pillow at the crescent moon.

"Stop it, Joey, stop it!" he heard her say just behind him. She looked frightened and alone, but he just kept waving his pillow and shouting at the moon.

"He did it, Ma. He did it!"

"I know," she said, leading the boy back to the heavy metal door that led down the stairs to the hot, airless apartments below.

CRATES

When my Mom yelled, "Get over to Grandma's house!" it meant two things. Take the bus to the Heights and, "don't tell anyone where you're going." On these special trips my grandmother would wait at the front window on the second floor until she saw me get off the bus. Then she'd duck back in and cut me a big chunk of apple pie. I'd run the half block, taking the stairs two at a time, listening for the low murmur of men's voices in the hall. Then I'd slow down so they wouldn't notice how anxious I was to get my piece of pie.

The men were always there. The smokers stood in the hall while the rest lined the walls of the apartment, waiting to pat my head as I went by. Their gentle brogues greeted me with, "Good to see you, Laddy," or "Lookin' grand, boyo." The smell of tobacco and whiskey clung to their clothes like a Dublin perfume. Some of them had fingers and arms missing, one was blind, another had no leg, but each one always had a warm greeting for a little boy looking for his piece of pie.

My grandmother would be waiting at the end of the line to lead me past the large wooden crates stacked in the living room. Four feet long, two feet wide, with DANGER, HANDLE WITH CARE and EXTREME CAUTION stamped all over them in bright red ink. Some were wrapped in blankets like children asleep in the corners. An acrid, oily smell seemed to be in the room when they were there, and Granny would rush me by them with a gentle push against the back of my shoulders.

Into the kitchen we'd go where that big piece of pie would be sitting on the table next to the sweating bowl of cold whipped cream. She'd pour the tea and look me straight in the eye. "You know what to do, Jack ... where to go ... who to see," she'd say. I'd just nod with my mouth full of the warm pie and whipped cream. "It's the same as last time and the time before that," she'd say in her lilting brogue. "See only Himself. If he's not there, you're to come straight back here."

"Is it for the six counties again, mum?"

"That it is, boy. Don't dawdle ... and go out through the backyard like last time." Then she'd stop talking, wait for me to swallow, and say, "You're to tell him —"

"The crates are in."

"You're a smart one, Jack," she'd say, pinching my cheek. Then she'd slip an envelope out of her apron, with funny looking stamps on it, and shove it into my hand. "And if he's there, give him this, and wait for an answer. If he's not ... bring it straight back here."

I never did have to go back to Grandma's house because he was always there in that dark apartment over in Eastchester. He was a giant of a man with a crutch under his arm and a missing foot. A man that never said, *please* or *thank you* or much of anything else.

"The crates are in, sir, and I'm to wait for an answer," I'd say, handing him the letter.

He'd nod at me, shove some loose change into my pocket and point to a little blue bowl of hard candy on the table. "Take a sucker, son. I won't be long," he'd say, and leave me alone in the gloom.

I'd take one of the striped peppermints from the bowl and sit on the bulky couch with its stained green slipcover. It was a dreary place with its worn out linoleum and mismatched furniture. A chipped green vase, with a drooping sprig of pussy willow, stood on a painted table. Under it was a neat row of left-footed shoes.

On that particular day I reached for another sucker and heard a high-pitched sound like the cry of a wounded animal. Growing louder it melted into a low litany that flowed under the door. Someone was crying in the next room. When I mustered the courage to peek in, I saw the one-footed man on his knees, his whole body heaving and wrenching with sobs. His crutch leaned against a rumpled bed and the rhythm of his chanting kept repeating, "Mary, Mother of God, pray for us who have recourse to thee."

"Did I do something wrong, sir?" I whispered.

He looked up at me standing in the doorway, then grabbed for his crutch. Rising like a mountain, eyes wet with tears, swaying back and forth like a madman, he said, "My only boy is gone. They've killed him."

"I'm sorry, sir."

"You better stay away from us from now on. Don't get wrapped up in these troubles, son."

"Troubles, sir?"

"We'll suffer them alone. They're ours ... not yours."

"Is it about the six counties, sir?" I asked, my little voice echoing in the dark room.

"It's best you run home now," was all he answered.

"Yes, sir," I said, backing away and running down the old wooden steps that led out to the street. And when I got back on the bus, I'd reach into my shirt pocket for the loose change he'd put there.

It wasn't until years later that I understood why I'd been bribed with money and whipped cream. In those apple pie days it was easy to make a little boy happy, and even easier to make a one-footed giant cry.

THE FIRE SEASON

An unspeakable curse had fallen on Nora Marlowe. Her last three films had lost money and she began to slip into the Hollywood void. Autograph hounds looked the other way, her phone calls went unanswered, and the usual lunch and party invitations had stopped in an abrupt silence. She made the usual adjustments: fired her agent, upgraded her car, and took sleeping pills to get her through the sudden empty nights.

In her Hollywood Hell she began to imagine things that weren't there until, on one of her overhung mornings, she heard a chorus of chop-chop sounds drift through the open window. The uneven rhythms grew louder and she crawled out of bed, flipped her blonde wisps in the full-length mirror, snapped a glistening red fingernail between her teeth, and grabbed her sunglasses to peek out into the stark southern California sunlight that seemed to devour everything under it.

A flash of metal gleamed near the rosebushes and a shadowy figure, with long jet-black hair, appeared from below. His hard, naked, sweat soaked chest came into view swinging a sharp glinting machete.

Nora lit a cigarette, slipped into her pink robe, and stepped out on to the patio. She headed across the bright Mexican tiles, taking her robe off in a long sweeping motion, and stretched naked across one of the long loungers as the dark figure cut his way up the hill toward her.

"Where the hell do you think you're going?" she yelled.

The surprised man put his hand up against the glaring sun and said, "Brush clearing. It's the fire season."

Nora quickly covered her nakedness and looked down the hill to where he was pointing, at the rest of the crew stacking brush into a red paneled truck.

"What's your name?" she demanded.

"Mando," he said, wiping his sweating face.

"Are you a gardener?"

"Sort of," he smiled, and one of the men called from below. "Sorry, ma'am," he said. "We have to go now."

"Go? You just got here."

"We're finished here, ma'am."

"Can you come back later? I'll show you what I need done."

"*Si*," he said, with a wave and a smile. The men in the truck shouted up to him again, and he began to roll the cut bundles of brush down the hill. Nora went back into the house and watched him from the window. When she finally reached the truck with the brush she crawled back into bed.

*

Ron Goode had been a Hollywood agent most of his life. He loved the circus of cynical writers, manipulating directors, fast-talking producers, and insecure movie stars. He'd worked for the Morris Office nearly twenty years until one day his lawyer convinced him that he should move up in the world and open his own agency. Renting a suite on one of Sunset's newer buildings he got the usual congratulatory telegrams, headlines in the trades, and was slapped with a respectable amount of lawsuits. He was off to a great start.

Nora Marlowe sent her congratulations and inserted a little blue card asking if he'd be interested in being her new agent. Ron had been a fan of Nora's ever since he saw her first film, *The Enchanted Goddess*, long before she'd turned into a movie star that no one wanted anymore.

"My knight in shining armor," Nora cooed, curling up on his new coffee colored leather couch in her new torn jeans, black tee shirt, and open-toed white heels.

"Did you read my contracts?" Ron asked.

Nora pulled the folded sheets out of her Gucci bag and sighed, "Signed and delivered."

"I've already got a line on a couple of projects," he said.

"The wronged woman?"

"How did you know?" he said. They both laughed and she waited for the details. "This role is much more interesting than just being the wronged woman," he said. "It's the *mother* of the wronged woman who has gotten —"

"The mother?"

"Yes," he said. "A mother wronged by a man whose about to do the same thing to her daughter. Isn't that fantastic?"

The suddenness of his proposal began to smolder in her stomach, and turned into a scorching hatred for the prissy little man on the other side of the coffee table. She had a sunken feeling about handing him her signed contract. It had been a mistake, and she wanted to grab it back out of his hand and head for the door.

"How old is the daughter?" she asked in a calm voice.

"Let's just say she's young," he said.

"I've never played a mother before. Is it the lead?"

"It's the title role. Every actress in town is after it. But we have an inside track because —"

"What's the other thing?"

"Other thing?"

"You said you had a *couple* of things."

"The *other* thing depends on you taking the role in *Sins of the Mother.*"

"*Sins of the —*"

"*Mother.*"

"Never heard of it."

"Bestseller. Cost ABC a fortune. They're thinking of turning it into a series after this initial —"

"I've never done TV. Less money ... isn't it?"

"All depends. We represent the director."

"Who's directing?"

"Gina Dreyfuss."

"A woman?"

"She did *State of Affairs* and *Long Time Gone* ... a TV movie and a mini-series. The *Sins* producers would love to talk with you about the project. They think you're perfect for the part." Nora stared back at him. He crossed his legs and said, "Cliff Bloom and Arnie Bellows love your work, darling."

"They should. I've done three pictures for them. I can't believe they're doing TV."

"Everyone does TV now, darling."

"You still haven't told me about the *other* thing."

"We've got a manufacturer who'll put out a perfume with your name on it."

"You mean like Cher and Liz?"

"Even better. It'll be cleaner ... if you know what I mean. We're debating what to call it. *Marlowe* or *Deirdre.*"

"Who the hell is Deirdre?"

"That's the name of the character you're going to play in *Sins of the Mother*. Won't be a big payoff up front," Ron droned, "but there's a lot of promise at the back end. When I tell Arnie and Cliff you'll take the part we'll start the perfume negotiations," he said, signing the contract and handing her back the copy she'd already signed.

*

Nora took another sleeping pill, turned on the air conditioner, crawled into bed with all her clothes on, and put the vodka sea breeze on the night table. She kept smelling something burning and getting up to check the kitchen. Each time she did she poured another vodka from the cold container in the fridge. On her fifth trip she heard a knock at the front door. She peeked out at the messenger the studio had probably sent over with *The Sins of the Mother* script.

"I'll sign for it," she said.

"I'm Mando," the young man said. "Remember ... this morning? You wanted me to garden."

"Of course ... cutting the brush," she slurred.

"Just in time. The fire's bad."

"Fire?" she asked, noticing a thin sheet of ash along the stone path.

"*Mira*," he said, pointing to the potbellied copters pouring water on the rising flames running up Mandeville Canyon like a rushing stream.

"It won't come over here, will it?" she asked.

"They're trying to stop it from jumping the freeway."

The lights in the pool popped on in the sudden darkness and it gave a pastel glow to the smoky air. A strong licorice smell rose out of the burning chaparral and made her nauseous. The thumping helicopters seemed to overpower her and she began to shake. Mando managed to help her into the house and then it all dropped into blackness.

*

Nora dangled her arm over the bed and reeled in the ringing phone. "Did I wake you?" the voice asked. She mumbled something unintelligible and had the phone upside down. "It's your new agent, darling. We've got an appointment at Kings Way. Two o'clock."

"I'll be there," she mumbled.

"Don't be late," he said and hung up.

She dropped the phone and it hit the floor with a dull thud. The clock read 11:36 in the morning and her clothes were still on. She tried to stand up, grabbed the headboard, and stared into the mirror. A swipe of mascara smeared her cheek. Her diamond ring and gold bracelet were still on, even the Tahitian pearl necklace. She swallowed the dryness in her mouth, tried to remember what had happened, and undressed on the way to the shower.

*

Ron Goode's arm steadied her as they walked briskly toward Kings Way Productions where Arnie Bellows waited at the door. "You look fantastic," he said, kissing her on the cheek. Nora smiled, moved towards a large easy chair, and tried to shake off another attack of dizziness. "Got some bad news," Arnie said. "Cliff's house burned down last night in the Mandeville fire so he can't be here. I know it's a bad time to talk business, but I'm excited about this new casting idea and we want you both to know we haven't committed on the part. I'm hoping Nora will test for us right away."

"Jesus, Arnie ... a test?" Nora said. "I've done three goddamn pictures for you."

"You'll do fine, Nora. The director just wants to see if you and this kid can make sparks together."

"You're using some kid?"

"She's probably scared stiff," Ron said. "We might even squeeze some publicity out of it. Nora coaching her in a scene ... that kind of thing."

Nora took in a quick breath, waited for the nausea to fade, and said, "I don't mind testing under certain conditions."

"Anything you want, darling," Arnie said.

"And I'll even let what-ever-her-name-is direct it ... but it has to be a scene from the script."

"Then it's done," Ron said. "Book the time, let us know what scene it is, and give my best to Cliff. We've got two other meetings this afternoon," he lied, taking Nora's arm and heading for the door just as a tall, distinguished looking man walked in.

"Nora," he said.

"Cliff." She threw her arms around him. "I heard about the house. So sorry."

"What are you doing here?"

"Arnie wants me to test for your new film."

"Gina wants to see Nora work with the kid," Arnie added.

"Why didn't I think of that?"

"Apparently, it was Ron's idea that I play Deirdre."

"Playing mothers could mean a whole new career for you."

Nora began to realize that the whole thing was playing out like it'd been scripted before she'd gotten there. Only her part was optional and unrehearsed. She'd been caught in another under-the-table deal and her hatred for these men who pulled and pushed her into whatever they wanted began to surface again.

"I don't need a goddamn screen test," she blurted.

"You're right," Cliff answered with a little laugh and it surprised her.

"But I promised the director —"

"To hell with the director, Arnie! Let's sign Nora for the part immediately," Cliff said. "Give Ron what he wants … within reason. There's a tight budget on this one, kids."

"I'll be kind," Ron said.

"We'll have lunch and work it out," Cliff insisted.

"I'd love it. Call me," Nora said, heading for the door.

Ron caught up with her at the elevator. "I'm sorry. I didn't know you were so tight with Cliff," he said.

"It all went exactly as planned, didn't it?" she mumbled.

The elevator doors sprung open and they got on with the end-of-the-lunch-crowd. The dizziness hit her again. She bit hard on the tip of her tongue, squeezed her hands into fists, and anticipated the elevator's drop. She needed a drink.

*

The musty smell of birds hit Mando even before he went through the large doors where the tethered cocks strutted in front of red painted walls. A fat man waved him to one of the benches and asked, "You the guy Tuto sent?" Mando nodded. "I'm Eddie. Tuto told me you speak English." Mando nodded again. "What do you know about cockfights?"

"My father ran a *Plaza de Gallo* where it's legal."

This time the fat man nodded, and said, "Tuto also told me you were a wiseass."

"Sometimes," Mando laughed.

"I don't need a wiseass, kid. I need someone to collect the bets. I get a bunch of old guys in here that think the place is a social club. If they don't bet I need you to throw them out. Think you can do it?"

"You have to speak English for that?"

"You take their bets in Spanish, you throw them out in English."

"Where do I bring the bets?"

"First, you write the bet down and make them sign it. If you don't they'll say it's wrong if their cock loses. Always give them a copy, keep one for yourself, and give the bets to the guy in the cage behind those boxes. We work Friday and Saturday nights. The cocks go at each other at nine. You start at eight."

"I get one dollar over minimum," Mando said.

"I'm paying fifty cents *under* minimum. You're an illegal. Take it or leave it."

"I'll take it for now. Then we'll see."

"Be here tonight ... eight sharp. One more thing: Only the customers call me Fat Eddie. Nobody else."

"Whatever you say, Boss," Mando said, quickly figuring that if he could get extra work out of *la senora bella* up on the hill he could go back to Mexico sooner than he'd planned.

*

It was Cliff Bloom that called and invited Nora out to lunch, forgetting that she didn't like to do *anything* on Fridays. Mondays were her lucky days, not Fridays. It'd been on a Monday when they wrapped their first hit movie and the day he admitted he'd fallen in love with her. Their affair lasted through that year with clandestine meetings in small hotels along the coast. Nora kept asking him to get a divorce but Cliff kept avoiding it. She'd worked her way into another Hollywood trap and began to hate him for it.

She started stealing little things he had just to annoy him but he either didn't notice or chose not to complain. It started with whatever was in the car's glove compartment when he stopped to get gas. She stole the car's maintenance records, then the maps, and a small flashlight. She had even taken a pack of cigarettes out of his jacket. It was always little things that he wouldn't necessarily notice. But one night, while he was asleep, she undid the gold medical bracelet he wore whenever they went out of town. It had his name engraved on it with a list of the medications he needed. The odd thing was that he never mentioned it missing ... so she kept it. Their affair was over and they both knew it.

Cliff produced several films after that. One of them had done quite well, and she hated him even more for not casting her in it. This time it'd be different. She'd make sure of that.

"Are you free this weekend?" Cliff asked on the way to the garage. "Thought you might like to take a drive to Del Mar."

"Sorry, I have plans," she lied, as her new Lexus came squealing down the garage ramp. "But call me in the morning," she said, and drove out into the Rodeo Drive glare just as her cell phone began to ring.

"I just talked to Cliff and I think we've got a deal," Ron said on the other end.

"Someone just told me that they're going to start shooting as soon as I'm signed for the part," she told him.

"You're getting inside info."

"Still haven't seen a script though."

"Let's concentrate on the important things. I got you fifty grand a day. Guaranteed two days, but I figure there'll be more. You'll have special appearance credit, a honey wagon, your own parking space, and guaranteed casting if there's a sequel. I'm also cutting a deal with a perfumer. And the production company will pay for your star on Hollywood Boulevard the same day the show premieres. Your career is about to take off," he said. "I'll call you when I get the contracts."

*

Ron Goode changed his clothes and headed downtown to The Cage on Fifth. He wore his new leather jacket, torn expensive jeans, and shiny cowboy boots. But none of it got him past the muscle at the door.

"Clive's expecting me," he said.

"She's getting dressed for the show. AIDS benefit tonight. Twenty buck cover. Clive does a great job ... raises a lot of money for the cause." Ron slipped the guy a fifty. "Go past the bar. Back door," he said.

"Thanks," Ron said, and headed into a sea of smoke where large cages hung from the ceiling with bright feathered macaws and parrots squawking in the haze. Men in leather leaned on the oval bar and talked over the loud music coming from the lighted jukebox in the corner. The muscle at the back door hung up the phone when he saw

Ron coming. "You the one looking for Clive?" Ron nodded and was led through a back alley to a red door. He stepped into the funk of perfume, cigarettes, and sweat.

"Hello, Clive," he said, edging his way behind the men at the long, cracked mirror putting on makeup.

Clive was tall and thin with long flowing red hair and sharp features. When he finished lining his large brown eyes he threw a blonde wig over his head and winked at Ron in the mirror. "And who the hell are you promoting this year, Mate?" he asked. Ron whispered Nora Marlowe's name in his ear, and Clive snapped to attention. "The ice queen?" Then Ron leaned over again and whispered Cliff Bloom's name. Clive's mascara brush stopped in mid-air. "They've started that up again, eh?" he asked. Clive caught Ron's surprise. "You didn't know? I thought the uptown crowd knew everything about those two. They tried so hard to keep it private. Pity."

"I just signed her to do Deirdre in *Sins of the Mother*," Ron said. "Cliff Bloom's producing. It'll hit the trades in the morning."

Clive stopped powdering his nose and raised his thin arms in supplication. "Hallelujah! Perfect casting at last."

*

Mando borrowed Tuto's red pickup and drove up the hill to *la casa de senora bella's* house on the hill. He parked across the street, behind a dented convertible with Nevada plates, and had to ring the bell several times before Nora came out to the locked gate.

"I'm Mando. We never got to talk because you — "

"I remember," she said, opening the gate.

They headed down the stone path to the patio on the other side of the house. Nora pointed at some dead plants and dried undergrowth. "All this has to be redone," she said.

"Maybe some birds of paradise here. Some *hosta* for shade."

"Sounds wonderful, errrr ..."

"Mando Zapata ... and you?"

"Nora Marlowe," she said waiting for his reaction. He stared blankly back at her. "When can you start?" she asked.

"Tomorrow."

"Sunday?"

"How much do you pay?"

"I pay my maid twenty dollars an hour."

"I'll take the same," he said quickly. "You got tools?"

"In the shed," she said, opening a door just off the veranda. An array of shovels, loppers, and rakes hung along the walls. "I'll have the nursery deliver —"

Nora's cell phone rang. She stiffened, snapped her fingernail between her teeth, and listened to it. Mando stared at her. "Hello," she finally said into the phone. "Oh, Cliff, thanks for that lovely lunch yesterday. I would've gone to Del Mar with you but my mother's in town for the weekend," she said. "She's visiting a sick friend and decided to stay here with me. By the way, I've been trying to get a copy of the script. You know, *Sins of the Mother.* Of course I read the book but scripts can be so different. Thanks, darling. Let's get together soon," she cooed and hung up.

"My mother's not really here," she said to Mando. "You can work as long as you want."

"I'll start at eight. If that's all right?"

Nora nodded and he thanked her. When he opened the front gate he heard clicking and a whirring sound. It stopped when he got into the truck and he saw a movement behind the wall when he made the U-turn to go back down the hill.

Clive slipped into the grandstand, causing a stir among the old Latino men sitting at one end of the stands. Mando collected their bets, took the money to the cage, and went looking for Eddie. "We got a visitor," he told him. "A gringo with red hair."

"He looks like a woman," Eddie said. Clive smiled when he saw them coming. "Listen to what I tell him so you can do this when I'm not here."

"Do you throw them out in Spanish or English?"

"Don't be a wiseass," Eddie said. Clive stood up to greet them. "This is a private club," Eddie told him. "You can't come in here unless you're a member."

"I just want to make a bet like everyone else."

Eddie gave him an annoyed little laugh. "No way. You've got to be a member."

"I've got pretty good connections," Clive said.

"Mando," Eddie said, switching to Spanish. "Throw this faggot out and tell him if he comes back I'll cut his heart out and eat it!" Then he pushed his way back through the growing crowd, leaving Mando alone to deal with Clive.

"What'd he tell you?" Clive asked.

"You better get out of here," Mando told him.

"Is he the owner?"

"We don't want any trouble."

Mando began to shoulder him toward the door but Clive broke away, pulled out a camera, and aimed it at the brightly lit area where the cocks were getting ready to fight.

"What the hell is this?" Mando shouted in Spanish.

Clive lunged backwards through the crowd. A car door slammed, a motor started, an old convertible spun backwards, slammed into a pickup truck, then roared down the road. The last thing Mando saw was the Nevada license plate and remembered that same car parked on the hill at *la casa de senora bella*. He walked back to the rows of men waiting for the cocks to be dropped on the dirt floor, collected their bets, took the money to the cage, but kept thinking about the pale man in the convertible with the Nevada plates.

∗

Nora lit a cigarette, started her morning exercise, and listened to the howling Santa Ana winds knocking over garbage cans and blowing grit through the hot streets. A car door slammed. The red paneled pickup was parked across the street and a shadowy figure moved on the stucco wall behind it. A few minutes later the doorbell rang.

"What do you want?" she asked.

"It's eight o'clock," Mando said. "I've come to work."

"What were you doing over there on the wall?"

"I was looking for a redheaded man with a camera. Yesterday he was over there and followed me to work. Took pictures ... then ran away. You know who he is?"

"He's come back," she said, pointing down the street.

The man he'd thrown out of Fat Eddie's the night before was walking up the hill with cameras around his neck. He looked up and down the empty street, snapped several pictures of the red-paneled truck, and jumped the stucco wall across the street.

"He's after me," she said.

"Why?"

Nora looked up at him in disbelief. "I'm a movie star," she said. "They hate us."

"But why would he come to where I work? And why would he take pictures of my friend Tuto's truck?"

"We better go inside," she said, pulling him into the cool shadows. "There's only one way to deal with them," she said, dialing her cell.

"Hello. This is Nora Marlowe. The actress. Yes. 1135 Chantilly Road. Bel Air. There's a man outside with long red hair. He's been stalking me for days. Yes. He's hiding behind the wall across from my house. Thank you so much."

"I better go," Mando said. "That's not my truck. If the police come they'll want to see my license or a green card."

He started for the door, but she grabbed his arm. "Just go to work like nothing happened," she said. He nodded at her as he opened the door. "You know where the tools are, don't you?"

"Yes," he said, running down the stairs to the patio.

There was a slam of car doors. Two cops circled the beat-up convertible parked down the street. A cracking sound behind the wall made them look up and draw their guns. Clive came over the wall with his hands extended like he'd been in the same kind of predicament before. One of the cops cuffed him and shoved him into the police car. The other cop, in street clothes, came to the gate and Nora went out to meet him.

"Is everything all right?" she asked.

"Yes, ma'am," he said. "We'll book him for trespassing. Do you know who owns the red truck?"

"My gardener. He's also been bothered by that man."

"Really? Can I talk to him?"

"He's working on the lower patio. Mando," she called, but there was no answer.

"We can do it some other time," the detective said, holding up his report book. "Would you mind giving me your autograph?" She smiled. "To Frank Benedetti would be great," he said. She wrote his name on the report sheet and signed it. "We'll have that convertible towed. He won't bother you anymore."

"Thank you," she said and watched them leave with Clive staring out at her from the back of the patrol car as it went down the hill.

Nora stood in front of a blazing set of mirrors while costumers sewed her into a tight red gown. A hard rap hit the dressing room door. "Two minutes!" Activity became frenzied. They led her out onto a spacious sound stage. Cliff Bloom took her arm. Ron Goode moved in next to her on the other side.

"The announcer will enter from the center. We'll meet him out there about halfway," Cliff told her.

"This is going to be a blockbuster," Ron said.

A resounding voice on a loud speaker introduced, "the wonderful cast playing these classic roles." Nora heard her name. Cliff led her through the curtain into the hot lights. When they got downstage she smiled at the applause. Cliff did a quick two-step and spun her so the crowd could see the gown. The loud speaker boomed, "Nora Marlowe plays the sensual, desirous Deirdre. Her Versace gown is worn in the dramatic climax at the Governor's Ball."

Nora moved along the edge of the stage above the rows of photographers jostling for positions. She spun, started back, and heard a high voice calling her. She turned toward it and heard the snapping cameras. Then she saw the gaunt, pale face and the flowing red hair. A sudden fear rose in her stomach and she headed for the wings.

"Nora. Nora. We're supposed to stay out here," Cliff called to her. The costumers scattered as she ran offstage to the dressing room.

Cliff rushed in behind her. "What's the matter?"

"I want to know why that pasty-faced sonofabitch is slinking around my house. Bothering my gardener. Stalking me until I had to have the police come and arrest him. That redheaded shit is out there now. They let him go. He just took my picture!"

"I'll take care of this immediately," Cliff said.

"And when the hell am I going to get a script?" she yelled, but he'd already gone.

They were cutting brush when the drab green government cars pulled up with the men in blue uniforms. "Hee-laar! Heeee-laaar!" they shouted. Mando ran through the brush, gulping the hot dry air until his lungs burned. He stopped in a blur of pastel colored houses, braced himself against the hill with his machete, and snaked across the narrow canyon toward the large Spanish house on the crest. He threw himself over the wall and into the shade of the orange-tiled overhangs, landing in an exhausted heap. Before he could catch his breath, Nora stood over him in white pants, a thin black blouse, and a haze of cigarette smoke.

"You didn't come back yesterday. Was it because of this?" She held up a newspaper with the headline, NORA MARLOWE IN LOVE TRIANGLE WITH TV PRODUCER & COCKFIGHTER. "That's me," she said, pointing to her picture. "And that's you."

Mando stared at the picture of the young man with the surprised look on his face. "I come to work, that's all," he said. "I swear it."

"That's all been fixed," she said, pulling out a green card with his name and picture on it. "All you have to do is fill in the blanks and sign it. My agent will take care of the rest."

He looked down at the newspaper again. The front of Nora's house was spread across the entire page. Below it were pictures of Tuto's truck and Fat Eddie's little plaza de gallo.

"This is why they came today. They arrested my friends and I have no place to work now."

"Don't worry. We'll set up something in the shed for you," she said, handing him the green card.

He felt his legs cramping as he went up the stone stairs, dropping the machete behind a large yucca plant, and following her into the coolness of the house. She angled the venetian blinds and pointed to a large couch. "You better get some rest. We'll fix up a place for you later," she said. "Don't worry, you'll make even more money than before." He stretched out in the shuttered light, smelled the jasmine, and closed his eyes. She nervously snapped her fingernail between her teeth and waited for the steady sound of his breathing, then picked up the phone, and hit the automatic dial.

"Ron Goode here."

"It's me," she said. "He came back exhausted. Had a run in with Immigration."

"Where is he now?"

"He's here. Sleeping."

"Did you give him the green card?"

"Yes. But I'm frightened. Cliff must've done this. He'll do anything to promote himself and his lousy movies."

"The trick is to make the situation work for us. The whole country's going nuts over you and this cock-fighter. In the past two hours I've had five blue chips begging for endorsements and every talk show is screaming for you. It's time to splash the perfume, honey. Incidentally, *People Magazine's* been crying on my shoulder. They keep whining about you not giving *them* the story first after they gave *you* all those fluffers."

"I didn't have anything to do with this."

"I know you didn't but I gave PEOPLE an exclusive for next Monday anyway. We've got the cover too. Your price will go through the roof after that. Think long term and give them what they want. Never fails. Got to put you on hold."

The telephone dropped into its soundless void. Nora studied herself in the mirror, fixed the edges of a curl, and Ron's voice snapped on again. "Just got off with Apple. They want you for their Euro market. Told them I'd get back in ten days. That'll be the week you're on the cover of *People.*"

"I've never done a commercial."

"That's why they'll pay plenty."

"What am I supposed to do with the gardener?"

"Keep him working. Don't let him out of your sight. If things keep rolling like this we'll have to hire bodyguards for the both of you," he said with a giggle, and hung up.

*

Nora waited for the chunk-chunk sounds to stop. She'd listened to its dull repetition for hours, watching the fog seep over the patio and spill into the pool lights. It'd been a hectic week. Her scenes for *Sins of the Mother* had wrapped. She sold out her first run of *Marlowe* perfume, did two commercials, posed for three magazine covers, and had to hire bodyguards to protect her from the fans who knew where she'd be before she got there. Every night Mando brought in the warmed dinners the cook left in the oven and they'd watch television. Then he'd go down to the refurbished tool shed. The only time the ritual ever changed was on that particular night.

"I'm going back to Mexico," he told her. "I've saved enough money to buy a house for my mother and I'll get work down there."

"You'll be coming back though … won't you?"

"I don't think so."

"You can always use more money," she said, but he just stood in the doorway staring at her. "When are you going?"

"Soon," he said, and walked out into the fog.

*

Mando stretched across the narrow bed and watched the mist roll up the stairs. He thought about his mother and the trip back, and had almost fallen asleep when the smell of jasmine hit him. He got up and walked out into the warm air wondering if *la senora bella* had been there or if he'd only dreamt it. He checked the front door. It was locked. Then he heard something at the bottom of the stairs, made the sign of the cross, and hoped it was just a stray cat or passing coyote. He crouched on the wet stairs when he heard the clicking sounds and a pale face came toward him through the fog.

"Took some good stuff here. Your fans will love it. You're a big celebrity now," Clive said, taking pictures of Mando as he came up the stairs. "I've created a whole new career for you. Just go with it, kid, 'cause it won't last long." Mando lunged at him. They crashed against the tool shed and struggled in a clumsy, groping dance. "What the hell are you doing? I'm trying to help you," Clive shouted, slipping easily out of Mando's grip. A spray of heavy rain suddenly splattered across Mando's head and shoulders. Clive moaned, fell backwards, and blood gushed across his face and down into his shirt. The split in his neck disappeared somewhere behind his bleeding ear and ran up into his matted red hair. Mando reached to help him, but Clive fell across the stone steps into a contorted heap and didn't move.

Just above him in the shadows he heard *la senora bella* ask, "Is he dead?" Bright splotches of blood ran down the front of her robe and his machete hung in her hand. "He's definitely that same sonofabitch," she said. "I can tell by the lousy dye job."

Mando nudged Clive with his foot, but he didn't move. "We better call an ambulance," he said.

"He must've parked his car down the road so we wouldn't see it," Nora mumbled, lifting Clive's bleeding head, taking the cameras from around his neck, and slipping something shiny into his jacket.

Mando saw what she did, and said, "You're not supposed to touch the body."

"Pick him up," she said. "I'll show you where to put him."

"But we're not supposed to —"

"Pick him up!"

Mando heaved Clive's body up on his shoulder and followed her down the stairs. She stopped to get a shovel from the shed and they went down the path that led under the house. She pointed to a spot. "Dig straight down along the cement pillar and make sure it's deep," she whispered. "If he's standing up against the pillar when you cover him they'll never suspect a thing. I'll get rid of these cameras." Mando leaned against the pillar and eased the body off his shoulder. When he looked back she was gone.

The hours passed and he kept digging. He could hear her hosing down the stone steps and saw the water running off into the soil below. He stared at Clive's body, slumped in the half-light, and remembered her slipping something into one of his pockets. He kneeled down, reached into Clive's jacket, and found the ID bracelet. Cliff Bloom's name was engraved on it but part of the chain and the catch was missing. A few of the links had been loosened and he separated them and slipped some into his pocket. He wiped the rest of the bracelet clean with his bandana and put it into the *gringo's* fist. He rechecked the links he'd put in his pocket and knew they'd be searching for them when they found the main part of the bracelet that he'd squeezed into the *gringo's* hand. *La senora bella* would pay plenty for the few pieces he'd kept. She'd have no choice.

He looked up at the thin light beginning to break through the heavy mist. With his last bit of strength he rolled Clive's body to the hole and dropped him head first against the pillar. His shoulders barely fit but Mando forced them down against the pillar, and mumbled a quick prayer. Then he filled in the upright grave, hung the shovel back in the shed, and went up the stairs to look for *la senora bella*. He found her standing naked in the shallow end of the pool, washing the blood out of her pink robe.

165

Cliff Bloom and a burly man in a red and yellow Hawaiian shirt came through the front gate. Nora heard the bell ring but didn't answer it. The door lock turned, and she remembered giving Cliff a key when they were going together. She slipped back into the bedroom, staggered out as if she'd been asleep, and surprised the two men coming in her front door.

"I'm so glad to see you, darling," Cliff said, kissing her on the cheek. "I got worried when you didn't answer my phone calls."

"Hello again," the man in the Hawaiian shirt waved.

"Back for another autograph?" she asked, recognizing him.

"I'm flattered you remember me. In fact, I just came by to ask you about the man we arrested that day."

"Is he still bothering people?"

"Not exactly," Cliff said. "He's missing."

"We found his car down the street with his keys still in it," Detective Benedetti said. "We were wondering if you'd —"

"I think he's a photographer," she said. "The last time I saw him he was taking pictures of me at a pre-production party."

"Yeah, that happened right after we arrested him. By the way, I just loved you in *Sins of the Mother.* I'm glad it was such a hit." She nodded her appreciation. "I never did get a chance to question your gardener. It might help if —"

"He's putting in ice plants along the hill near the south patio," she said, walking him toward the door.

"Thanks, I'll find him," he said.

She edged toward the kitchen window and avoided snapping her fingernail or appearing nervous. Benedetti flashed his badge, and Mando reached for his green card. She turned away, opened the fridge, and took out what was left in the sea breeze pitcher.

"I hope you aren't upset about us barging in like this," Cliff said. "Benedetti just showed up at the office. When he mentioned coming up here I thought I'd better tag along."

"How's your wife?" Nora asked.

Cliff looked surprised at her question and smiled. "We've decided to get a divorce," he said. "She wants to rebuild but I'm looking for a house." Nora glanced back through the window at Benedetti talking to Mando at the bottom of the stone steps. "I figured we could pick up a nice piece of property if we bought it together," Cliff went on. "Tie the knot, so to speak." She looked over at him. He had a slight smile on his face, but his eyes looked frightened. "I know it's all rather sudden to bring this up. Especially with this paparazzi business going on."

"Stalkers will be stalkers," Nora said, draining the sea breeze and letting her tongue linger on a piece of ice. She could see Benedetti pointing at something under the house.

"No one seems to be concerned about a missing drag queen anyway," Cliff said. "Particularly the cops." Benedetti and Mando had disappeared and Nora stared down the empty steps. "We're about to close a deal and start on a new movie," Cliff went on. "We're drawing up the contracts now. This time you can be part of the production company. Thought we might talk about it over dinner tonight. That new Samoan restaurant up the coast might be nice."

She watched as Benedetti turned the corner and came back up the stairs. This time he opened the door without knocking and had an odd expression on his face. "There's a patch of disturbed earth under your house," he said. "The gardener doesn't seem to know anything about it. I'll bring back a couple of men to check it out," he said. "Probably just some coyote or a neighbor's dog."

The front door closed, and Cliff said, "He's certainly efficient. He ought to be in the movie business."

"How did you get in?" she asked.

"I remembered that I still had your key on my chain, so I used it."

"Of course," she said, smiling and pouring herself another drink. Benedetti's car started down the hill and she noticed a quick movement behind the house at the same time. A figure jumped the low fence and stopped to look back. She recognized Mando. He looked up and saw her at the window. They stared at each other for a moment and when he turned away she knew he'd be on the night bus back to Mexico.

"Got anymore of those sea breezes left?" Cliff asked.

"Help yourself," she said, watching Mando running through the cut brush below.

"Guess I ought to introduce myself to the cock fighter," Cliff said, pouring himself another drink. "The three of us seem to be part of a Hollywood triangle. It's amazing how Ron Goode works these things, isn't it?"

"What things?" she asked.

"That publicity crap he creates in those magazines. You know: the cock fighter, producer, and the beautiful actress. It works wonders with the viewers."

"I thought you and Arnie did that?"

"Producers always get blamed," he said. "That's because we take the free publicity. Why not? It certainly helped *Sins.*"

She looked down the hill again, but Mando had disappeared into the brush below. Nothing moved except the shimmer of sunlight on the orange tiled roofs. Cliff finished his drink and headed for the door. "While I'm here I better take a look at that loose patch of dirt Benedetti found under the house."

"Good idea," she said, and followed him out.

When he disappeared around the tool shed she took the links from Cliff's broken ID bracelet out of her pocket, and threw them behind the Yucca plant with Mando's machete so Benedetti would be sure to find them

"A little publicity never hurt anyone," she mumbled, went back into the house, picked up her drink, and began to plan the evening. She'd wear something dazzling ... for the paparazzi.

THE MINOTAUR

The Cave

Scattered weights, jump ropes and leather headgear seemed to be forgotten in the heavy smell of sweat and green liniment. Motionless punching bags hanging like stalactites along stained walls and overturned spit cans. In the center of it all is the squared boxing ring. A pair of leather boxing shoes lay abandoned on an old stool in the champion's favorite corner. The ring itself seems to rise above the debris around it like a pagan altar amidst the empty lockers and jumbled benches.

Yesterday the place had been filled with the murmurs of an expectant crowd watching the Champion prepare his mind and body for the struggle ahead, but it's quiet now. The dull conversations of secret body punches, hooks, and combinations, have turned to the odds on who will win the gaudy belt tomorrow night. Gamblers, wise guys, and reporters, have all raced back to the city to await the brutal contest that will last about sixty minutes, or less, in some other arena far from the smells of this ancient, cavernous place.

The Combatants

A shrill voice, like a sharp left hook, rushed out of the swinging doors on the far side of the cavernous room. "WHERE THE HELL IS EVERYBODY?" a wiry little man shouted in a high raspy voice, and burst into the gym squeezing shiny new leather luggage in both fists. A glinting gold crucifix bounced under his open blue Hawaiian shirt, and he looked around at the scattered equipment for something, or someone, that wasn't there.

"THOSE CLEANUP GUYS WERE SUPPOSED TO BE HERE OVER AN HOUR AGO," he yelled into the emptiness, dropping the luggage and swiping at his bulbous nose with a tissue. "AND WHERE'S THE

CHAMP?" he shouted in that quick-jabbing way, surprised that no one was there. "WHERE THE HELL ARE YA, HAROLD? I GOTTA GET THE CHAMP INTO TOWN FOR THAT FUCKING WEIGH-IN!"

A large, round-shouldered black man, carrying several orange athletic totes and his own beat-up overnight bag, pushed his way through the swinging doors. His white t-shirt fit like a second-skin across his broad chest. He started to say something, but the little man in front of him just kept talking in that same quick delivery. "You got all the bags, Harold? I don't take chances anymore. At least two of everything's my motto. Be prepared. Look at me! I've turned into a fucking boy scout with hay fever," he said, waving a damp tissue. "This sneezing shit is driving me crazy. I hate these trees, the fucking grass, and that goddamn lake out there. I need a good hit of bus fumes to straighten me out."

"Hey, Renz," Harold managed to get in before another rush of the little man's tirade started. "You thinking about taking on any new boys these days?"

"I'm always looking for new blood. Bring the kid around. I'll run him through some stuff and let you know if he's got anything," Renzo mumbled, wiping his nose.

"I meant me!" Harold piped, dropping the bags. "I thought we could do a few bouts together," he said, taking a few quick shuffle steps. "I'm ready to fight again."

"Yeah, sure," Renzo replied, with a wave of his wet tissue. "We'll talk. Right now I gotta find those goddamn cleanup clowns ... *and* the limo guy. We'll never make the weigh-in at this rate."

"I need a manager," Harold said quickly.

"Jesus, you had a whole week for all this. I got things going on here, man."

"But I need to know now ... before you go."

"Still think you got a few fights left, eh?"

"I got years, Renz. Years. I can feel it."

171

"Call me in a few days after the Champ finishes with Montoya. We'll do contracts ... the whole *schmeer.*"

"I knew you was a right guy, Renz," he said, picking up the totes again.

"Forget those bags. That's the limo guy's job. I'll get his ass moving. IF YOU SEE THE CHAMP, TELL HIM I'M OUTSIDE," Renzo yelled over his shoulder, and headed under the exit sign like a sudden gust of wind that hits and is gone.

Harold looked around, sat down in one of the folding chairs at ringside, and stretched his legs to ease his morning stiffness. It had been almost five days since he showed up at the camp. He felt slighted when the Champ didn't recognize him, but when he finally did they talked and drank like old times. Good scotch and the Champ drinking his special vitamin water. They drank to those days when they struggled to get the rent for some dump they shared on Lenox Avenue. Harold never even had to tell the Champ that he needed a job. The Champ just handed him a roll and said they were "winding down for the Montoya fight." Then he told Renzo to give him something to do. It felt like old times again.

Harold leaned over, opened one of Renzo's orange totes, and pulled out a few rolls of half-inch tape. From another bag he took a couple of mouthpieces and stuffed them into his own bag, checked the room again, and went back for a pair of boxing gloves he'd seen Renzo shove into the bottom of another bulging tote. He didn't think it was stealing because he'd need all the equipment he could get for his comeback. By the end of the year he'd be in shape again. All Renzo had to do was book him a few bouts and he'd be back in the game.

"How would *you* take him, Harold?"

The deep low voice seemed to come out of nowhere and it resonated through the cavernous room like a growl. He turned too fast, raising his hands in a clumsy way that

172

made him look like he was frightened, or had done something wrong. He didn't see the Champ in the deep shadows and wondered how long he'd been standing there watching him, and if he saw what he'd taken from the other bags.

"Champ? That you?" he asked, still not seeing him.

"How would you take him, Harold?" came at him again, and he caught a glimpse of the Champ in the shadows. He looked great in his gray pinstriped suit, light blue shirt, and red tie. His brown sugar skin glowed in the dim light as he headed straight for the ring in that hypnotic, direct way he had that could rivet a crowd's attention to his every move.

"Take who?" Harold asked.

"Montoya," the Champ said, brushing by him.

"The big Cubano?" Harold asked, slipping into a hunched fighting pose. "I'd crowd him. Keep him off guard. He'll play Ginger Man, for sure. I'd go easy in those early rounds. Take him out into deep water past the fifth, sixth ... seventh round. Make him fight *your* fight."

"Sounds like you been figuring this one," the Champ said, jumping lightly up onto the ring apron.

"Yeah," Harold answered with a short laugh. "Just remember, you got what he wants, Champ. All you have to do is look for his weak spots."

"I did that the last time I fought him. I won, but it felt like I'd been hit by a tank. Didn't find too many weak spots."

"Everyone's got to be wobbly in there some place."

"Are you wobbly, Harold?"

"Aren't you, Champ?"

"Never," the Champ replied.

The punching bags along the wall swayed imperceptibly as the Champ stared back at Harold with those dark eyes that pierced through a man. He took off his jacket, folded it, and draped it over the ropes. "This whole game's got its weak spots," the Champ said. "Hiding yours and finding the other guy's is the trick."

"You talking about fighting or those fancy threads you got on?"

"The threads are just one of the wrinkles. You've got to look good or they won't believe you're the Champ. Blue and gray's for the TV cameras. The latest style is to let them know that I'm still the one on top."

"You mean like that last Montoya fight?" The Champ stared down at him. "I figure you made that fight close so you could get the crowd back for another shot. Make *him* look good ... pick up a bundle on the rematch."

"I don't carry anybody. Never have, never will," the Champ said, slipping through the ropes and into the ring. Harold laughed in a loose, nervous way. "You earn every inch in this game. This isn't Wall Street, or Main Street. It's Blood Street. You have to do the heavy work yourself when you're up in here." He threw some easy jabs and danced across the flat expanse of the sweat-stained boxing ring. "Montoya's weak spot is that he thinks he knows more about me than he really does. In this game that's a weakness that can get you killed."

"How you figure that, man?" Harold asked, climbing up into the ring with him.

"That kid, Montoya," the Champ said, doing a quick dance step along the ropes. "He's inside the numbers."

"Numbers?"

"All those numbers that make up the game, Harold. They're everything. I crawl inside those numbers every time I step through those ropes. It's the numbers that take me through the maze," the Champ said, moving out into the middle of the ring.

"You talking about fighting, Champ ... or dying?" Harold asked, with that same nervous laugh, moving in closer, and looking into the Champion's bottomless eyes.

"It's all in the numbers," the Champ repeated.

"You talking money numbers?"

"I'm talking the only numbers that really matter," the Champ said, dancing around the ring throwing quick combinations into the space between them.

"You're talking crazy, Champ."

"I'm talking numbers. Ten rounds. Fifteen rounds. Three minutes each. One minute to rest. Three minutes again. My measurements. His measurements. The odds. The hours. The days. The weights. The big-ass cash register. The only numbers that count," the Champ said. "They're talking to me right now. I'm so inside those numbers I can't get out of them anymore. They're part of me. Montoya's in those numbers too, an I got him figured." He began to shadow box around the ring. "It's when you're outside those numbers that makes it hard to figure," he said, shuffling from side to side, pursuing his imaginary opponent.

"What do you mean ... *outside* the numbers?"

"My wife. The kids. The lawyers, the limo-guy, those dumb reporters, even the referee," he said. "They're all *outside* the numbers."

"But you say you're caught inside those numbers."

"You got it," the Champ said, dancing across the canvas. "Up here in the ring ... I understand things," he said, stopping in front of Harold. "Sometimes I even get lost in them. That's when everything comes back. The confusion becomes clear. The order. The numbers. They come home ... and everything falls into place again."

For a moment, they just stared at each other in the middle of the ring. "I think I know what you mean, Champ," Harold finally said. "About being *inside* the numbers. I remember a kid that could tell exactly when the round would start. When it got to be half over. When it would end. Like some kind of clock was in his head. This kid could even guess your weight and was never off more than a pound or two. It was hard to beat that kid. Know what I mean? Then one day he just walks out. Never comes back to the gym again. He quit. Never could figure that kid."

"That's 'cause you *think* a guy is inside the numbers … then you realize he's really outside. And he's been outside all the while. That's the guy that'll burn you," the Champ said in a whisper.

"But Montoya's inside the numbers … isn't he?"

"Montoya's *deep* inside the numbers. I don't worry about him," the Champ said, brushing up against the ropes and heading back into the center of the ring again.

"If it's not Montoya … who else is there?"

"You," the Champ said. "I worry about you."

"Me?"

"You're *out*side the numbers, Harold. That makes you dangerous."

He never saw it coming. The Champ just laid it out there and danced away, his body shifting under his shirt and tie, jabbing the air. "I know you went looking for work over at Montoya's before you came here," he said. "I knew it even before you showed up. That kind of talk runs fast between training camps."

"Hell, yeah," Harold said. "I went over to Montoya's looking for a sparring job. I figured it'd be a lot easier sparring for him than for you. Just trying to protect my end a little and not get hurt."

The Champ stopped bobbing and weaving. "But you ended up here, didn't you?" he said.

"The kid didn't have any work so I figured —"

"He had plenty of things for you to do though. The minute he saw your eyes he could tell you were *out*side the numbers scratching to get back in."

"I ain't outside nothing. I'm ready to go again."

"What kind of numbers did you get, Harold? A hundred? A thousand? Ten thousand?" The Champ picked his jacket up off the ropes and slipped it back on. "What kind of numbers did he give you, Harold?"

"You're talking crazy," Harold said, taking a short step back towards the edge of the ring. "Ask Renz," he said, pointing toward the exit. "He's waiting for me right now. He knows I'm straight. Ask him!"

"Renzo's been onto you ever since you got here," the Champ said. "He knows who you've been calling ... what you been dealing."

"He just said he'd represent me. Get me some fights."

The Champ buttoned his jacket, straightened his tie, and started for the ropes. "Renzo knew what you were after, and he gave it to you. He let you think we were worried about that dumb left-hand combination of Montoya's. He also told you that I'm out of shape and can't go past ten. You forgot the basics, Harold. It'll take Montoya about five rounds to figure out I can go the distance. That's when he'll try that dumb left-handed combination. And I'll be waiting for it. You gave him *exactly* what we wanted you to give him ... no more, no less."

"You got it wrong, Champ," Harold said, staring into those dark, penetrating eyes.

"You got inside my numbers and tried to burn me."

"I didn't burn anybody. That Cuban kid's gonna whip your ass. And after that he'll fight me. And I'll nail him cause I got him figured. I got him cold!"

"You couldn't beat Montoya with an army. You're out of the numbers, Harold. Been out for years."

"That's bullshit! I'm the guy you could never get by, you sonofabitch," Harold snarled. "We used to be friends before you stuck me out on a back burner."

"The Champ isn't allowed to have friends. When they hand you that belt it's like being shoved into a dark, lonely cave where you just wait to fight again. They wouldn't let me work up a sweat over you. You're not worth it. You're out of the numbers."

Harold moved across the ring toward the Champ in a quick shuffle. "You're a liar!" he shouted. "You gave that Cuban cock two shots but you never once looked my way. You kept me down!"

"You're the only one keeping you down, Harold. And it's been that way for a long time."

Harold shifted his feet and hooked his fist upward. The Champ winced and took the punch under the heart. He didn't move. A soft cry came out of Harold as he swung out with both hands, his fists pounding the Champ's chest, his cry turning into a long moan.

"Don't fight the numbers! Take them as they come! ONE! TWO! THREE! FOUR!" Harold's arms began to weaken, his legs slipped away on him, and he held on to keep from falling. "I should've taken you out a long time ago. Ended your numbers," the Champ said, as Harold swung again. "SIX. SEVEN. EIGHT. NINE." Harold's knees buckled and he dropped to the stained canvas. "TEN!" the Champ said. "It's over! Get out! Don't come back!"

Renzo's squeaky voice yelled up at him, "CHAMP, YOUR HANDS! YOU CRAZY? YOUR HANDS! I told you to stay away from him. He's a loser … all wrong!"

"I just finished his numbers," the Champ said, while Renzo checked his hands for broken bones. "I never touched him. It was the numbers that ran right over him. Didn't leave a mark."

"WHAT'RE YOU TALKING ABOUT?" Renzo yelled, but the Champ could only hear the numbers clicking in his head and the sharp blare of a car horn. "It's the limo guy, Champ. We gotta go."

He stepped over the man sprawled at his feet, slipped through the ropes, and went out past the hanging punching bags along the wall, still inside the numbers.

FULL CIRCLE

Michael D. Robbins was given the missing piece to his entire life when a movie producer asked him to star in a film about a man who loses his faith after the death of his wife. After years of playing gangsters, and guys who didn't get the girl, Michael D. Robbins (aka Morris Rubinski) had been validated like a punched parking ticket. Contracts were signed, schedules set, and on the first day of shooting a scrawny kid in a seersucker suit showed up at his hotel room, catching Michael getting dressed for his once in a lifetime part.

"I'm from the office, sir," the kid said, trying to look casual standing in the doorway.

"Hope there aren't too many rewrites in that pile of papers you got there," Michael said, giving him his famous actor's smile. "Got it all up here in my head. Memorized from front to back. Up. Down. Sideways too."

"Oh, I don't have anything to do with that," the kid said, handing Michael the papers. "I'm just the —"

"Helluva script," Michael said.

"Yes, sir," the kid muttered. "But this has nothing to do with that. These are printouts. Copies, actually."

"Printouts?"

"Uh-eh, the script's been frozen since last Tuesday."

"Have we met before?"

"Yes, sir. I'm one of Mr. Cameron's assistants."

"You're not with the hotel?"

"No, sir. Mr. Cameron is your New York agent. Remember? The Morris Office?"

"Of course. Errrr, Sammy, isn't it?"

"Yes, sir," the kid said in a short squeak, surprised at being remembered.

Michael waved the kid toward a mustard-colored chair in the middle of the room. "Can I order you some breakfast, Sammy?"

"No, sir. I've eaten, thank you. Special blend. Cereal. Fruit. My mother makes it for me every morning. Health thing."

"How 'bout some coffee?"

The kid shook his head. "I'm not allowed." Michael tried to give the printouts back to the kid. "That's your copy, sir. The originals are at the office."

"Look, kid, I've got a lot to do this morning and —"

"I know, but you better check those over, sir."

Michael glanced down at the loose papers, as if they were stuck to his hand. "Just a lot of numbers," he said.

"The last page, sir. Under Summary."

"Summary?"

"Insurance stuff, sir," the kid said, and got up to show him the exact paragraph. "Right here, sir. Defined risk. I'm supposed to wait for any message you want sent back to the office."

"They're expecting me over on the set. Ready to roll. Got the whole script up here," he repeated, tapping his head and giving the kid that smile again.

"I know, sir, but the computer says —"

"Computer?"

"Right here, sir. It's under Summary. See?"

Michael stared down at the numbers and noticed the boy's hand was shaking.

"Basically it's saying you won't make it through the picture, sir. That's why they can't insure you," Sammy said, sitting down again.

"What the hell are you talking about? The computer's not doing the movie. I am!" Michael said, throwing the printouts into the kid's lap.

"It's your heart, sir."

"I'm in perfect health! Do you know how many movies I've made? Forty. Fifty! More! Big hits!"

180

"You don't understand, sir," Sammy said, looking for the summary page again. "You see? Right here. Your rating is a two point five with a little black minus mark."

"Yeah? So? What about it?"

"When the computer puts in that little black minus mark it means ... Actually, it rates you as dead. See? Two point five. Little black minus mark."

"Do I look dead to you?"

"Please, don't yell."

"Why are you curling up like that?"

"You threw the printouts at me and now you're yelling. I have a problem when people —"

"Screw your printouts!"

"Don't yell. Please."

"Sit up like a man and tell me who sent you."

"No one at the office would do it —"

"Are they cancelling the picture?"

"They're using the backup, sir."

"Nobody backs up Michael D. Robbins!"

"You're yelling again."

"I'm not yelling!"

"Solly Morton's doing the picture, sir."

"He's too young. A lightweight. All wrong."

"That's right, sir."

"You agree? Now we're getting somewhere!"

"I agree but ... but ..."

"But what?"

"I'm just one of the assistants, sir."

Michael stared down at the boy curled in the mustard chair like an overdone hotdog. "Stop cringing," he yelled. "Some agent. You're nothing but a messenger boy."

"I don't want to be an agent. And I don't want you getting a heart attack. I mean, right now, right here. In front of me."

"What the hell kind of an idiot are you?"

"I needed a job and my uncle —"

"Oh, so Cameron's your uncle?"

"No, sir. Levitz is my uncle."

"You're Izzy Levitz's kid?"

"His nephew."

"That's it! Izzy is playing a joke on me. I knew it! He's out in the hall right now, laughing his head off. Great kidder," Michael said, starting for the door.

"My Uncle Izzy never laughs. Not ever."

"You're right," Michael mumbled. "Not a muscle in his body moves. We were dragged up in Brooklyn and he never laughed at anything. But he's a big honcho now. We'll make him work for a change." Michael picked up the phone. "Get me Beverly Hills. 310-555-2856."

"That's my uncle's home number."

"That's right. From me to God's ear."

"Please, don't tell him I'm here. He might think —"

"Izzy? This is Michael. What do you mean, *Michael who?* I know it's four AM out there, but this is an emergency. I'm in New York trying to make a goddamn movie and they want to break my contract. The bastards are going with Solly and he's not right for the part. I know Solly's your client! But so am I!"

Sammy slumped in the chair like he'd been shot. He was watching Michael D. Robbins go through the same anger and denial he'd witnessed when they told Gloria Bishop she'd made her last movie. That same vacant look had come into her eyes and she'd gone back to her apartment, taken an overdose of sleeping pills, and on a wet afternoon in midtown Manhattan, she'd faded into movie history.

"You knew about this and didn't tell me?" Michael yelled into the phone. "You should've called. Instead you send your nephew? I don't want to see a doctor. I want to make this movie. It's important to me. I'm perfect for the part. This movie completes my entire career. Brings it full circle!" Sammy could hear his Uncle's voice trying to explain the unexplainable on the other end. "We go back a long way, Izzy," Michael shouted. "I know they'll pay all my expenses. Yeah, he's still here. Nice boy."

Michael dropped the phone in the kid's lap. "He wants to talk to you."

"Me?"

"Aren't you Sammy the nephew?"

"Yes, sir," the kid said, picking up the phone. "Uncle Izzy?" he stammered. "No, sir. No, sir."

"Try saying *yes* to something!" Michael yelled.

"Don't, please," Sammy whined, squeezing the phone. "No, not you, sir. Mr. Robbins here was just yelling —" There was a sudden silence. "Yes, sir. Yes, sir," he said, and hung up.

"And what did Uncle Izzy tell you?" Michael asked.

"He told me to bring you home."

The early morning traffic stirred in the streets below. A siren wailed somewhere uptown. Michael stared at the kid curled in the mustard chair. "They want to put me out to pasture," he said. "Buy me lunches. Give me plaques and pats on the back." He knew it was going to take a lot of schmoozing and fast-talking to get through this mess, but he'd never expected to get fired by a computer. "Ever been to Hollywood?" he asked the kid.

"I've never been out of New York City."

"You can stay with me."

"I don't drive."

"You'll learn."

"I don't like the beach."

"You don't have to go to the beach!"

"Don't yell. Please. Remember your heart."

Michael knew that news about this would spread fast. In this business, if you sneezed at eight you had pneumonia by noon and the newspapers were pulling out your obituary by three. "Don't say anything to anybody," he said to the kid. "It'll be our secret. You, me, and Uncle Izzy."

"My uncle said they've got the best cardiologist in the world out there. He also said you shouldn't worry. He'll take care of everything. No matter what it costs."

"Izzy said that?"

"Yes, sir. He said, 'You'll be able to make another forty movies after this guy sees you.' I forget his name, but Uncle Izzy's making an appointment for you right now."

"Feingold. His name's Feingold," Michael said.

"That's right! Dr. Feingold. You know him?"

"Yeah, I know him."

"You've been there?"

There was a sudden knock and they both turned to stare at the door, as if some terrible force might be on the other side. Another knock and Michael went to open it. A short bald-headed man wheeled in a cart with breakfast on it. Michael signed the bill, tipped him, and closed the door. He lifted the plated lid and said, "Hope you like scrambled eggs and bacon. I've lost my appetite."

"I don't eat bacon. I'll just have a little of the orange juice and a small piece of the bagel," the kid said.

"Good," Michael said, heading for the bedroom.

"Where you going?" Sammy asked, jumping out of the chair.

"I'm going to put on that dark blue suit I got for the movie I'm not going to make," Michael said, closing the door to get away from the fear in the boy's eyes. He sat down on the bed and stared into the large framed mirror over the dresser. An old man stared back at him. Pale, small, and frightened. He knew he was sick but now everyone would know. He went into the bathroom to kneel at the bowl. He wondered if this was the way it ended. Down on your knees at the toilet. Not praying, heaving.

A light tap hit the bathroom door behind him. "Would you do me a favor?" the kid asked from the other side. "It's my mother. She'll never believe me if I tell her I have to take you back to Hollywood. She'll think I'm running away with some floozie. But if you come home with me and explain the situation, it might help. My mother's a big fan. Seen all your movies."

Michael's head hung over the bowl. "Where do you live?" he managed to ask.

"Flatbush."

"Haven't been back there in years."

"Hasn't changed much."

"Two story brick?"

"How did you know?"

Michael flushed the toilet and traces of blood rushed around the bowl and disappeared down the drain. He leaned toward the door and listened to the kid's frightened breathing on the other side.

"Maybe you better call your mother and tell her we're coming," he said. The pain in his arm got worse.

"You all right?" the kid asked.

"Don't forget to make those plane reservations," he said, and waited until the kid's footsteps faded away before pulling himself up off the floor and opening the door. The kid was on the phone in the next room. Michael went to the closet, took out the dark blue suit, and laid it across the bed. "Not everyday you get a tailored suit like this," he said. "Needs a carnation. White," he muttered, smoothing the lapels.

*

His past pressed in on him as they drove through the Brooklyn streets. Balancing the large bouquet of yellow roses in his arms, he squeezed out of the taxi. Houses with walls and porches cemented to each other, like rows of Siamese twins, ran up and down both sides of the street. A slightly overweight, middle-aged woman hurried down the brick stairs to greet them and Michael handed her the bouquet of roses.

"Happy to meet you, ma'am," he said.

"Welcome," she answered, a bit flustered, nearly dropping the flowers when Sammy brushed by her.

"This is Mr. Robbins, Mamma. We have to —"

"I know who Mr. Robbins is," she said, extending her hand like Michael was a visiting prince. "Before you were born I knew about Mr. Robbins. I'm Rhoda ... Sammy's mother."

"I would've never guessed," he said, taking her hand. "It's so good to be back in the old neighborhood."

"You're from Brooklyn?"

"Flushing Avenue," he said.

"Come in, come in, we'll have tea and mandelbrot," she said, pulling Michael up the stairs. "If I knew *you* were coming I would've cleaned," she mumbled. "Sammy didn't tell me."

"Believe me, it's a pleasure to come into a beautiful home like this after those boring hotel rooms."

"We have to catch a plane," Sammy yelled from the bedroom.

"You're going somewhere?"

"Back to Hollywood for our next assignment," Michael told her.

"I thought your movie making was right here?"

"There's been a snafu," Sammy yelled, peeking out of the bathroom. "Mr. Robbins has to go back to California and Uncle Izzy wants me to accompany him."

"Sorry to bother you like this," Michael said. "Something's come up and it has to be handled in Hollywood."

"You need Sammy for this?"

"He's my agent."

"Since when?"

"This morning."

186

"He's been promoted?"

"You could put it that way," Michael said.

"He's my youngest," she said, putting water up for tea. "He's delicate. I worry."

"Wonderful boy. Knows just what to do and say at the right moment. A natural agent."

"Really?" she said, taking a large blue vase from the cupboard. He caught the suspicion in her voice.

"I never knew Izzy had a sister," he said quickly.

"Izzy's from the other side of the family. I come from the Westside. We're Sephardic," she said, shoving his long-stemmed roses into the blue vase one at a time.

"You married Izzy's younger brother. The one that —"

She cut him off with a curt "Mmmmm-eh," poured the tea into the delicate porcelain cups, and served him a piece of mandel cake on a matching plate. "I've seen all your movies," she said. "The funny ones, the gangsters, even the fancy ones with the coming attractions that were better than the movie. Loved them."

He could feel the weakness coming back and the cold sweats hitting him in short dizzying waves. "Sammy wants you to know that he's taking me back to California and isn't running off with some floozie," he said, trying to give her a funny delivery.

"Hmmmm-eh," she muttered and looked away. He felt nauseated and short of breath, and wanted to get to the bathroom but couldn't move. This was the way it ended, he thought, having tea and mandelbrat with a stranger. He'd come to that moment where he was expected to show what he could do. Death is what they remembered. When it came he'd hit the table, glance off the chair, ease onto the floor, spill the tea as he went down, letting the porcelain cup break at the perfect moment. Close-ups later.

MOON CHILDREN

NEW MOON RISING

Long rays of headlights crisscrossed Manhattan and plunged northward towards the dark patch they called The Heights. The steel herd picked up speed and disappeared into winter trees, frozen grass, shopping malls, and flickering suburban living rooms. Hector looked down at the stream of lights as he moved across the tenement's roof. It'd been about a year since they'd worked. No moon. Perfect.

He pulled his collar up against the wind and headed down the stairs to have another look at the building's insides, checking the corners for anything that might get in their way. Broken walls, cracked ceilings, pipes ripped out for the brass and copper. Even the structural cables had been exposed and they hung over him like a giant spider web. The wind whipped in low across his legs. He moved up the stairs with it, crossed the roof to the next building and went back down to the street from the other side. If the weather held they wouldn't have anything to worry about. A good fire lived off the wind. But they'd have to be quiet. People were still living there.

*

The Cadillac purred its way into the traffic along the Henry Hudson Parkway. "I can't believe there's no moon tonight," Stella said. "I wanted a moon."

"It's up there," Jason said.

"I *know* it's up there. I just want to see it."

"Is all this moon-phase bullshit coming off your new wristwatch?" he said with a laugh.

"It tells me exactly what to expect."

"But only from the moon," he said.

They rolled past the George Washington Bridge, hugged the rail, and swung onto the Westside Highway.

Stella lifted her cashmere skirt across her thighs to look down at her new shoes. She hated heels, but wore them for Jason. He loved to look at her legs. She presumed he looked at other women's legs too. It was one of his few admitted weaknesses.

"You know, we don't really have to go to this damn thing tonight," he said. "I could make some excuse —"

"I don't really mind," she said.

"It's just another one of his dumb parties."

"Your brother's parties are never dumb. In fact, your brother's parties are smart."

"What's that supposed to mean?"

She smoothed out a wrinkle in her stocking. "A smart party always has smart people," she said.

"They're not smart. They're successful. There's a big difference," he said.

"You mean connected."

"Connected?"

"Attached to each other," she said. "Same neighborhoods, summer camps, private schools, colleges, clubs. Connected. To each other."

"Are you saying that I don't have any connections?"

"Your brother's the one with the connections, Jason. That's why he throws the parties. We just go to them."

"Eli's parties suck," he sneered.

"You're not getting it," she said with a sigh.

"You're talking about having connections."

"The people at Eli's parties don't need connections. They *are* the connections."

"You don't know what you're talking about," he mumbled as they rolled down the narrow ramp. "Connected is connected," he said. "Period."

"Not really. You see, the connected ones have each other's unlisted phone numbers. And they *do* call each other."

189

"So what?" he said. "Eli would give me any one of those phone numbers if I asked him."

"Wanna bet?" she said.

"Sure I'll bet. How 'bout fifty bucks?"

"I forgot. I don't bet with you anymore."

They sat quietly and rolled across Seventy-Ninth Street toward Central Park.

"Has Eli ever given you any of his friend's phone numbers before?" she finally asked.

"Of course ... lots of times."

"Really?"

"Don't you remember that time he helped me when I needed to talk with someone in city housing?" He looked her way but she didn't answer. "And what about the car leasing problem I had?"

"He gave you their *office* numbers, Jason. Office numbers don't count. They're listed in the phone book," she said.

"Then what the hell does count?" he asked.

"Unlisted home numbers, Jason. That's all that counts."

They drove across the park without saying anything. Jason made the turn on Fifth, cruised for a place to park, and found a spot about five blocks away. Stella didn't like walking in the cold wind, but she didn't complain. Walking up Fifth Avenue still rated as her favorite sport, even without a moon.

*

The cold wind pierced Hector's mask and a sharp gust rushed through the open doors. The slap of gasoline sloshed across the landing and streamed down the stairs. The fuel led directly to the rags they'd stuffed in the walls. He heard the clang of an empty gasoline can that meant Shadow and Bee were nearly done. Their staccato barks came at him from below. If it didn't work tonight they'd

190

have to wait weeks before trying again. That'd be bad for business. He had a reputation to protect.

Hector snapped a wooden match against the dry wall, looked for the gasoline stain trickling down the staircase, and waited for the next rush of wind. It gusted up the stairs behind him. When it hit, he dropped the match. The roar pushed him back as the flames ran up the stairs. Then the blast carried the fire up over the cracked walls.

Another sharp bark came from below. The halls were lit from the blaze above. The three of them were running and banging on doors as they raced down the stairs, howling like wild animals. Hector looked back at the upper floors to make sure the fire kept moving, and they poured out into the street. The cold air hit Hector's chest like a hammer as he ran with them through the snow.

*

Stella thought they'd stayed too long at the party even if Jason was socializing more than usual. He'd even danced with the Park Avenue dentist's wife. The one that laughed too loud and too much, but had nice legs. When Stella mentioned what a good time he seemed to be having he said that he'd "finally felt connected." She apologized for what she'd said in the car but that only seemed to make matters worse, so they avoided each other for the rest of the evening.

The politicians were the first to leave and then the psychiatrists. Jason shook hands, kissed cheeks, and said *goodbyes*. Even his brother noticed the difference and encouraged it.

"We'll do lunch," Eli kept telling his departing guests. "I'll bring Jason."

A small clack of young lawyers lingered in the kitchen with their dates. Most of them had just graduated from high-priced law schools. The music had finally stopped. Those who remained talked about the ones who had gone. The party had ended.

The heated Cadillac rolled through the light snow flurries. Stella listened to the pluck of violins playing *Holiday For Strings*. Then the smooth tones of Nat Cole drifted in singing *The Christmas Song*. Jason reached over to touch her leg. He asked if she wanted to stop for coffee.

"No, let's go straight home," she said. He smiled, made the turn onto the Westside Highway, and headed the big car northward with one hand on the wheel, the other on her leg.

*

The light snow reflected in the growing fire from across the street. Gusts blew the pink flurries into the air and dropped them like crystal sheets across the dark rooftops. A heavy metal door creaked on its hinges. Charley Johnson slipped out on to the roof and crunched across the untouched snow. He stopped every few feet to look behind him at the crisp white sheet that he'd broken with his Charley boots. Shivering in his pea coat he watched the blaze growing larger across the street. He sniffed at the fiery air as the hot pieces of tarred roofing sparked, exploded, and fell back again into the burning structure. The first wail of sirens began to echo through the canyons of empty tenements.

A sound came from behind him. He moved back from the edge but couldn't see anything through the falling snow. Standing frozen in the wind he watched the roof's metal door swing back and forth. The only tracks he could make out were his own and he remembered closing the door before he came out.

"Hector?" he whispered. "Hector? That you?" Something moved just above the door. He looked for a place to run but the only way out was the way he came in. "Hector? It's me," he said. Nothing moved except the slight swing of the open door. He started to circle it but stopped when he saw the figure move. "What're you doing?" he said in a shivering voice. "I've been looking for you, man."

Hector lifted the ski mask over his head. "We been looking for you too," he said.

That's when Charley noticed the two catlike figures behind him. "You guys been up here all the while?" he asked with a nervous giggle. "*Mysterioso*, man, *mysterioso*."

Shadow lifted the loose fitting hood over his head to reveal a young black kid. Bee, closer to the stairs, stopped moving. Charley could see her eyes watching him through the ragged slits in the stocking mask.

"Long night," Hector said.

"Yeah," Charley answered, edging toward the edge as the moaning fire engines turned the corner. "The blaze looks beautiful, man. It's like a fucking postcard. That's a great touch signing the front of the building like that. *Moon Children '86*. Fucking poetry, man." He stuffed his hands into his pockets and watched the fire below. "You did a great job, Hector. Except for one thing. You torched the wrong fucking building," he yelled over the sirens. "You fucking dummies!" The dark figures stared silently back at him as he moved along the edge of the roof yelling at them. "Four-sixty-two! Not the one on the corner. The one *next* to it!"

"They're *both* going," Hector said.

"What're you talking about?"

"We started the burn on the corner, 460. Made sure it'd spread next door. This way the report lists 462 as an accident," Hector said. "You got a perfect burn, Charley. Your client collects. No questions. 460 will get the rap."

Charley stepped back to take another look into the street. Firemen were running heavy hoses into both buildings. The flames had already cut through the top floor of 462. "Yeah, I see that now. It's definitely on the torch, man. Wow! You're the best, Hector. I can tell my client that he has a burned out building. A scorcher. Totaled. Nothing left. No questions."

Hector moved up behind Charley and put his hand out. "Pay time," he said.

"What're you talking about? I *paid* you, man."

Charley sensed a slight movement from the two others and Hector moved in closer. "You were shy five hundred in the first payment," he said in that same monotone voice.

"I promised I'd —"

"Make it up in the second payment," Hector said. "Now you owe us five grand. Payment on delivery." Charley glanced behind him but there was nowhere to run. "No sweat, I'll get it," he said. Hector grabbed the front of Charley's coat. Nothing moved except the falling snow reflecting in the fire across the street. "I can explain," he said in short breaths. "The guy ... the client ... still hasn't paid me. This all happened ... you know, so fast. I'll get it from him today. First thing."

"That wasn't the deal!" Hector said, and in one quick motion he pulled out a long, crude shiv and cut one of Charley's pockets. A few coins fell out into the snow. "First payment on agreement. You were five hundred short," Hector said waving the glinting piece of steel in front of him. "Second payment, right after fire is set. Remember?"

"I just wanted to make sure you guys did the job," Charley said. "It's confidential stuff. The client agreed to pay on delivery. The dump burns. I get paid. *You* get paid."

"The dump is burning," Hector said, pulling Charley's sleeve up. Small scabs of blood ran along his arm.

"Is that where the money went?" Hector asked, pinching him just above the vein.

"No, no, man," Charley said. "I'd never do that. Deal's a deal. The client *wants* to pay you."

194

"Let's leave this shit with the garbage," Bee said. "He's nothing but a junkie-whiner."

Hector pulled Charley to the edge of the roof and they looked down at the firemen wrestling their hoses in the street. "Tell me who the client is," Hector said, twisting his ear. "We'll deal direct. That way there's no fuckups."

"Let me do it, Hector. I *know* these people. Who they are ... how they think." Hector threw him in the snow and the others grabbed him from behind.

"Who's the client?" Hector said.

"I'll get the money for you. I swear it."

They began to drag Charley through the crusting snow. Hector threw a knotted loop around Charley's chest, and kept pushing him toward the edge of the roof until he fell off.

The rope tightened as Charley swung into the mist that drifted up from the fire below. He hit the side of the building, the rope jerked, and a loud grunt came out of him. He reached up to grab the rope, almost fell through it, and watched the buildings roll in the flickering light as he swung through the darkness. Sounds of fire trucks and sizzling water faded as the pressure on his chest grew tighter. He was falling again.

*

Stella woke up in the car and looked out at the snow that angled through the trees. Dimly lit lampposts reflected off the water below. She knew this place. They used to come here after Jason's fraternity parties, before they were married.

It had stopped snowing but there were fresh tracks leading away from the car. She got out and followed them down through the naked trees to the footbridge. A lone figure stood just beyond the lights along the path. The cold crept up under her cashmere skirt, edging its way along the tops of her stockings. The wind murmured through the leafless trees like someone crying. When she reached the flat stones that led out onto the bridge, she saw someone staring down into the lake.

"Jason?" she called, moving in closer.

He wiped his eyes as she came across the bridge.

"Are you all right?" she asked.

"Fine."

She felt the warmth of his breath on her neck. "You're not fine. You're crying," she said.

He didn't answer. She felt him tremble as she held him in the cold. He seemed frightened. Needy. When she looked up he kissed her and began to unbutton her blouse. She opened her mouth to his kiss. For a moment, they stopped breathing. His coat brushed across her cheek. She looked up to find him staring at the traffic on the parkway. It began to snow again.

He edged her in against the low wall of the bridge as they'd done so many times before. Only this time it felt distant, lonely, and detached. When he kissed her neck she dug her heels into his back to brace herself against the wall. A chill ran through her. He lowered his head across her belly. Her legs tightened around him and she watched the rushing headlights dance through the trees along the parkway. His tongue moved to the small space near the top of her thighs. The clear, cold air rushed into her. She felt the sudden warmth between her legs. Then she leaned back to let herself float up into the icy web of bare branches, and rocked to the rhythm of his breathing. His tongue went deeper. Her vision blurred. It started snowing again.

*

Charley couldn't stop shaking. He kept repeating the name in Hector's ear. "We ever do a burn for this guy before?" Hector asked. Hugging himself, Charley shook his head. "I want to talk to him," Hector said. "Now."

"The office is closed, man," Charley stuttered.

196

"Take me to his house."

"That's up in Westchester," he said, trying to get up.

"You know where he lives?" Charley looked up in surprise. Hector's dark eyes stared coldly down at him. Shadow and Bee grabbed him from either side. He tried to get to his feet but this time they wrapped the rope around his neck. "It's still early," Hector said. "Why don't we go for a little drive?"

"I don't have that much gas, man."

"We'll fill it for you. Take it out of what you owe us," Hector said. He lifted Charley up by his hair so he could stare down into his drugged eyes. "You ain't in any shape to drive, Charley. Gimme the keys."

NEW MOON FALLING

A sharp bark bit the cold air. Hector answered it with a low, growling yelp. A deep shiver ran through his body as he stood in the brisk wind that cut through the naked trees. They were in so close he could smell the smoke from the chimney. The client's old stone house was well built. It'd be hard to torch a house like that.

When the second bark hit he came out from behind the trees, dragging Charley with him. "You're gonna wake up the whole neighborhood with that crazy barking shit," he said. "It's stupid, man. They'll call the cops and we'll end up getting grabbed for walking on their dumb lawn."

Another bark came and Hector pushed Charley toward the house. They were in so close he could see the Christmas wreath on the front door. "You can't bother these people at two in the morning," Charley pleaded. Hector pushed him up on the porch.

*

They'd hardly said a word on the ride home. Stella felt like she had made love with some stranger in the park and didn't quite understand it. She turned the glass of brandy in her hands as Jason threw another log on the fire, sending a cluster of sparks up the chimney. Then she leaned over and clicked on the Christmas tree lights, turning the color of the room into a pale blue moonlight.

"We ought to sleep down here tonight," she said.

"Like old times," Jason answered with a little laugh. "Remember the look on my mother's face when she'd find us curled up on the couch? She never understood the younger generation."

"I miss her," Stella said, offering him her brandy.

"I miss both of them."

"I miss that little twinkle in your father's eye," she said. "Whenever I saw it I knew something would happen."

"It usually meant he'd closed a business deal."

"Funny, I always thought the twinkle was for me."

He laughed. "His first love was the deal. After that you got whatever you could out of him."

"He adored your mother."

Jason raised the brandy glass in a toast. "I'm glad they didn't have to live too long without each other."

"Do you think we'll be that lucky?"

"Lucky enough to retire to San Diego?"

"You know what I mean."

He put down the glass and kissed her. His hand moved up along her slim waist to her breast as a distant bell began to ring in his head along with her breathing. Her body tensed. "There's someone at the door," she said.

The chimes rang again. "Don't answer it," he said.

"It might be one of the neighbors."

"At this hour?"

"Someone might be in trouble."

For a moment it was quiet again. Then a desperate pounding hit the door. Stella fumbled with the buttons on her blouse.

"I don't want to see any more people tonight," Jason said, peeking out the window to see another face staring back at him.

"Hey, man," Charley called, waving his fingers in a childlike greeting.

"What're you doing here?" Jason asked.

"It's okay, man. Everything went down."

"What's the trouble, Jason?" Stella asked, but when she tried to look out the window he blocked her view.

"It's nothing, darling," he said. "Just the boy from across the street."

"Why don't you let him in?"

Jason waved her off. "We're about to go to bed," he said through the window.

"We gotta talk."

"Tomorrow," Jason said. "Call me at the office. Anytime. I'll be there all day."

"No, no," Charley yelled, his breath clouding the cold window. "Gotta see you now. It's about the building."

"What does he want, Jason?"

"Honey, go upstairs. Let me handle this."

"Something about a building?"

He opened the front door and Charley tumbled in, pushing Jason up against the heavy oak table at the entrance. They had to hold on to each other to keep from falling. Two children, a black kid and a white girl with stringy auburn hair, came rushing in behind them.

Then a handsome boy, about fifteen years old, moved into the doorway. The light from the porch glowed behind his curly hair making him shine like an ancient icon. His deep, dark eyes scanned the room and stopped when they reached Stella. She held her breath as the boy's gaze took her in.

"Tell him to close the door, Jason," she said. "He's letting in the cold air." Hector stepped in and the door closed by itself as if a force had come in behind him.

"What the hell's going on here?" Jason demanded. "I don't have time for this kind of —"

"Who are these children?" Stella asked.

"It's okay, Mrs. Grimsky," Charley said. "We've got a little business to straighten out with your husband."

"I'll make some tea," she said.

Hector motioned Bee and Shadow to follow Stella into the kitchen and moved to the fireplace. Jason watched him and switched on a bank of lights, wiping out the blue glow from the Christmas tree.

"You know I wouldn't come here if it wasn't important," Charley said quickly.

"Who the hell is he?"

"I'm the supplier," Hector said, staring down at the burning log in the fireplace.

"The *what?*"

"He's the one that did the job, Mr. Grimsky."

Jason put his hands up to cover his ears. "I told you I didn't want to hear anything about this until —"

"It's done!" Hector said.

"What did he say?" Jason asked, dropping his hands.

"You can notify your insurance company first thing tomorrow morning," Hector told him. "It's over."

Jason almost laughed, but when he saw Hector staring at him he picked up Stella's glass and finished her brandy.

"The job's also guaranteed," Charley said. "The supplier started the fire in the next building so there won't be any investigation of your dump. You're clean, Mr. Grimsky. Absolutely spotless."

"That's great," Jason said in a rush, waving Stella's empty glass in the air. "Sounds like you do terrific work. Thanks for dropping by," he said. "Sorry I got angry but I've had a long day and —"

"There's more," Hector said.

"More?" Jason asked. "No one got hurt … did they?"

"It's about your payment, Mr. Grimsky. That's why we dropped by. The supplier still has to get paid."

"I *paid* you," Jason said.

"You paid front money. Now there's back money," Charley said, pushing away his straggly hair.

"I gave you everything I had."

"And I got you the best."

"You told me that money would cover everything."

"You got it wrong, Mr. Grimsky —"

Hector made a quick turn, grabbed Charley, and reached into his coat. A bent spoon, a hypodermic needle, and a plastic bag of brownish powder fell out across the deep reds and blues in the carpet.

"Charley had himself a busy night," Hector said. "Bought a good high, watched a great torch, then had a nice ride up to nowhere land. All this good shit in your arm, but it *still* ain't happening, is it, baby?"

Charley moaned and Jason glanced nervously at the kitchen doors. "Pleeeease," he begged. "Can't you settle this somewhere else? I don't want my wife —"

"We ain't moving 'til you pay us for that sweet-ass deal you got tonight!" Hector demanded.

"I don't have anymore money!" Jason said. "That's why you had to burn down the goddamn building. I owe *banks!*"

"You're fucking building's gone. You owe *me!*" Hector said, moving in closer.

"Once the fire is verified and my insurance —"

"The supplier wants it settled now," Hector said.

The room got quiet except for the crackling of the burning logs in the fireplace. Jason took in a deep breath. "Get out, or I'll call the police," he said. "You're just a lot of snot-nosed kids."

"Take it easy, Mr. Grimsky," Charley pleaded. "You call the cops and it'll blow your whole insurance thing."

"I don't care," Jason said. "Get out!"

Hector grabbed a Turkish vase off the sideboard and held it up over his head. Thin glints of light reflected off it from the fire. Then a dull thud hit the marble along the edge of the fireplace and slivers of color flew across the room as the vase shattered.

"This's bad, man ... bad," Charley muttered.

The kitchen doors swung open and Stella stumbled in with her hands tied behind her back, her mouth taped, eyes in a panic, and her blouse partially opened. Jason tried to reach her before she fell but Hector slipped quickly between them and caught her.

"Leave her alone! She's got nothing to do with it!"

"Don't move," Hector said, helping Stella to a chair.

"This won't take long, ma'am," Charley said, and Stella tried to answer but only a muffled squeal crept out from under the tape.

"She bit my goddamn hand," Shadow said. "It's bleeding." He took a quick step toward her but Hector cut him off.

"We got business here," Hector said.

"She tried to call the cops."

"What do you want from us?" Jason asked.

"You owe us five thousand dollars! Not including collection fees," Hector said.

"I'll get it for you when the insurance company —"

"We want it now," Shadow said, flexing his bitten hand. "You got money all over this fucking place. I can smell it."

"Just give me a little time."

"If we wanted the money tomorrow we wouldn't a showed up tonight," Hector said.

"That means empty your pockets and open the drawers," Shadow drawled. "Otherwise I'll do your fancy bitch so bad you won't be able to put her back together again."

Hector caught the sudden terror in Stella's eyes as she tried to figure out what the broken pieces of pottery were doing on the rug. Then she glanced toward the staircase where a little boy in pajamas, pushing sleep away with the back of his hand, moved down the stairs. He took in the strangers, jumped the last few steps, and ran toward his mother tied in the chair. Shadow caught him just before he got there.

"Let him go. She's all finished fighting," Hector said. The little boy tore the tape off his mother's mouth.

"Don't let them frighten you, Michael," Stella said. "Give them what they want, Jason. Get them out of here."

"You got a smart mamma there," Hector said.

"I'll pay you twice as much if you leave us alone."

"Sounds pretty good," Bee said.

"He's all bullshit," Shadow told her with a wave of his sore hand. "Let's just grab what we can and get out."

"What're they doing here, Jason?"

"It has to do with that last building of my father's. The one on The Heights."

"Didn't Eli tell you to sell those buildings?"

"I thought we could get a better price on it because of the location. We were close to cutting a deal but it fell through."

"What do these *kids* have to do with it?"

"They burned it down tonight," he said.

"Oh, my God."

"Get outta my house!" the little boy said. Hector smiled down at the little boy.

"Don't stare at him like that. You're frightening him," Stella said.

"I'm not afraid of them," the kid said.

"Go back to bed, Michael," Jason told him.

The kid stared back into Hector's dark eyes. "I don't like you," he said.

"Kid's tough," Hector said with a laugh.

"For God's sake, Jason, give them what you owe them before something terrible happens."

"I gave them everything I had," Jason said.

"What about the money you keep in the drawer?"

"I used that for the payroll a few months ago. I'm three weeks behind! I'm even late on my quarterlies. Why the hell do you think I had them burn the place down?" Tears began to well in his eyes. "The insurance kept going up. I had to find someone crazy enough to buy the place … or burn it down."

"Nice family stuff," Hector said, grabbing a bottle of wine off the sideboard. "Open this. We could all use a hit," Hector said, handing the bottle to Jason.

"Suppose I don't want to?"

"You take care of your family, I'll take care of mine," Hector told him in a cold, vacant tone.

"Open it, Jason," Stella said. "A nice glass of wine might change the atmosphere in here."

Jason took the bottle and searched for the opener. When he found it, the phone began to ring. Shadow jumped across the leather couch to get it.

"Don't answer that!" Hector said.

The ringing clicked into a woman's voice, telling the caller to leave a message. "Are you there, Jason? Pick up," a man's voice demanded. "I just got a report that one of our buildings burned down on The Heights tonight. Didn't we sell those? Call me back immediately. If I don't hear from you, I'll drive up. We've got to talk."

"Let's get the fuck outta here," Shadow said.

"You and Charley tie up the clients," Hector said.

"*Me?*" Charley said.

"You do the kid," Shadow said. "I'll do this one."

"I'm doing this under protest, Mr. Grimsky," Charley assured him.

"You're even worse than they are," Stella said. "I know your parents. You're from a decent home."

"Lady's pissed," Hector said.

"It isn't my fault these guys don't take credit, Ma'am. I told your husband that a hundred times."

"Once we get what you owe us," Hector said, "you can all go back to being one big happy family again."

Shadow wrapped the ball of twine around Jason's legs, up across his chest, then down behind him. "You don't have to do this," Jason said. "I'll pay you."

"I'm tired of listening to your bullshit, Grimsky," Hector said. "If you can't get the money we'll take it another way." He spread the tablecloth across the floor, and Bee began rolling in bottles of wine and throwing in the pillows off the couch. Shadow grabbed Jason's glittering tennis trophy, the open bottle of brandy, and some silverware.

"None of this shit is enough to cover what you owe us," Hector said, wrapping a piece of tape over Jason's mouth. "We'll just call this stuff a collection fee."

The others had already headed out the door, dragging the tablecloth with them. "Don't change the locks or the phone number. We're coming back," Hector said, turning off the lights. "Count on it!" The rattling sound of the loaded tablecloth grew fainter. Then it was gone.

Jason stiffened in the straight chair. When he tried to reassure Michael his words came out in a muffled grunt that seemed to frighten the boy even more. Stella began to hiccup. The only other sound was the crackling logs in the fireplace beginning to die in short bursts of sparks. Stella tried to turn and face them but she couldn't quite make it. She shook her head, took a deep breath, and her body jerked with another hiccup.

A sudden cold draft rushed into the room. Jason tried turning the chair and caught sight of the dark boy again. He was standing in the Christmas tree's pale blue light, taking a sharp piece of metal out of his pocket.

"There's no way I can trust you shits," Hector said, holding the steel piece out in front of him. Stella struggled against her bonds and a high squeak crept out of her, making her body jerk forward in the chair.

Jason began to rock from side to side as Hector bent over Michael with the piece of steel. Stella leaned forward, her head straining against the tape on her mouth, as the dark boy cut Michael's ropes and pulled him towards the front door. When Hector heard Jason's garbled cry he spun around and came back across the room.

He leaned down so close that all Jason could see were the dark eyes staring into him. He heard a low, rolling growl and looked into the uncontrolled rage rushing at him like a wild animal, and he sunk into its fiery smell.

"I'm just taking a little Christmas present. You get the money up and put it into one nice pile. Call the cops, you got no kid." The words rushed out like cold numbing water. A door slammed and Michael's chair stood empty. Cut ropes lay in pieces on the floor. He was gone. So were Stella's hiccups.

MOONSCAPE

Charley's compact slipped through the snow packed streets. Abandoned buildings, graffiti walls, and broken windows blurred in the storm. Hector looked for Christmas lights but the streets were dark. The few diehards left in the neighborhood had gone to sleep. He leaned over and tapped Shadow coiled on the front seat. Shadow shook himself awake, opened the door, and rolled out onto the blanket of new snow.

"Turn the corner and park," Hector said.

"I hate this *mysterioso* shit, man," Charley said, pulling over in front of a darkened building.

"Turn off the headlights," Hector said. The street vanished into an umbrella of whiteness that covered the windshield.

"What the hell we doing?" Charley asked.

"Waiting," Hector said, slumping back into the seat between Bee and the sleeping kid.

*

Shadow hugged the wall and climbed up into the heart of the old building. The tenement's deadening cold clung to him like an icy sheet. He stopped near a heavy metal door and slammed it. The echoing sound exploded through the deserted building, making the rats scurry back into the walls.

Rushing through another door he dragged a trashcan with him, rolled it up onto the broken cement blocks in the middle of the room, and filled it with pieces of wood from a pile near the window. His fingers were numb and he fumbled with the matches. He lit one and its small light tore across the empty room. He waved the lighted match from right to left across the window and ran back to drop it on the wooden slats. The match licked at some half burned paper near the bottom of the can and he pushed down on the wood so the flames could spread. The fire started to smoke and he threw in some longer pieces of the flooring until it crackled to life. Three short yips came from below. He yelped back and the hollow sound of his bark echoed through the darkness. Looking around to make sure he hadn't forgotten anything, he threw another piece of the flooring into the fire.

Charley came in first. He stood in the doorway holding one end of the bulging tablecloth. Then someone shoved him from behind. "Let's warm this fucking place up," Hector said, pushing past him into the room.

"Yeah, yeah," Shadow said, going for more wood.

Bee came in holding Michael's hand and pulling the other end of the tablecloth behind her. She slid the cloth from under the clattering wine bottles and wrapped it around the little boy. Leading him closer to the fire she began rubbing his body to get him warm.

"I don't like this place," the shivering kid said.

"Who cares what you like?" Hector said.

"You said you were taking me to your house."

"This *is* my house," Hector said, heading for the dark pile of blankets on the other side of the room.

Shadow laughed at the surprised expression on the kid's face and went back to poking at the fire until its sparks popped against the blackened ceiling. Hector shoved a blanket at the kid and pointed to a dark corner.

"What am I supposed to do with this?" Michael said, holding up the stained brown blanket with the smell of fire on it.

"Roll up in it and go to sleep," Hector said.

"That *my* blanket?" Shadow asked.

"It's *mine*," Hector said.

"What're you giving him your blanket for?"

"Cause I'm staying up all night."

"I'll stay up with you," Bee said.

"It'll be your turn tomorrow."

"I don't like the kid taking your blanket," Shadow said, stirring the fire.

"The kid's only got pajamas," Bee said.

"I still don't like it."

Hector pulled him away from the fire, and said, "That's the one giving us the trouble ... not the kid."

Shadow glanced over at Charley. A thin piece of tubing lay in his lap and he opened his bag of powder and dipped in his spoon. He bent his left arm and tied the rubber tube around it. "Hey, I'm okay," he said when he saw them watching. "I'll sleep right here next to the fire."

Shadow started towards him but Hector pulled him into the far corner. "That's why we didn't get paid," Shadow said. "He bought that bag of shit with our money and paid what he owed."

"Get some sleep," Hector said.

Shadow threw his blanket down across the cold floor, and mumbled, "I don't like guests."

"Want a hit, kid?" Charley asked the staring little boy.

"I don't think so," Michael said, as he watched Charley suck the dull liquid up into the needle.

"Looks like you could use some."

"It does?"

"Take a hit and you'll stop shivering. Be like you were back in your own little bed again."

"Really?" the kid said.

Hector grabbed Charley's arm below the rubber tubing and stared across the open fire at Michael. "Get over in that corner with Bee and stay there!" he said.

"Hey, man," Charley moaned. "I wasn't really gonna —"

"Go to sleep and shut up!"

"I'm the Lone Ranger, man."

Hector let him go. "Keep that shit to yourself," he said moving back to the fire.

Charley stuck the needle into his arm and pushed down on the plunger. His body shook as he drew it out, loosened the rubber tubing, and rubbed his arm.

Bee moved across the room from the other side. "Make him go down to the river to do that," she said.

"If I let him go we'll never see him again. That shit he just put in his arm will put him out for the night."

"I don't like him doing drugs around the kid," she said, heading back to the corner.

"You were too much out there tonight, Hector," Charley said with a laugh. "Incredible. The Iceman. I could hardly believe it when I saw you coming back out with the kid."

Michael got up, wrapped in the tablecloth, and moved along the edge of the flickering light toward the fire. "Is he really a junkie?" the kid asked. "I saw a guy do that on TV. One a those cop shows that —"

"How come you're not doing what I told you?" Hector asked.

"I don't like it here," the kid said.

"Get to sleep."

"I'm hungry," Michael said.

"Maybe you should've left the little shit at home, eh?" Charley asked.

"You gonna entertain us all night with your druggie-bullshit, or what?"

Charley raised his hands defensively. "Don't get mean on me, man. I'm away, baby," he said, curling up on the floor.

"Now you," Hector said pointing at Michael. "I don't give a shit if you sleep, or not. Just roll your ass up in that blanket and shut up!"

"Don't you know you can't trust junkies?" the kid said. Hector stared down at him. "That's why you didn't get my Dad's money from him. Maybe you ought to —"

"If you don't go to sleep your ass is gonna be in deep shit with me!" Hector said.

The kid swallowed hard, trying not to cry. "How am I supposed to sleep if I'm not tired?" he asked.

"Just *do* it!"

"I'm cold and this place is like being outside."

"All you gotta do is face the fire. It'll feel like you're inside," Hector said, throwing in more wood.

Michael pulled the smelly blanket closer to him as he edged toward the fire. "You going to sleep too?" he asked.

"I'm not going anywhere," Hector said.

"You protecting us?"

"Yeah."

"From what?"

"You ask me one more fucking question and I'm gonna punch you out."

Michael looked down into the fire as the new wood caught the flames. The uneven shimmer glowed against the walls in the stark, empty room.

"Stop worrying," Hector told him. "This place looks a lot better in the daytime. You'll get used to it."

"I don't think so."

"You got three things to do here. Don't ask dumb questions. Keep warm. And three … go to sleep."

The kid started back to the corner but stopped when he saw the tennis trophy on the floor with the bottles of wine. The nameplate glistened in the flickering light. JASON GRIMSKY PINE RIDGE HOTEL SINGLES CHAMPION 1982.

"How long do I have to stay here?" Michael asked.

"Another dumb question."

Michael picked up the tennis trophy. The leaping tennis player glowed. He rubbed its rough edges and started back to the dark corner with it.

"Shadow will get pissed if you take that," Hector said.

"It's my Dad's trophy," Michael said.

"Not anymore. Everything in that pile belongs to us now. That's the way it is here. Shadow took the trophy. It goes in his pile. Same goes for you."

"Me?"

"I took *you*, didn't I?" Hector said. "You go in *my* pile."

"What do you mean?" the kid asked.

"It means you do what I tell you."

"Suppose I don't," he said.

"Around here, if you get your ass in trouble it can be the end for all of us. But if you do like I tell you, it can be the beginning of something. You know what I'm saying?"

"No," Michael muttered.

"Just go to sleep and think about it," Hector told him.

Michael put his father's tennis trophy back where he'd found it and looked around the room at the sleeping lumps in the dim, fluttering light. The air had gotten warmer and heavier. Hector held his hands over the fire, waiting for the kid to close his eyes and nestle into the roughness of his mother's lace tablecloth.

*

The old stone house looked deserted except for the blue light from the Christmas tree. Eli parked the car and walked up the path. He rang the bell but nothing happened so he took out his cell phone.

"It's me again," he said to the answering machine. "We've got to talk before the fire investigator shows up. I'm outside. Open the goddamned door." He tapped on the window but couldn't see anything. Then he rang the bell again, tried the handle, and to his surprise the door swung open.

It wasn't until he crossed the living room that he noticed the broken pieces from the Turkish vase strewn across the floor. When he turned, Stella was staring up at him.

"Oh, my God," he said.

When he finished untying her he moved to Jason who had fallen over in the chair. Stella ripped the tape off her mouth and picked up the phone.

"Don't call the police ... not yet," Jason said.

Stella put the phone down and turned on a lamp.

"What the hell's going on?" Eli asked. "Does this have anything to do with our building?" They didn't answer. "Somebody say something," he said.

"I don't know where to begin," Jason said.

"Begin at the beginning," Eli told him. "You must've got my message," he said. "Start there."

"Tell him what happened," Stella said.

"That building ... tonight. I had it burned down."

"Burned down? You know what you just said?"

"Arson."

"It's against the law."

"The supplier showed up looking for more money."

"You mean the arsonist came here tonight?"

"Tell him," Stella said in a tight shout.

"Tell me what?" Eli said.

"They've taken Michael. Kidnapped him," Stella said.

Eli's mouth went dry and Stella began to cry.

*

The fire had nearly gone out. Hector couldn't tell how long he'd been asleep. Something had wakened him. He heard a sound on the stairs but it might've just been the rats getting closer to the fire. He rubbed his arms to wake himself but stopped when he heard the sound again. By the time he got to the door Shadow had moved in behind him. They waited in the chill air listening to the scuffling noises coming out of the darkness.

"Yo! Hector! You up there?" a thin voice called out.

"It's Toozey with his kids," Shadow whispered. "By now they're all over the place."

Hector took in a deep breath. "What do you want, Tooz?" he called into the darkness.

"Need to talk with you, bro."

"It's late," Hector said.

"Nobody sleeps in the ghetto, baby. I got my kids watching both sides. That okay?"

"Come on up. Real slow," Hector said.

A gray shadow rose like a ghost from below. A tall thin black man moved soundlessly up the steps and a tableau of little faces emerged behind him. Hector waited until he heard the wheeze of Toozey's chest before he stepped out of the shadows.

Toozey stopped on the stairs when he saw him. "How 'bout talking inside near the fire?" he said.

"I got people sleeping in there," Hector said.

"Yeah, we know. You got a deal goin' down," he said. "Ain't like you to sleep with junkies though. An that kid you dragged in looks like he'd be better off hanging out with us."

"What do you want, Tooz?"

"That fire you lit tonight was a beaut, baby," he said. The low murmur of children's voices rippled down the stairs behind him in agreement.

"You come to talk money, a job, or what?"

"Hey, don't get uptight, man," Toozey said. "We ain't trying to move in on anything. We're just clocking you. Keeping things straight in our little village. No surprises."

"Thanks for the interest."

"I got more," Toozey said moving up the stairs. His head hung suspended in the darkness. "I come to talk. What you got. What I got. I'm talking assets, liabilities, that kind a shit. It's time the night fox got together to fight off the wolf."

Hector could see the kids more clearly now. They were on either side of the stairs. They'd even come in over the roofs. Toozey just kept moving up between them. Never looking at them. He finally reached the landing. "I wanted to let you know I was coming, bro, but the word is that you got rid of your fax," he said with a wheezy laugh. His eyes gleamed over the short dark beard that hid the delicate features. He had on a baggy, torn topcoat that covered him like a brown paper bag. Toozey smiled then gently hugged Hector, moving his hands to feel for weapons.

"All I got is my old friend," Hector said, taking the shiv out of his pocket to show him. The kids on the stairs looked up at the gleaming piece of metal. A rustling ran along the walls as they pushed one another to get a better view.

"Where's my main man?" Toozey asked.

"Right here," Shadow said from the darkness.

"Damn," Toozey said with another laugh. "See that, kids? That's the kind a thing you gotta learn. Be like Shadow. He's my finest graduate. We miss you, Shadowman."

"What's this shit about foxes and wolves?" Hector asked.

"The night fox must come together in peace," Toozey said. The children giggled and their laughter ran through the empty building. Toozey raised his hand and the silence returned. The rings on his fingers glistened in the dim light. "The wolf sleeps," he said. "But we've got to be ready. He'll wake up soon and want to eat again."

216

"Juicer's the only wolf I know," Hector said. "Ain't you working for him?"

Toozey wheezed, then shook his head. "We don't deal that shit anymore," he said. "Drug people can't be trusted."

Hector watched the frieze of dirty faces along the stairway. No one moved. "Are you saying you're out of the drug business? No more pickups ... no more deliveries?"

"You got it. I want to merge. One operation."

"What happened between you an the Juicer?"

"We parted company."

Hector looked straight into Toozey's dark eyes, trying to read them. "You got anybody on drugs?" Hector asked.

"No," Toozey said, glancing at Shadow. "I've lost my share of good people that way. You never know with drugs."

"I don't deal with druggies," Hector said.

"What about Charley?"

"Who told you that?"

"That's what he told the Juicer when he came in to pay off what he owed. Never saw such good timing. We were about to take the prick's car," Toozey said. "Charley laid down some big money and I know that boy ain't worked in awhile. You guys must've cleared a bundle."

Hector could feel Shadow tense behind him. "We try to stay away from the junkies," Hector said. "They hustle their way into everything."

"If you and me merged we could cut a lot of that shit out. More jobs. Get things done faster. Wouldn't need junkies."

"Who'd run the game? My people look to me. Your people look to you."

"The night fox must look to each other," Toozey said. "I don't know how Shadow might take it. Or Bee. I wouldn't expect you to be handling my man Crazy Eyes either, or my kids. I'm saying we should try moving together a little at a time. See how it works."

"What do we tell Juicer? That we're going into business for ourselves? Pushing him out?"

"Juicer is the first business we take care of, baby."

Hector started to answer but stopped when he saw another dark, slim figure moving up the stairs between the kids. Crazy Eyes. Toozey turned in a frightened way until he saw him. "*Que pasa,* man?" he asked.

Crazy Eyes waited until Toozey came down the stairs, and whispered something to him. "It seems that me an Juicer have officially come to a parting of the ways," Toozey said.

"Looks like you got custody a the kids though, eh?"

Toozey laughed as he started down the stairs. "It's time to go out on our own, bro," he said. "We might even think about moving the operation to some place like L.A. or Miami."

"I could go for warm," Hector said.

Toozey kept laughing as he disappeared between the rows of suspended heads. Then they were suddenly gone too.

"Toozey's in trouble," Shadow said.

"Divorces ain't easy."

"Especially when the Juicer's on the other end," Hector said, and went back inside to put more wood on the fire.

MOON CHASERS

Adeste Fidelis rose out of the blaring traffic on Thirty-Fourth Street. Bee pulled Michael in closer as they crossed Herald Square. The wavering music started up again and the Salvation Army band segued into *Silent Night*. Michael had to hold his pants up as they plunged through the crowd toward the buxom woman hitting the jangling tambourine with her fist. Bee had found some clothes for Michael and tied them together with ropes to make them fit. She'd also given him sneakers but they were also too big and had holes in them, and his feet were numb from the dark lumps of ice and snow that covered the ground.

"Stay close," Bee said as she pushed her way into the revolving door behind a fat woman carrying a shopping bag. The woman's feet began to drag but the crowd pushed them past the bored security guards and into the crowded elevator. Another little boy, in a chesterfield coat and cap, stood eye-to-eye with him as the doors closed. By the time they got to the second floor the smell of fire on their clothing permeated the elevator. The little boy next to Michael tried to turn away but his mother squeezed his shoulder so he couldn't move.

A little girl with braided, mousey hair peeked around an adult's legs and wrinkled her nose at the stench on Michael's clothes. The little boy began struggling to get out of his mother's grip and two more people pushed into the elevator on the next floor and knocked the little boy's cap off. The cap fell between Michael's feet and he kicked it away.

"Stop squirming," Bee told him.

The kid in the chesterfield coat reached down for his cap, the elevator jerked upward, and Bee pulled the kid up like a flopping fish. "Thank you ... oh, thank-you," the boy's mother said, while Bee held the screaming kid in the air. Then the elevator doors burst open and the crowd poured into *Santa Land*.

*

"What're we going to do?" Jason asked.

"I'll get you a good criminal lawyer."

"I'm not a goddamned criminal! *They're* the criminals!"

"*You* had the building burned down, Jason. *That's* a criminal act. You need a criminal lawyer."

"I'm scared, Eli. Everything's falling apart."

"Don't panic," Eli said. "Where did you meet the contact?"

"I mentioned the old building at a party up the street. The next day this kid shows up at the house. He asked me if the building was insured. Said he could have it torched for a reasonable price."

"Is that when you paid him?"

"He wanted cash so we met on the upper West Side."

"How much did you give him?"

"Twenty thousand."

"You just handed some kid twenty thousand dollars?"

"In a paper bag."

"What's this kid's name?"

"His name is Charley Johnson," Stella said. "His parents live down the street."

"They must've told their son about the building you mentioned at the party," Eli said. "They're involved."

"Several people were there when I mentioned it. Could've been anyone."

"I doubt it," Eli said. "The Johnsons know what their son is. I bet they know where he is too."

"There's a lot more to this than just tying us up and taking Michael," Stella said. Her eyes flashed at them in short averted glances. "The whole thing was like an accident. It just *happened*. That's what makes it so frightening."

"You're talking crazy!" Jason said. "You just don't burn down a building. It takes a certain amount of expertise."

"They might've planned that part," she said. "But they were unsure of themselves with us. When they realized we didn't have any money in the house they started taking things."

"Like Michael," Eli said.

"No. Not even Michael. He'd left. Gone out the door."

"Who did?"

"The dark boy ... their leader. He came back to get Michael. They hadn't planned on taking him. He just did it," she said. "As an afterthought."

"So what?" Jason said. "He did it."

"Don't you see?" she said. "If they didn't plan it then we're not dealing with the usual. That's what's *frightening*."

"You're saying they might do anything," Eli said.

"They're like wild animals," she said. "You can't be sure what they'll do next." Her eyes glazed over as if someone had hit her. "Wild, lonely animals," she said, and the tears began to well in her eyes again.

*

Michael had lost track of what floor they were on. Bee kept moving up and down the escalators making sure they weren't being followed. They finally stopped in an aisle filled with racks of children's clothes. "The dark ones won't show the dirt," she said, holding up a pair of navy blue corduroy pants, measuring their length against Michael's legs. "Perfect. Now we have to make sure it fits the other way."

"Can I help you?" a tall man in a double-breasted suit said, peeking at them over the piles of pants.

"You sure can," Bee said. "My Momma wants my little brother here to get some clothes he can grow into. I could sure use your measuring tape ... if you don't mind."

"Maybe I better measure him," the man said.

"My Momma don't like strangers touching us," Bee said.

The man extended his measuring tape to her, and said, "If you need me I'll be at the cashier's desk."

"We'll pick out a few things and be right over," she told him, wrapping the tape around Michael's waist, pushing two fingers against his belly, and checking the measurement.

"He's gone," Michael said.

Bee stood up to look out over the stacks of clothes. "Yeah, but we have to work fast." Her hands moved rapidly through the stack of pants until she found the right size. "Keep your head down and follow me," she said, heading for the next aisle with the pair of pants under her arm. She stopped at a rack of sweatshirts with planets floating on them. Guessing at the size she stuffed it under her arm with the pants.

"That's a dumb little kid's shirt," Michael said.

"Shut up!" she said, reaching out to grab several pairs of socks on her way to the rows of coats.

Michael watched the man at the cashier's desk looking over at them. "He's watching us," he said.

"Just do what I tell you an we'll be all right."

"What're we going to do?"

"We're going to walk out of here with something that'll keep you warm," she said pulling out a dark green louden coat with a large floppy hood. "This looks even better than what I got on," she said, helping him into it. "Too small. Take it off." Michael dropped the coat so he could put his arms through the next one she held out. Bee slipped the wooden pegs into the loops, then pulled the hood up over his head. It had to be the softest, warmest coat he ever had. "You look great, Mikey," she said, just before the loud banging and shouting started on the other side of the long room. "They're right on time. Just do what I tell you." The sounds grew closer and Bee pulled him to the end of the aisle where Hector chased Shadow up and down between the racks of clothing. The two men at the cashier's desk converged on them. Shadow gave another whooping yell and ran straight at the approaching men.

Bee edged Michael towards the main aisle. Someone yelled for a security guard as Hector rushed past the cashier's desk going the other way. "Let's go," Bee said, pulling Michael toward the escalators. "Don't look back!"

*

Eli spread his pile of notes across the dining room table. Jason sat slumped in a chair, a half eaten egg sandwich and a cold cup of coffee next to him. Stella stared down at Eli's papers. They'd given him a detailed description of the kidnappers but couldn't remember what they'd taken except for Michael.

"We'll have to report this," Eli said.

"He warned me not to go to the police," Jason said.

"Who warned you?" Eli asked.

"The dark one. The one who *took* Michael."

"What did he say?"

"That he'd kill him if I went to the police."

"Then all we've got are the Johnsons," Eli said, looking at his notes. "Let's start with them."

*

Bee pulled Michael through the door after her. "This is the ladies room. I'm not supposed to be in here," he said.

"You're with me."

223

Several women stood in front of the large mirrors putting on lipstick and combing their hair. Bee dragged Michael into one of the open stalls and slammed the steel bolt into place. From inside her jacket she pulled out the pair of blue socks. Michael took them, slipped out of the sneakers, and put his cold feet on the warm floor. "Least you'll have socks now," she said. "Stand up on the seat." Michael stood on either side of the open bowl as Bee pulled at the ropes holding up his oversized pants. She reached behind him, gave a tug, and it all unraveled. He was standing in his pajamas again. "Now put these on," she said, handing him the corduroy pants.

"Why don't we do this in the dressing room like everybody else?" Michael asked.

"Cause we ain't *everybody else*," she snapped. "Besides, nobody does it in the dressing room anymore. They do it in the toilet now." He closed the zipper and buttoned the top. "They look great," she said. "How do they feel?"

"Okay, I guess."

"Now put on the sweatshirt ... even if you don't like it," she said, ripping off the tags. He slipped it on and retied the old sneakers over the new socks. Bee worked the coat's price tag between her teeth before setting it into the steel lock on the door. She pulled down until it started to give. Then she took out Hector's shiv to cut through the rest of it.

"Want to take a leak, or anything?"

"No," he said.

"Then just flush the tags down the gazoo."

He pressed the handle and the heavy rush of water hit. The tags swirled, rushed around the edge, and disappeared.

"We got one more thing to do," she said.

Bee squeezed Michael's hand while people flowed below them in a jumbled stream of bobbing heads. When he looked down to the next floor Shadow and Hector were standing in front of them. He felt Bee's hand tighten around his shoulder.

"Something's wrong," she said. "Hector has his collar up. The security guards must be watching them. Just keep going to the shoe department."

A man in a blue sport jacket leaned in behind them. "Can I help you?" he said.

"Could you please show us some sneakers like that boy is trying on over there?" Bee asked. "Take off those old things, honey." Michael undid the laces, and the expressionless man lowered the measurement rack to let Michael slide in his foot.

"Those sneakers you're wearing are too big," the man said, checking the gold line where Michael's big toe stood in the new blue sock. "He's a five. The boy over there is trying on Nikes. They're on sale," he said. Then he straightened up, without looking at them, and disappeared into the back.

"I don't like this," Bee said.

"What's wrong?" Michael asked.

"Hector should've been here by now."

"They gonna run around here too?"

"They're supposed to cover us so we can grab the sneaks. Put your old shoes back on and meet me by that escalator. I'll check things out."

"You're not buying me any sneakers?"

This time they took the elevator. When it hit the main floor they headed straight for the exit. Halfway through the perfumes they hit the crowd at the front door. Hector and Shadow were up against the wall being searched. A large, black policeman stood over them with security guards on either side.

"You can't arrest us," Hector yelled at the guard.

"Shut up!" the black policeman told him.

"You shut up!" Shadow yelled back. "What the hell kind of brother are you anyways?" The black policeman glanced back at the growing crowd.

"We didn't steal anything," Hector said. "I can have your ass for this!"

"Let's get out of here," Bee said, pulling Michael towards the revolving doors.

"What about —"

"They'll be all right. They didn't take anything. Hector's too smart for them." She knew exactly where she was headed and pulled Michael across Seventh Avenue into the warm smell of food. "Two dogs," she told the man behind the counter. Michael watched the heavyset man slip the greasy ladle over the griddle. Bee lifted him onto one of the stools just as the glistening hot dogs, in their warm buns, slid across the faded counter.

"Everything's over there," Bee said, and paid the man. "What do you want on yours?"

"Mustard … relish."

"That's it?" Michael nodded as he reached for the mustard. "I put everything on it. You know, catsup, onions, pickles, relish, sauerkraut, and mustard. The works."

Michael spread the mustard carefully, added the relish, while Bee shoveled on everything she could find. Then she held the overloaded hotdog out in front of her, like some sacrificial totem, before taking a large bite. The excess onions, mustard, relish and catsup squished out the sides of her mouth. Michael began to laugh, making it even harder for her to swallow. They laughed so hard they didn't notice Hector and Shadow come up behind them. "What's so funny?" Hector asked. Bee put the laden hotdog down and threw her arms around him.

"She got worried when she saw you with your collar up," Michael said.

"Kid looks good in the new clothes," Hector said with a laugh, playfully mussing Michael's hair. "Too bad about the sneakers. We'll get you a pair somewhere else."

"That's okay. I got them myself," he said, pulling out a new pair of Nikes from under the louden coat. Hector quickly pushed the sneakers below the counter before anyone saw them.

"This kid's too much," Shadow muttered.

"Shut up and order a couple of dogs," Hector said.

"I didn't know, Hector. I swear it," Bee said.

"I thought that's what you wanted?" Michael said.

"It's okay, Mikey," Hector told him. "You did good. Only next time listen to Bee. You understand? We gotta watch ourselves. All the time."

Shadow handed Hector his hotdog and he took a quick bite. "This's pretty good," he said, rubbing the little boy's head.

"You want me to put the sneakers back?"

"You gotta be kidding," Shadow said with a laugh.

"How do you know they even fit?" Bee asked

"I saw it on the box. Size five."

"You did great, kid. Just don't do it anymore," Hector said. "From now on just do what we tell you."

Michael squeezed the sneakers under his new coat, finished his hotdog, shared an orange drink with Bee, and followed Hector out onto Thirty-Fourth Street. A cold wind blew in off the Hudson as they walked with the crowd of Christmas shoppers toward the subway. Michael could see the Empire State just ahead. The late copper glow of the sun hit the top of it like a torch. He felt tired and hoped Hector would let him sleep in a real bed when they got home.

*

The big white house sat on a rise just off the intersection. Eli took a deep breath before opening the heavy metal gate. Stella stepped in ahead of him and started for the house. When she rang the bell there was an immediate response from behind the door. "Who is it?" a woman's voice asked.

"Mrs. Grimsky from down the street," Stella said, leaning in closer to the door.

"Who's that with you?" the voice asked.

"This's Jason's brother. We want to ask you a few questions about Charley."

"Where's Mr. Grimsky?"

"At home. Waiting for a phone call."

"My husband's not home."

"We want to talk with you, Mrs. Johnson," Eli said.

"About what?"

"We're looking for your son."

"I don't know where Charles is," she said.

"We'd like to talk with you anyway," Stella said, taking in a quick breath. She started to speak again but heard the loud snap of a deadbolt behind the door, followed by the scraping of a chain lock. The heated air from inside rushed out at them. Stella peered through the crack in the door. "It's only me, Mrs. Johnson," she said.

"I don't think I can help you," the thin voice answered. "We don't know where Charles is and haven't heard from him in—"

"We're desperate, Mrs. Johnson," Stella said.

There was no answer. Then the door opened all the way and they stepped into the dimly lit foyer. The smell of burnt logs and cigarettes hung in the air as they moved across the marble floor. The woman turned to them in the dim light with a glass in her hand. "Can I get anyone a drink?" she said. When they refused she extended her glass and filled it from a line of crystal decanters. "Please, sit down," she said. Eli sat in one of the upholstered chairs near the fire. Stella sank into the couch and crossed her legs.

"You haven't heard from your son, Charles, in awhile?" Eli asked. The woman nodded and looked at him for the first time. "Doesn't he have a phone?"

"No," she said. "But sometimes he ships out to work on the freighters and that's probably —"

"He was at my house early this morning," Stella said.

The simple statement seemed to stun the woman. She hesitated, and then muttered, "It's been difficult for Charles. You know young people. Don't know what they want to do."

"We know about Charley, Mrs. Johnson," Stella said. "About his problem with drugs."

The moment hung in the room as they waited for her to say something else. A burning log shifted in the fireplace and made a dull thud as it fell across the logs below it. The woman nervously smoothed her gray wool skirt, and said, "I'm sorry. I hope he hasn't been any trouble to you."

"We've got to talk to him," Stella said. The woman seemed to withdraw into herself, sipping her drink.

Eli shifted uncomfortably in the chair. "Were you the one that told Charley about my brother's problem with a building he owned in the Bronx?"

"I don't know anything about that," she said.

"Then it must've been your husband."

"No, no. He doesn't know anything about this."

"Maybe he *should* know about it," Eli said. "Your son came over to my brother's house the day after the party and offered to burn down a building for him. He could've only known about that if you told him what you'd heard at the party."

"I don't think so," she said, fighting back the tears.

"You did tell Charley about that building, didn't you, Mrs. Johnson?" She stared back at him with a foolish smirk on her face. His question seemed to sober her for a moment.

"Yes, I told him about it," she said. "I thought he might be able to help Mr. Grimsky."

"Then you must've called Charley to tell him," Eli said.

"No. He was here at the house. But I haven't heard from him since," she said, reaching for the glass again.

"You're facing very serious charges, ma'am," Eli said.

"Charges?" she said, looking up in a daze.

"Accessory to arson, kidnapping and —"

"Kidnapping," she said, glancing up over the whiskey glass at Stella. "Oh, my God," she moaned and took in a deep breath. "I haven't heard from Charles since he went over to see Mr. Grimsky." She lifted her hand to her face and Stella knelt down next to her. "He told me not to worry ... that there wouldn't be any problem," she said.

The fireplace popped and spit. "I'm sure you'll hear from him soon," Stella said. "Please call me right away when you do. We've got to talk to him."

The tearful lady on the couch nodded, took another long sip of her drink, but when Eli started talking again she looked up in a frightened stare.

"Don't tell Charley we've been here," he said.

"I'd never do that," she said.

"Tell him you've got some extra cash. He'll come running," Eli told her. "Then call us." She kept nodding but it was hard to tell if she was listening. "If we don't hear from you we'll have to tell your husband about this," Eli said.

Her back stiffened and she glanced at her watch. "He'll be home soon," she said. Her hand nervously brushed back a wisp of hair. "I'll do everything I can," she said, heading unsteadily for the front door. "G'night," she slurred as they stepped out into the cold again, and the heavy door closed behind them.

"We got absolutely nowhere," Eli said.

"I feel sorry for her," Stella said.

"You can't trust her. She's not responsible."

"She reminded me of myself."

"That's ridiculous. She's nothing but a drunk."

"I'm just younger than she is, that's all."

They walked down the path in silence. The early winter sky had darkened and they didn't notice Jason standing out in the street waiting for them.

HUMP - BACKED MOON

The tenement stood frozen in a thin wash of moonlight. A pale flicker edged across an upper window where a shopping-cart reflected in the dim light from a low fire. Above the cart a pear-shaped sack swung from an exposed girder throwing its odd-shaped shadow across the back wall. The sharp crack of a bark broke the quiet just before Hector and Bee appeared at the door. They began tossing more wood into the fire, sending a spray of sparks towards the hanging sack in the corner.

Hector checked the other rooms while Bee stoked the new fire. "I don't like it," she said.

"We got no choice. You gotta have connections."

"You call that prick a connection? Whenever we go over there we get fucked. I hate the Juicer."

"He came through with another job, didn't he?"

"A *couple* of jobs. Don't forget the freebee he wants," she said, pulling a hypodermic needle out of her pocket.

"At least we got a deposit out of him," Hector said, letting her see the roll of money he had in his coat.

"The prick's already made plenty off us. And you know he's gonna take his cut when we settle with that kid's asshole father," she said. "Juicer squeezes hard. And where's Toozey? Why ain't he doing this shit?" She shook her head.

Hector moved across the room to untie the rope holding up the sack in the corner. He felt the weight of it drop, braced himself against the wall, and lowered it to the floor. A low groan came out of the bag when he opened the top. Charley crawled out like a large bug.

"Hey, man, you didn't have to hang my ass in the air like that. Where's my stash? I'm starting to shake."

"You hungry? We're gonna eat soon," Bee said.

"Let me get straight first. Where you been?"

"Here's your boots," Hector said, throwing them on the floor. Charley pulled the rubber tubing out of the boot and tied it around his arm. Bee took out the hypodermic needle.

"Here," she said handing it to Charley. "Shadow mixed the shit for you."

"I bet he stole some of it too, didn't he?"

"Shadow's clean," she said.

"Hey, whatever," Charley said, brushing the needle across his arm before sticking the brownish fluid into his bulging vein. Hector watched him push the needle's plunger downward. The moment seemed endless.

"What's for dinner?" Charley asked, and fell over with the needle still dangling in his arm. A trickle of blood ran just below it and the smell of urine hit the room.

Bee leaned down to look at him. "What do you think?"

"Let's drag him into the other room," Hector said. "Don't forget his boots. Juicer doesn't fuck around when it comes to being dead. Charley just drowned in his own private river."

*

The moon had dropped so low that Stella thought it was going to crash through the window. She remembered her mother telling her that all the children in the world belonged to the moon and that Stella was her own private moonchild. Born on the fifth of July. The moon had become their link but her mother could never overcome the loneliness. The constant need to talk with someone. Stella remembered her mother's incoherent prayers pouring into the night like some crazed monastic monk's, and watched the large white shape move across the sky over her. All she wanted was the phone to ring.

There had been a few calls with no one on the other end. She'd shouted pathetic *hellos* into its uncompromising void. Christmas had arrived, and left. Jason finally believed her and gave in. If they didn't hear anything by noon she was going to the police. Whatever else happened didn't mean a thing. All she could think about was Michael and the moon.

*

Hector heard the bark, put the grates across the fire, signaled to Bee, then edged toward the door to wait for the footsteps. He could see them coming up the stairs. Close together. Laughing at something. He stepped back in the doorway. "What's so funny?" he asked.

"Him," Shadow said. "He's crazy."

"I am not," Michael said, throwing a loaf of bread at him. "You're the one that's crazy."

"They were on us every minute," Shadow said, as he tumbled into the room. "They would've caught us if we hadn't bought the bread. Good thing I had money on me."

"It took you long enough," Bee said. Shadow held his coat open so she could take out the frozen food packages stuffed in his pockets. "You got hamburger again?" she said.

"It was on sale."

"You stole it! Anyway, we can't keep eating hamburger."

"Why not?"

"What did you get, kid?" she asked.

Michael started taking packages out of his pockets. "I like macaroni and cheese," he said.

"So do I. But it's bad for you. What else you got?" she asked. Michael pulled a frozen pound cake out of his pants.

"That's more like it," Hector said, taking it from him.

"That shit's bad for you too."

"Everything's bad for you," Shadow said.

"Shut up and listen," she told him, putting the frozen packages on the grating over the fire.

"You did good," Hector said, rubbing Michael's head.

"Does it mean I can go home now?"

"Still asking dumb questions," he said, placing the package of pound cake next to the warm cement blocks to defrost.

"I just wanted to know if you talked to my father about the money he owes you. That's why you brought me here, isn't it?"

"Your father keeps saying he doesn't have any money."

Michael looked back at him in surprise. "What about my mother? She'll get you the money."

"All they care about are themselves."

"Not my mother."

"Your mother's got nothing to do with it," Hector said. "It's between me and your old man."

They listened to the crackle of the fire. Bee looked down into it and repositioned the trays of food on the grating.

"You could become a homeboy," Hector said.

"What's that?" Michael asked.

"Once you're in a place like this ... with us ... you've got connections. You're somebody. You belong."

"How do you become a homeboy?"

"You're doing it."

"I am?"

"Yeah. Just do what we do. Follow the rules."

"Rules?"

"We don't do drugs or lie to each other. If someone needs clothes, we get it for them. Need food, we find it. We do it together and take care of each other."

"That makes me a homeboy?"

"You still got a ways to go," Hector said. "But so far you're doing great."

"We definitely need you if we're gonna get the money from your old man," Bee said.

"If you let me talk to my Uncle Eli I can get the money for you right away. He gives me anything I want."

"The kid's into the action. He loves it," Shadow said.

"I want to help," Michael said.

"What do we have to lose?" Shadow said. "Let the kid talk to his Uncle."

"How much do you need?" Michael asked.

"Your old man owes us five grand. He's paying late, so we figure it's up to six ... maybe even seven by now," Shadow said.

"You've got to be exact," he told them. "If you keep changing the amount it mixes them up."

Shadow moved in closer to the fire. "Maybe that's what we're doing wrong," he said.

"You've got to know how much you need. Exactly!" Michael said. "Then go get it!"

"We already got some money hid away," Bee said.

"Don't tell him about that," Shadow said.

"I ain't telling him *where*. I'm telling him *what !*"

Bee gave a quick glance at Hector standing at the fire. When he didn't look back she went to get the papers from her blanket and spread them across the floor. "This's what we want to do with our money," she said.

Michael sat down next to her and stared at the worn pieces of paper on the floor. "An RV," he said. "They're neat."

"It's got water and faucets," Bee said. "There's even a toilet and a little kitchen where you can cook."

"My Dad rented one of them once. They're great. Got everything. We went on vacation."

"You can sleep in it too. Right?" Shadow asked.

"You can do anything."

"It's got TV. Right?" Shadow asked.

"That's optional."

"Few more burns and we're home free," Bee said.

"We'll almost have enough if we close this deal with your old man," Shadow said.

"Sounds great," Michael said.

"Hear that, Hector?" Shadow said.

"I heard," Hector said, poking at the fire.

"I still think we ought to steal one and get out of here now," Shadow said.

"We're gonna do it right. Legal," Hector said.

"Yeah, they can trace RVs real easy," Michael said. "Where you taking it?" No one answered.

Hector nodded to Bee and she said, "Arizona. I think I got a cousin out there." The three of them stared at Michael, waiting for his reaction to their plan. When he finally looked up from the brochure he nodded at their expectant faces.

"How much more money do you need?" Michael asked.

"We're pretty close," Bee said.

"Don't forget you're gonna need a lot of gas. It's a long way to Arizona. And insurance. You also need food."

"We can always steal that," Shadow said.

"And we don't need any insurance," Hector said. There was another long silence as Bee refolded the brochure and slid it back into her blanket.

"Why don't we let the kid call his Uncle?" Shadow asked.

"I'll give the kid back when I want to," Hector said.

"You want to keep him, don't you?" Shadow asked. They stared at Hector over the fire, waiting for his answer.

The long night slipped into a thin gray morning. Stella turned to look for the hump-backed moon, but it was gone. When her feet touched the floor she heard the door chime. It stopped when she snapped on the porch lights and opened it. Eli edged in past her. "Michael called," he said. She pressed her hand against her mouth to keep from screaming. He took a cassette out of his pocket. "You can hear it for yourself," he said.

"Where is he?" Jason asked, rushing in from the other room.

"He wouldn't tell me."

"Does he have warm clothes?" Stella asked.

"He didn't have much time," Eli said, putting the cassette into the machine.

The burr of a ringing telephone sounded.

"Hello," a little boy's voice said. "Uncle Eli?"

"Michael? Where are you?"

"I can't tell you that."

"You all right?"

"Yeah. Just don't trace this. OK?"

"Of course."

"Here's the deal. They want twenty-five thousand in small bills. Fifties, hundreds, and a lot of used twenties."

"I understand."

"Tell my father to bring it tonight. He has to come alone. If he brings anyone with him ... the deal's off."

"They with you now?"

"Yeah. But it's OK," he said.

"Where's your Dad supposed to bring the money?"

"4368 Brook Avenue. Got that?"

"Got it. That's in the Bronx."

"The front door will be open. Tell him to go up the stairs to the fourth floor at midnight. Apartment 4C. All he has to do is put the money in the shopping cart that will be there. After that he goes out the same way he came in.

That's important. If he does anything else you'll never see me again. I gotta go now —"

"Wait a minute —"

The phone clicked into a dead silence. Michael was gone. Jason took in a deep breath. "Where the hell am I going to get that kind of money by tonight?" he asked numbly.

"We'll get it," Stella said. "We've *got* to get it."

"Where?"

"I don't *know*! We'll just get it!" she said.

"That's probably why he called my number," Eli said. "He figured it'd be a lot easier for me to get the money than you."

"How much do you think you can raise?" Jason asked.

"I don't know," Eli said.

"Do you have that much?" Stella asked.

"I can get half immediately."

"Is that all?" Jason asked.

"There must be someone you can go to, Jason."

"The banks shut me off. And who knows when that insurance check will arrive?"

"We've got to get it somewhere," Stella said.

"I could probably come up with the rest," Eli said. "But we'd have to pay a high interest."

"How high?" Jason asked.

"Thirty percent."

"That could bankrupt the business."

"We don't have any choice," Stella said.

"Where would you get it?"

"Friends," Eli said.

"If they charge thirty percent they're not friends."

"That's what their money's for, Jason. It makes more money. They know that. They also know that if you have to go to them then you can't get it from the banks.

239

They trust you to pay it back. That's what friendship's all about with them."

"Michael is depending on us! My God ... he's out there all alone," Stella said. "Get the money anyway you can."

"Do you want me to make the phone calls?" Eli asked.

"We don't have any choice," Stella said.

"You'll have to vouch for the money. Sign papers."

"I'll pay it back when the insurance check comes in," Jason said. "But that could be months from now."

PERIGEE

A full moon slid across the sky and its satin glow covered the streets. A burned out Christmas tree, silver foil still clinging to its blackened branches, rocked back and forth in the cold breeze. Hector leaned against a corner of the building waiting for Bee to climb down the fire escape behind him. At the cry of a distant siren they paled back into the shadows. When the siren faded, Bee jumped down and helped Hector pull a shopping cart out of the doorway. At the end of the building, Michael and Shadow joined them, and guided the heavy load down an alley that led out to the avenue.

Hector raised his hand and the shopping cart came to a stop. They were in a well, facing the street, and Shadow crept up the stairs to peek through the iron grating. He took in a deep breath, waved a signal, and Hector ripped the paint-stained plastic off the top of the cart where Charley's body had been stuffed in an old army blanket with his feet sticking out of one end. A strong fetid smell hit them when they lifted the body up over the top of the cart.

"I broke the lock on the front door," Hector said. "All we gotta do is get him into the building. Bee and Mikey can get the cans. We'll come back for the shopping cart. Better check the street again." Shadow peeked out at the avenue all the way to the end of the block. His eyes lingered on the intersection before he signaled, and Hector said, "Let's get this shit inside."

They edged Charley up the metal stairs one at a time and had almost reached the top when a pair of headlights hit the building on the corner. They ducked behind the grating. Charley's body slid back down the stairs in a heap. "It's the cops," Shadow said in a whispered panic.

"Watch them," Hector said, hunching over Charley's body.

The car's lights widened as it moved down the street. "Shiiit, it's just some dude," Shadow said.

Hector climbed up to peek out over the edge as the car picked up speed. "It's a fancy foreign job," he said.

"Is it red?" Michael asked.

"Yeah, I think so," Hector said.

"German?"

"Oh, shiiiiit. It's your old man. What time is it?"

"Quarter after eleven," Bee said.

"Sonofabitch won't do what we tell him," Hector moaned.

They dragged Charley up the stairs again. Lugging the dead weight through the front door and into the cold darkness.

Headlights hit the building on the corner again. The car almost stopped when it reached them and Hector could see someone looking out from the passenger seat. He'd brought someone with him. "When he makes the turn, take the kid and bring in the rest of the stuff," Hector ordered. Bee nodded, put her arm around Michael, and headed for the door.

Hector and Shadow dragged Charley to the staircase. The body bounced across the floor as they dragged and pushed it into the blackness under the stairs. Halfway in, it hit something. Hector grunted as he tried forcing it the rest of the way and Shadow reached in to see what was blocking it.

"Something's there," he said.

Hector reached in and pulled out a pair of hands tied with shoelaces. When they rolled it over, Toozey stared blankly back at them through a clear plastic bag tied over his head.

"Shiiit," Shadow said, tearing open the plastic covering.

"You never saw him," Hector said. "We're just gonna walk away. Forget it. We got a building to burn. What's inside ain't our business."

"The Juicer jobbed this burn to get rid of Toozey and Charley at the same time. We're doing the prick's dirty work."

"It's also a warning. One more body around here don't make much difference," Hector said, pushing Toozey's body back under the stairs. "If you got a problem with a guy like Juicer you better do whatever you're going to do fast," Hector said, and they rolled Charley's body into the darkness on top of Toozey.

"I ain't forgetting this shit," Shadow said.

A cold draft hit them as Bee and Michael came in the front door carrying piles of rags and sloshing cans of gasoline.

"Did he drive by again?" Hector asked.

"No," she said, piling the rags and cans near the door.

"Make sure we got enough of that shit left for under the stairs," Hector said.

Bee nodded and took Michael to the back of the building. Hector looked out through the crack in the door at the empty street. "Don't say anything to Bee about Toozey. Just concentrate on the job," he whispered.

"We better get the shopping cart in," Shadow replied.

"Yeah, and watch out for the tourist. He's dangerous."

*

Jason drove past the building for a third time. Stella could see pieces of the full moon floating between the alleys as they went by. She'd insisted on coming and was the one that had found the building with the number 4368 chalked across its front. There was also a lot of graffiti over the door in a rainbow of balloon letters that read, *MOON CHILDREN '86.*

"I'll park the car away from the building so it'll be out of the way," Jason told her.

"Just make sure I can see the door," she said.

He turned and parked across the street. They sat quietly staring at the building. On either side of it were empty lots. A stained yellow sofa lay overturned on the sidewalk with its stuffing ripped out.

"You got Eli's number?" Jason asked.

The sound of his voice startled her. She squeezed the cell in her lap. "I'll call him when you go inside," she said.

Jason looked across the street at the empty building and opened the car door. The interior light jumped on. "God damn it," he said in surprise.

He turned off the light and Stella took in a breath of the cold air. "You've still got twenty minutes," she said.

"I'm going in now," he said, reaching behind the front seat for the overnight bag.

"Don't forget the flashlight."

"I put it in the bag with the money," he said, starting across the street.

"Be careful," she said, watching him go.

*

Hector had been standing at the second floor window when the Beemer's interior light popped on. He watched Jason try to put it out before anyone noticed Stella in the car with him. All they could do now was finish the dance and get out of there. Slipping the stocking mask on he watched Jason cross the street with the satchel twenty minutes early.

The front door creaked open and Jason's flashlight roamed the walls, playing along the empty staircase. Hector watched the beam of light move up the stairs and he trailed after it. When they got to the third floor Shadow took over and Hector felt Bee's hand on his arm. "Where's the kid?" he asked.

"Next to me," she said.

Hector stood frozen until Jason's beam of light disappeared somewhere on the upper floors.

"Looks like he's headed for the roof," Hector said.

"Should we make our move?"

"Let's make sure he's gone first."

"I'll check out the fourth floor," Bee said, and disappeared into the darkness along the stairs.

"It'll all be over soon," Hector said.

"It's exciting," Michael whispered.

*

Stella's hand shook as she dialed the cell phone. "Eli?"

"Where's Jason?"

"Inside the building."

"What's going on?"

"I'm not sure," she said. The clock on the dashboard clicked midnight. She glanced over at the building but Jason was nowhere in sight.

"All he has to do is drop the goddamn money in a shopping cart and come out," Eli said.

"Something's wrong. I can feel it," she said, noticing a movement in the shadows along the front windows. She hung up, got out of the car, and started across the street. She could hear the phone ringing in the car.

*

Hector had picked the apartment because none of its back windows could be seen from the street. A thin wash of moonlight poured in from the two windows that faced the alley. He set the shopping cart in the middle of the room and slipped Jason's tennis trophy into the wired mesh. Its gold veneer gleamed in the dull moonlight.

Midnight passed. The Beemer hadn't moved. Hector took Michael to the back stairs to cover the alley. They kept each other in sight and used hand signals to report anything. Hector heard a scuffling sound and slipped back into the apartment to check it out.

"Jason?" Stella called. "Where are you?"

Hector squeezed himself against the wall and held his breath as she went by. When she saw the empty shopping cart she reached down and touched the trophy. "Michael?" she whispered. A sudden noise made her jump. She stopped at the door when she saw a light moving up the stairs. It went out and someone grabbed her arm and led her back into the apartment.

"Did you lock the car?" Jason asked.

"Yes," she lied in a short, frightened breath. "You were gone for so long I thought —"

"I've been all over this goddamn building. It's empty."

"Michael said it'd be empty."

"You'd be amazed at what goes on in these buildings."

"I found the shopping cart," she said. "Right where he said it'd be. It even has your tennis trophy in it."

Jason saw it and ran back to check the hallway. "That cart wasn't there a few minutes ago," he said.

"Maybe you didn't see it."

"How the hell can you miss something like that? They've been here. They're here right now."

Stella stared across the room at him in the moonlight. "Put the bag in the shopping cart like he told you," she said.

"The smell's gotten stronger. Something's going on."

"Just leave the money and let's get out of here."

"When do we get Michael?"

"You've got to trust them, Jason."

"They're ripping me off for thousands with all the guarantees on their side. You want me to trust them?"

"Michael told you to go out the same way you came in."

"I just want to make sure everything's in order," he said, staring into the empty darkness.

*

The moon slipped out over the river, turning the shifting currents into a cold milky web. A shadowy blur moved through the building on The Heights, disappeared for a moment, than headed for the shopping cart.

"Where is he, you sonofabitch?" Jason hissed, clicking on his flashlight.

The figure lifted his arms to block the glaring light, and said, "You're supposed to leave the money and go."

"Michael ... is that you?"

"Why do you keep changing what I told you?"

"Are you alone?" Jason asked, swinging the flashlight. "You're one smart kid," he said, unzipping the bag and taking out the stacks of money. "All that stuff on the phone threw me, but now I see what you're doing. We'll leave the empty bag. They won't know the difference," he said, cramming the packets of money into his pockets.

"Keep it," Hector's voice said from the darkness. "You need it more than we do. Take it and get out."

"I want my son."

"You earn that," Hector said, coming into the room.

"Michael ... please don't," Stella's voice trembled.

Hector and Shadow came out of the darkness and put their arms around Michael. His whole body seemed to disappear into the smell of the gasoline on their clothes. Hector whispered something and they all disappeared into the darkness again. Stella looked over at Michael in a quick, frightened way.

"You have to go now," Michael said.

"Help me get this money back into the bag," Jason whispered from the shadows.

"There isn't time," Michael said, just before a flash of light bounced off the walls. A dull roar rushed up the stairs, smoke drifted into the room, and the popping sounds grew louder when the sudden heat poured from the walls.

A piercing bark bit the smoky haze and echoed up the metal stairs. A mournful wail followed. Michael answered it with three sharp staccato barks. Then a sad look came into his eyes as he raised his head and let out a long, primal howl.

"My God," Stella mumbled, as the high-pitched sound of Michael's voice broke the darkness and ran through the burning building like the plaintive cry of a wild animal. Its lonely wail echoed through the halls, up the stairs, and faded into the barking from below.

A trail of loose bills fell from Jason's pockets and Stella's fur coat caught fire and she beat at it with her hands. Michael opened a door and the night air rushed in like a cold tongue. The cry of sirens and a pale searchlight followed them. Their long shadows raced over the building's walls as they stumbled across broken sidewalks, and dodged through narrow alleyways. When they finally reached the street Stella realized that the light chasing them had only been the moon, and when she stopped to look back for Michael he was gone. She listened to the yips and howls fade into the wail of oncoming fire engines, and then they were gone too.

EDITING ACKNOWLEDGEMENTS

Chris Helvey (Trajectory)
Wendy Marcus (Drash Mosaic)
and
"The Lang Gang"
Susan Lang
Warner Dixon
Bert and Denise
Elaine Thompson
Layne Longfellow
And most of all,
Barbara Sassone
and always,
Stella

J.S. KIERLAND is a graduate of the University of Connecticut. He did postgrad at Hunter College where he won the New York City playwright award. He was given a full scholarship to the Yale Drama School and became the playwright-in-residence at Lincoln Center, Brandeis University and the Lab Theatre. In Hollywood he was resident playwright at the LAAT, where he founded the successful LA Playwright's Group, and went on to join Camelot Artists. He has published a novel, edited two books of one-act plays, written two films, and has had over forty publications of his short stories in literary reviews and magazines around the country. This is the first collection of his short stories.

www.ingramcontent.com/pod-product-compliance
Lightning Source LLC
Chambersburg PA
CBHW050730180626
46814CB00002B/687